THE SIGNAL

THE SIGNAL

SHADOW RAPTORS

VOLUME II

***

***

PAPERBACK ISBN: 979-8-9892919-1-5

EPUB ISBN: 979-8-2234821-9-2

***

WRITTEN BY SŁAWOMIR NIEŚCIUR

PUBLISHED BY ROYAL HAWAIIAN PRESS

COVER ART BY TYRONE ROSHANTHA

TRANSLATED BY WIESLAWA MENTZEN

PUBLISHING ASSISTANCE BY DOROTA RESZKE

***

THE SIGNAL

SHADOW RAPTORS
VOLUME II

BY SŁAWOMIR NIEŚCIUR

Table of Contents

1

Cruiser "Frontier"
The Epsilon Eridani planetary system

"Commander, the ammunition warehouses are almost empty, the gas level in the plasma generator chambers has dropped to less than twenty percent." The electronically distorted voice of the gunner rumbled from under his helmet. Most of the screens surrounding the gunner's position glowed red, while others were extinguished. "Activate the rocket launchers?"

"Cease firing." Commander Lupos decided. "We must have a reserve in case of surprises. The frigates will finish the rest."

"Roger." The gunner's hands, covered with sensors, moved, blue sparks flashed through the strands of fiber optics connecting them to the control panel, carrying with them the subatomic-level encoded commands issued non-verbally. One by one, more monitors went out.

Plasma cannon turrets stilled, then slowly disappeared, drawn into recesses in the cruiser's hull.

"Weapons systems deactivated."

"Contact Captain Sellige." Sitting at the spacious console, the radio operator nodded and reached for the switches.

"Redirect to your terminal?"

"Yes." The cruiser commander put on his headset, then adjusted the angle of the display with both hands. After a moment, Sellige appeared on the screen, sitting in a high-backed chair. The frigate commander looked monstrously tired. His puffy, almost round face had lengthened, while his cheeks had sagged to such an extent that it occurred to Lupos out of nowhere that the frigate's gravity generator had malfunctioned and instead of the typical gravity of a rocket ship of about one-third of a g, Sellige's body was being affected by a force several times greater. Even the captain's neatly groomed, ruler-like trimmed mustache was strangely crooked, as if something had pulled its ends down. The impression was compounded by a large hematoma adorning the man's left eye socket.

"Yes, Commander?" he asked ochrily.

"We were running out of ammunition, Captain." Lupos went straight to the point. "All we have left is a bit of mixture for the plasma cannons and a dozen or so short-range rockets, unfortunately. We need to retreat to the nearest supply point."

"Should I take over the operation?"

"Someone has to."

"Uh-huh." Nodded Sellige unenthusiastically and completely out of line. "Has to..."

"You will manage. Only the aft part of the Oumuamua, poorly armored and almost without defense systems, remained to be crushed."

"Almost makes a big difference, Commander," replied Sellige.

"But Captain, I don't suppose you are afraid of a few rocket launchers?"

"Yes, I'm afraid. My frigates don't have reactive armor or individual early warning systems." Sellige croaked. "Anyway, what am I talking about?" He retorted. "They don't have armor at all! Look, Commander." He moved the camera's viewfinder so that Lupos could see a massive breach in one of the control room's side walls. The room within a few meters of the bullet hole was stripped of literally everything, even the floor covering was gone.

"Oh!" Gnarled Lupos. "Did you get hit that badly?"

"Unfortunately." Sellige pointed the camera back in his direction. "And do you know what it was?"

"A kineticist?"

"In a way. More specifically, a piece of debris. The most ordinary splinting. Garbage of some kind, not big, barely thirty centimeters in diameter. Oh, just this one." Sellige placed a lump of slag in front of him, tarry black and glistening in the light of the lamps.

"This is the culprit. It pierced all the layers of plating like cardboard, trashed one of the missile compartments, fortunately already empty, and stopped at the main radiator housing. If it hadn't, it would have gone all the way through the ship, all the way out..." he fell silent for a moment. "Now imagine being hit by something, let's say, five times bigger and correspondingly faster. With a missile. With an enriched core..." he suspended his voice again. With his fingertip he touched his swollen lips. "It's one thing to smash a piece of rock with rockets, Commander, and another to stand up to a regular battle with an actively defending Oumuamua," he concluded grimly.

"A fragment of Oumuamua," specified Lupos.

"For my ships it is a giant. Deadly dangerous."

"Without exaggeration, Captain. Big because it's big, but now it's just a wreck drifting in space. A few salvos from the right distance and the job is done." Lupos waved his hand dismissively. "We have scanned it probably fifty meters deep, we know the location of all active battle stations. To make your task easier, the commander of my escort, Colonel Dressler, will illuminate the targets and, if necessary, also set up markers. Your ships will fire as if at a target."

Sellige again wiped at his swollen lips, then gently picked up a sizable scab on his lower lip with his fingernail. A trickle of blood dripped down his chin.

"You can try..." he muttered, wiping his fingers on the sleeve of his uniform. "I will discuss it with the others."

"Captain, I'm not asking you to consult!" Lupos straightened up and looked sternly into the camera lens. "I give an order and expect to be carried out!"

"Okay, okay..." Sellige raised his hands in a calming gesture. "After all, I didn't say that I refuse. I only expressed my objections."

"The remarks were accepted," replied Lupos stiffly. "As I said earlier, I will send you data on the wreck. All that we have at our disposal and I will assign a reconnaissance ship to help."

"Are you talking about that pile of scrap metal you have moored off the midship?" Sneered Sellige.

"This pile of scrap is a fully operational PF-2 hybrid torpedo ship, equipped with additional weapons systems."

"What kind of systems?" The frigate commander was suddenly interested.

"Plasma throwers, coupled kinetic cannons and an anti-missile system."

"Coupled, you say..." Sellige reached his hand somewhere outside the frame, then turned that way with his chair. "Interesting... May I know what caliber?"

"Wait a minute..." Lupos furrowed his eyebrows and looked back.

"Lieutenant Moss!" Said over his shoulder toward the officer, slumbering at one of the side terminals.

The man twitched, quickly rose from his seat, then limping slightly walked to the commander's station and stood behind the high back of the chair.

"Yes, Commander?"

"This is about the kinetic ammunition on Dressler's torpedo ship. What caliber is it?" Asked Lupos, without even turning his head.

Moss thought about it.

"The cannons were dismantled from the wreckage of the gunship..." he replied after a while. "So regular. Twelve centimeters."

"Five hundred each in a cartridge, Lieutenant?" This time the question was asked by Captain Sellige. He continued to glance at something off-screen, probably checking the technical specifications of the torpedo ship on some screen.

"That's right," nodded Moss. "The containers are double; one battery includes three sets of cannons." He explained, moving closer to the desktop.

"Will you sit down?" Lupos looked meaningfully at the wads of bandage gauze peeking through the fabric of the officer's uniform, taped with dark tape.

"No, thank you. It hurts less when I'm standing." Moss smiled faintly. At the same time, he shifted his body weight from leg to leg to relieve the pressure on his injured ribs. "He shifted his gaze to the screen."

"A total of three thousand bullets, Captain," he said.

"If added twice that much, it would be enough to put up a kinetic shield for my entire squadron," Sellige said. "What do you think about it, Commander?"

Instead of answering, Lupos looked at Moss questioningly.

"Personally, I don't see a problem," the lieutenant shrugged. "We have enough standard bullets. They were intended for our now defunct unmanned escort."

"It's settled then." Lupos said. "Did you hear that, Captain?" He turned to the microphone. "In a few hours, a torpedo ship loaded with kinetic ammunition will join your ships. I'm placing it under your command."

"Thank you." Something like a smile appeared on Sellige's bruised face. "I will report on an ongoing basis," he added, a bit more cheerfully.

"Then I wish you good luck." Lupos ended the conversation, then turned off the screen and took off his headphones.

"Lieutenant, you will make sure that additional kinetics cartridges are loaded," he said to Moss. "Then please go to the medical section and finally take advantage of the benefits of the medcom."

"Commander, but I feel quite good!" Moss protested.

"No buts! It's an order," Lupos said.

"Yes, sir!" The officer gave in. Pressing his elbow against his aching side, he shuffled towards the exit, followed by the envious look of engineer Sniegova, who was still standing at the control panel of the cruiser's propulsion systems, surrounded by monitors and barely visible from behind a pile of printouts.

"Communications, please call Colonel Dressler to the bridge!" Lupos said.

The operator's fingers immediately danced on the console keyboard.

"And establish contact with the service dock master's office." Added the commander, glancing at Sniegova.

Taking advantage of the moment of respite, he took out the previously opened tube of conditioner from the glove compartment, squeezed its contents into his mouth and swallowed quickly. Three full days had passed since they had set off at full speed to meet Oumuamua as it slid deeper into the system, and in that time, he had only managed to take a nap once, and that was while sitting in the captain's chair. It wasn't that he was particularly exhausted, because the stimulants and regenerative additives contained in the supplement provided the cells with a constant supply of necessary substances, but he began to feel more and more tired.

A few minutes later, Colonel Ian Dressler appeared on the bridge. Tall, muscular, with a crew-cut, wearing a brand-new two-piece jet black uniform and a thigh holster with the butt of a hand-held plasma thrower sticking out, the cruiser's escort commander looked like someone out of a recruiting poster.

"I report on orders!" he said, standing at attention at Lupos' desk.

"Well, I see you've already pulled yourself together," said the commander with undisguised admiration.

"Depends on what you mean," Dressler replied. "There's nothing wrong with me physically, at least that's what the doctor says. As for the effects of the coupling with the rover..." he fell silent for a moment, and a shadow passed over his handsome face. "Well, I'm holding on somehow. It wasn't the first time I had to say goodbye to a comrade in arms."

"I see," Lupos nodded. "By the way, it's amazing how much such AI can..."

"Commander, I don't want to talk about it!" Dressler interrupted him unceremoniously. "Not yet," he added.

"All right, Colonel." Lupos said conciliatingly. "Please sit down." He pointed to a small frame on the side of the desk, with a seat attached to it. The entire structure was screwed to the floor slabs.

"Do you know our current tactical situation?"

"More or less." Dressler looked back at the main screen, where the simulation of the disaster area generated based on lidar data was again displayed. "Current reports indicate that we are continuing the operation to clear the impact area of those Oumuamua fragments that are reasonably suspected to still be active and potentially dangerous," he recited from memory a fragment of the latest on-board bulletin. "I see that there is still quite a lot left..." he added after a while, pointing to the multitude of markers on the screen.

"It's just garbage, Colonel. Well, maybe we'll need to re-examine a few of them. First of all, we need to take care of this... um... little thing." Using the electronic pointer, Lupos enlarged the lower left corner of the screen and moved the cursor over the yellow pulsating square and additionally marked with a large red exclamation mark. "This is our biggest problem. The stern section of Oumuamua," he explained. "Seven hundred and fifty meters long, estimated weight three million tons."

"Well, well, well," Dressler whistled. "Does it have power?"

"This is another problem." Lupos enlarged the image even further.

The previously flashing point turned into a spatial grid of green lines, forming a geometric shape, somewhat reminiscent of a large cigar butt.

"We detected emissions coming from the thruster jets, so even if the main drive is down, they can still fly broadside forward. Some artillery positions are also active." Said the commander.

Dressler rose from his seat and walked closer to the display.

"Seven hundred and fifty meters..." he muttered under his breath. "Subtract from this about a hundred for the destruction zone... and another fifty, most likely cut off from the rest by security bulkheads... That will still leave us with half a kilometer of potentially intact sections, including the engine room." He said. "Not good."

"Even very bad, Colonel." Lupos agreed. "While the Skunians did not change the existing design assumptions specific to this class, on Oumuamua, apart from the engine room, the hangars and, who knows, maybe quite a large part of the living quarters, survived."

"What is its current trajectory?" Dressler asked.

"Fortunately for us, the collision with the habitat threw it off course, quite specifically. It drifts perpendicular to the ecliptic plane."

"Then there is no problem as such." The colonel's wrinkled forehead smoothed out. "Let's give them the big push and let them go." He smiled broadly. "In a few months, we will send one or two mining installations and a bulk carrier to collect the spoil. Unionists and Sigilians will be delighted."

"The problem is that this damn wreck is now flying towards the Fold." Lupos also got up from his seat and walked over to the display. "Even while drifting, it will theoretically still be able to fire at the installations there. Please take a look at this."

He moved the pointer and a dashed line appeared on the screen, connecting the Skunian wreck and the Fold marker in the opposite corner of the screen.

"According to our calculations, it will fly less than ten thousand kilometers from the edge of the anomaly, close enough and slow enough to target major transfer stations, not to mention minor installations. We have to sort this out here and now, Colonel."

The pointer cursor circled the visualization of a fragment of the enemy ship, moving slowly along the line drawn by the commander.

Signal lights flashed above the communications console.

"Commander, we have a connection with the repair shipyard master's office," the radio operator announced. "Delay ten seconds."

"I'm sorry, Colonel." Lupos returned to the command chair and put on his headphones.

Left to his own devices, Ian walked to the observation slot and looked at the rows of reactive armor plates stretching out beyond the window.

Slightly convex ovals filled with an explosive substance were intended to weaken and dissipate the energy of enemy kinetic projectiles, thus minimizing the effects of direct hits and protecting the ship's plating underneath.

In some places, where rockets fired from Skunian fighters had recently hit the cruiser's side, damage was still visible. In the resulting gaps, exposed steel gleamed with living metal and bent fragments of mounting bolts and hooks stuck out.

The ship's bow, a large horizontal plane containing the forward plasma cannon turrets and kinetic missile batteries, was bathed in the harsh light emitted by Epsilon Eridani, several hundred million kilometers away. At the peak of its cyclical activity, the young cosmic star had been glowing furiously white for months, emitting enormous amounts of high-energy radiation particles, mercilessly frying its only planet, AEgir. The globe, buffeted by X-rays, was visible from this distance as a small speck of blue, shining against the blackness of space.

Sigil, its natural satellite, a rocky, mineral-rich globe similar in size to Earth's Moon, although unlike it more compact and with a still liquid core, also received its dose of radiation.

"Please watch your eyes, Colonel," said the voice of engineer Sniegova. "This glass has no filters."

She handed him safety glasses with smoked lenses. She had the same one on her nose.

"Beautiful, isn't it?" She said, turning her head towards the upper right corner of the viewfinder, where a fragment of Epsilon Eridani's shield was visible.

"Yes, beautiful," he agreed. "But also, deadly."

"Just like all of them." The girl moved closer to the window, with a brush of her finger she increased the polarization of the glasses, which immediately darkened and became almost black.

He repeated her gesture. Filtered through the nanocrystal layer, the star's blinding glow softened, transforming into a soothing, bright orange aura.

"And to think that even the coldest, dead and burnt out stars still have enough heat inside them to turn everything around them into slag..." she said thoughtfully.

"You forgot about brown dwarfs, lady engineer." He said. "For example, WISE-1828... It's like a star, but it's as cold as you and me."

Sniegova covered her mouth with her hand and giggled. Moments later, the giggling turned into loud laughter.

"Did I say something wrong?" He asked, confused.

"No, of course not... You're right, Colonel... I forgot about brown dwarfs..." she choked out. Still giggling, she took off her glasses and wiped her eyes.

"I'm sorry," she added, trying to sound serious, though her lips were still twitching with suppressed mirth. "I was visualizing this and that unnecessarily..."

Ian smiled broadly.

"You have a vivid imagination, lady engineer. Very vivid," he commented, handing back the glasses.

The girl's dark cheeks darkened even more, this time with embarrassment. She slipped her glasses into her hip pocket and walked briskly back to the control station.

"... I don't care... they must wait ready for loading... if you want no problem write to the chief of staff... everything you have in stock... I repeat, I don't care about your limits..." Ian heard fragments of the heated discussion led by Lupos. He looked away from the peephole and looked in that direction.

The cruiser's commander, red with anger, sat in his chair and, clenching his hands on the movable microphone stand, said something through gritted teeth. His gray hair, usually perfectly parted, was now ruffled by the wire headband of his headphones, which kept sliding down towards his wrinkled forehead. Purple spots appeared on the commander's flushed cheeks, partially covered by his impressive sideburns - a sign of an overdose of stimulants, already well known to Ian. The commander's ash-gray uniform was wrinkled, and on one of the sleeves there was an ugly dark streak, most likely a grease stain, stretching from the shoulder to the elbow. The cuff of the other sleeve was stained with something furiously green, looking from a distance like lumps of jelly.

"Conditioner," Dressler thought.

"End of discussion!" Lupos growled, then pushed the microphone away and jumped up abruptly from his chair. The headphones slipped off his head and fell to the floor. He kicked them under the chair. Angry, he glanced angrily around the bridge, as if he were looking for someone else to talk to. The heads of everyone present in the room leaned over the desks, and the hushed conversations fell silent.

Seeing that the commander's negotiations with the shipyard management were over, Ian quickly went to his desk.

"Let me guess," he said, smiling slightly, completely unfazed by Lupos's ominous expression. "Another skirmish with the official machine?"

"A machine?" the angry commander huffed. "Just an ordinary pen-picker who fancied that he can decide about anything! No way!" he growled. "Lady engineer, please start the braking procedure immediately and set a new, most optimal course possible. We're going back to the shipyard!" He threw towards Sniegova, and then took a deep breath once and twice to calm down. "As for the wreck," he resumed the previously interrupted thread, "Captain Sellige's frigates will take care of it. Your job, Colonel, will be to provide cover for them once they are in position." He pointed his finger at the main screen, where four more symbols appeared next to the previous ones.

"Cover?" Dressler had the impression that he had misheard. "This rickety, crudely armed torpedo ship? How?!"

"You will put up a kinetic shield." Lupos replied. "I ordered additional containers to be loaded on board."

"The shield is good, but for rocket fire or against fighters." Dressler objected. "Fire from kinetic cannons, no matter how intense, will not stop plasma and thermopills or classic missiles! What these frigates need is not cover, but a full escort, and one that will both clear the approach and eliminate enemy artillery."

"I'm sorry, Colonel, but we don't have such forces." Lupos grimaced. "The gunships and patrol ships from Sigil are busy convoying all the civilian mob that wanted to get off the planet to their home bases. We must deal with what is. You have one hour to prepare for takeoff. You will receive the coordinates of the meeting point and details of the operation from Captain Sellige."

"All right." Ian gave in. "Can I ask you something else?"

"Of course."

"Have you finally located the Fleet?"

"Unfortunately, no," Lupos replied. "They went down the gurgler."

2

Cruiser "Pandemonium"
The Solar System

"Commander, do you see what I see?!" Kravchenko turned the display towards Tsugawa, who was standing at the side of the console.

A gigantic object was moving on the screen, consisting of several dozen metallic shimmering balls, connected by vast spiderwebs of massive grids. Visible against the background of this huge structure, the cruiser "Ukulele" looked like a bumblebee hovering next to a large bunch of grapes.

The repair trawler that was towing the damaged cruiser was not visible at all, even with the image intensification system activated.

"Amazing construction!" Tsugawa smacked his lips appreciatively. "It's not even a single ship..." he said, moving closer to the screen. "...just a conglomeration of units. Please look." He pointed at one of the spheres. "The maneuvering engines, and the protrusions under them, are probably the main drive's pulsation jets. The bulges around the perimeter," he touched the screen, "look like artillery turrets to me... Amazing construction," he repeated. "Why our engineers didn't think of it either?!" He shook his head in disbelief.

"Commander." Kravchenko looked at him sternly. "I don't need a rapporteur. For now, my eyesight is still good. Please tell us how we can get away with this and avoid confrontation."

"I have no idea, Admiral." Tsugawa spread his hands. "They caught up with us easily and considering the number of these modules and their armament, they have more firepower than all our ships combined. Maybe if we fell apart..." he thought for a moment. "No, that's not an option either," he answered immediately to himself. "These girders appear to be movable, so they will most likely be able to release individual modules quickly."

"And then we will have not just one ship on our backs, but a whole swarm of them, each of them the size of our cruiser." Tsugawa finished for him.

As if to confirm the commander's words, one of the spheres broke off and, spitting streams of gases from the nozzles of the maneuvering engines, flew majestically towards the "Ukulele". Even far from the cruiser, it seemed almost half its size.

The men watching the scene groaned in unison.

"Oh shit!" Kravchenko gasped. "It's a kilometer in diameter!"

"One thousand three hundred meters, exactly." Tsugawa informed.

He leaned even lower and enlarged the window at the bottom of the screen that displayed the telemetry data.

"How many of them are there on this damn scaffolding?"

"Twenty-four. The whole thing is eight kilometers long, not counting the transmitter spiers."

"And this is the Dragon Seven?! Just a battleship?!" There was disbelief in the admiral's voice.

"This is what the identification data we received shows." Tsugawa replied. "Phobos District Security Service auxiliary."

"WHAT?!" The admiral's disbelief turned into something like shock. "An A... AUXILIARY unit?!" he choked out. "It's a fucking giga-carrier, with battleships as fighters! If it's a support ship, what is their main force?! Jupiter's moons?! Planets equipped with propulsion?! Where the hell did they get the funds and raw materials to build such a monstrosity? That's twenty million tons of steel!"

"Estimated mass of the structure: twenty-four and a half million tons..." Tsugawa read from the screen. "A lot, that's a fact." He admitted calmly. "However, please remember that they have a lot of raw materials at their disposal here. Planets, an asteroid belt and about two hundred larger and smaller moons... This is not our humble arrangement with one planet, a moon riddled with holes like Swiss cheese and asteroid belts completely exploited by the Skunians. Moreover, they do not have to complain about the lack of labor, unlike us. And no one steals their machines like Skunks do."

"I'm aware of this." Kravchenko grumbled.

He stared at the screen with furrowed brows.

"Not responding to transmissions? " He asked after a while.

"No. No reaction. It just repeats the request to deactivate the weapons systems and sends the anchorage coordinates repeatedly."

"Were you able to contact the local authorities?"

"We tried with the district commissioner and the headquarters on Mars. Without result. McReady most likely activated the jamming systems. To communicate with anyone, we would need to obtain access codes to the network of relays here." Tsugawa explained, while glancing at the communications officer on duty listening to their conversation.

The man nodded to show that he agreed with him.

"Admiral, this sphere just targeted the Ukulele." The gunner reported. "Captain Karpinski asks for permission to open fire."

"I refuse!" Kravchenko almost shouted, jumping up from his chair. "Commander, please keep your eyes on this... this leviathan!" He said over his shoulder to Tsugawa, and then quickly walked to the platform, above which was a sensor cocoon with a gunner immobilized inside.

"Let them release their moorings and join the main formation!" He ordered, jumping onto the dais and taking a seat behind a small console that was a smaller copy of his command post. Then he turned on the small displays placed around the console. All of them flashed messages about the detection of foreign radar and lidar beams.

"Please activate the pulse drive. Full sequence. We'll try to jump back!" He called to Tsugawa, and then entered the appropriate command for the command harmonization system, which immediately sent his order to the other ships.

"What about the Ukulele, Admiral?" Came the question from the cocoon.

"We'll find out soon," he replied. "Are you able to activate any of his weapons systems from here?"

"Anti-missile system only. Activate?"

"Yes. I understand that the tracking systems also don't work?"

"Unfortunately, Admiral. The anti-missile launchers are powered by an emergency generator and have their own target guidance modules, the other systems drew power from the main reactor, just like lidars."

"That's tough! Please run everything that can be run remotely. So that it shines brightly into their sensors."

"Admiral, the tug has joined the main formation!" Tsugawa reported.

"Excellent." Kravchenko's fingers danced across the keyboard once again. "We're making a getaway towards the Fold," he announced, fastening his harness. "Commander, you can start the countdown."

There were clicks of buckles on all sides of the bridge, and here and there the seat adjustment pneumatics hissed. The lighting dimmed, and a scarlet alarm lamp lit up above the entrance to the bridge.

"I'm starting the procedure." Tsugawa announced.

"The countdown has started," the security system announced after a while from the loudspeakers. "Pulse sequence in one hundred and twenty seconds. Decreasing value."

Kravchenko made himself more comfortable. The perforated, unupholstered metal backrest pinched his back, and the tight harness pinched his shoulders. For a moment he considered returning to the main desktop, but when he saw Tsugawa, wired, covered with a pile of graphene data plates and already strapped to the chair, he decided against it.

"Pulse sequence in sixty seconds. Decreasing value."

It was almost dark on the bridge. The only source of light was the glow of the main and smaller displays, which were not extinguished while the power reserve was accumulating. The bow visor covers closed silently.

"Pulse sequence, first pulse," the automaton announced in a mechanical voice.

As soon as the message echoed, the ship jerked. For a few seconds the gravity disappeared, and the kinetic energy absorbers groaned.

Kravchenko, pushed into the hard chair by the acceleration, clenched his jaw with all his strength so as not to scream in pain. Deprived of self-regulation and protective foam, the backrest frame dug into his back, something angular pressed into his right hip, the edge of the seat dug under his knees, almost crushing his calves. The structure of the chair creaked dangerously and one of the harness buckles came loose.

After a while the pressure eased. Taking advantage of the moment's respite, the Admiral straightened up as much as his seat belts would allow. Wincing in pain, he reached for the console and activated the handheld tactical screen. To his disappointment, the display remained solid black, not even a command tree appeared.

"Pulse sequence pulse two in twenty seconds," the security system announced dispassionately.

"Commander, please put the Ukulele orbiter feed on the main screen," the admiral groaned, reaching behind his back to check what had stabbed him in the kidney. The culprit turned out to be a loose screw with a rounded head. He tightened it with his fingers, being glad that the seat designers hadn't thought of using screws with pointed heads to stiffen the frame.

"Pulse sequence, pulse two, in ten seconds."

The screen occupying almost half of the front wall of the bridge, larger even than the one below the bow observation slit, glowed with a familiar green, which after a moment faded to grainy gray, and then to deep black, against which the slightly deformed but still slender silhouette of the damaged cruiser appeared.

"Pulse sequence, second pulse."

This time, Kravchenko did not allow himself to be surprised by the forces released by the acceleration. As the ship shuddered again, torn apart by the gargantuan energy of a directed nuclear explosion, the admiral grabbed the armrests with his hands and straightened his legs at the knees. When the overload pressed him to the chair again, he felt only the discomfort typical of such situations.

During the subsequent half-minute intervals between pulsations, he carefully watched the screen, which continuously displayed the image of the drifting "Ukulele" and the spherical ship flying right behind it. Fortunately, the leviathan from which the smaller element had separated still did not accelerate, but continued to move parallel to the damaged cruiser, at less than twenty kilometers.

The distance between the group and the large battleship was constantly increasing and after the last, fifth impulse it was almost four million kilometers. Less than sixty million of them remained to the edge of the Fold and the installations guarding it.

"Pulse sequence completed." The system finally announced.

The lamps brightened, the omnipresent whine of the kinetic energy sinks quieted, and dozens of gigawatts of energy flowed into the backup energy cells to power systems that did not draw power directly from the Pandemonium's propulsion system.

Kravchenko rose, bent down and, ignoring the warning jab in the small of his back, rubbed his sore calves.

"How did you know they wouldn't chase us?" He heard the muffled voice of an artilleryman above him.

The Admiral straightened and looked at the sensor cocoon. First the operator's wired hands emerged from between the folds of fabric, then his arms. A moment later, the cocoon opened like a flower, releasing a figure covered with hundreds of sensors in a tight, tight-fitting suit and a spherical, opaque helmet.

"They will chase us, Sergeant," Kravchenko replied, stepping aside so that the operator could safely jump from the cradle onto the platform. "They will come after us as soon as they receive such an order from the headquarters, but it will take a while."

"I don't understand?" The gunner took off his helmet and placed it carefully on the platform. Beads of sweat beaded on his shaven skull. On his temples and above his forehead, there were circular traces imprinted on his skin from the suction cups of the psychosensory transmitters through which he communicated with the intelligence controlling the combat systems.

"They were supposed to intercept and escort us, which they did. If we tried to escape, a fight would most likely break out." Kravchenko explained. "However, since we waited for them politely and, what's more, we allowed them to fly to their largest ship, they decided that everything would go smoothly from there. Routine, Sergeant. In this profession, a person's greatest enemy is routine. And now they have a problem, because to follow us, they would have to leave the Ukulele unattended."

"After all, the smaller one is keeping an eye..."

"Yes, it's keeping an eye." The admiral agreed. Seeing the consternation on the gunner's face, he smiled wryly. "And it will keep an eye, and this entire Dragon will start chasing us, but..." he smiled a little wider, "...but only when his commander receives clear instructions. Bureaucracy, Sergeant, is a double-edged sword. Now do you understand?"

"Yes, Admiral," confirmed the gunner. A smile also appeared on his haggard, pale face. With professional skill, he freed himself from the sensors and wires, which he then placed carefully next to the helmet so that it would be easier for the deputy to connect them to the sockets in the cocoon.

"Admiral, Constable McReady on the line. He wants to talk to you," said the communications officer. "Switch to your terminal?" he asked, pointing to the commander's desk, where Commander Tsugawa was still sitting.

"Switch." Kravchenko walked slowly to the main desk. "Take it easy, Commander." He put his hand on Tsugawa's shoulder as he started to get up to make room for him. "Please log out calmly and collect your stuff. It's not on fire." He winked knowingly.

Tsugawa, who immediately realized that from this point on they would only be playing for time, obediently sat back down at the desk, opened the small case and began to insert the data disks into it, completely ignoring the persistent buzzing of the incoming transmission beacon that came from the tabletop loudspeaker console and ignoring the scarlet flashing light on the device.

After about two minutes he stood up.

"Please, Admiral," he pointed to the desk with a polite gesture.

"Thank you." Kravchenko replied equally politely. He slowly settled himself in the chair, carefully straightened the headphone cable, blew some non-existent dust from the plastic boom, adjusted the ear cups, and then equally carefully leveled the microphone.

"Admiral Sergei Kravchenko. Hello." He said, turning on the speakerphone.

"Francis McReady, Senior Constable. Phobos District Security Service," an officer's voice, distorted by interference, came from the speakers. There was an impatience in his voice. "You did not follow my orders."

"So, what about this?" Kravchenko asked indifferently.

"I'm forced to change your status to HO."

"Meaning?"

"Hostile Objects. Please check the regulations for details. As far as I remember, you have this text in your data bank."

"You have a good memory, McReady."

31

"Yes." The other one nodded, again dispassionately.

"I understand that the procedure does not provide for appeals?" Kravchenko opened the file with the text of the regulations on the monitor.

"Not at this stage. We do not negotiate with criminals." Even though it seemed impossible, the officer's voice became even more dry.

"We have not made a single hostile move against you." Kravchenko replied calmly. "I mean, we haven't done it yet," he added after a short pause. "But if your ship doesn't stop probing our ships with its scanning beams, that could change at any moment. Some of our combat systems operate in automatic mode and there is a real risk that one of the intelligences controlling them will classify your actions as an act of aggression. Just as your defense system on Mercury considered our group a threat. I loyally inform you that the fleet you see on your screens is a group of warships. Any confrontation may bring disastrous results."

"Is that a threat?" This time there was something like amusement in the constable's voice.

"Just information." Kravchenko replied immediately, remembering the course of their earlier conversation.

The speakers were silent for a few seconds.

"Admiral, let's be serious." McReady finally nodded, and Kravchenko was pleased to note that this was the first time the officer had addressed him using his military rank. "You probably have our battleship on your screens and see what class it is and are aware of the weapons it has?"

"Three times yes."

"So please slow down and let me escort you to the anchorage."

Kravchenko looked back at Tsugawa, who, resting his hands on the top of his console, still unrepaired from the short circuit caused by the moisture from the holoprojector nozzles, was listening (like the entire bridge crew) to the commander's conversation with this implacable system police officer. The commander smiled slightly and pointed his thumb at the rangefinder display behind him. The number representing the distance between the front of the formation and the edge of the Fold was constantly decreasing.

"Please slow down." McReady repeated. "I'm giving you an additional five minutes to initiate the braking procedure and enter the course indicated by the escort ship. If you do not comply, your status will change."

"Why are you jamming our signal?" Kravchenko asked unexpectedly. "We cannot establish contact not only with your authorities, but even with the commander of this battleship."

"Procedural requirements. UO-class objects can contact central government bodies only through lower-level bodies, contact with operational units is not an option at all."

"No exceptions?"

"None. Jamming systems are activated automatically when the UO status is assigned."

"Do you realize, constable, that if an inter-system conflict occurs, you will be the direct cause of it?"

"I act in accordance with the procedure and within its limits."

"I understand that you are aware that at this moment the Epsilon Eridani system is under attack by Skunians, and the group you want to arrest is the only armed formation capable of effectively facing hostile forces? If you don't believe me, please contact the Fold listening stations. I'm more than sure they picked up the distress messages from the warning systems in our system." Kravchenko glanced at the rangefinder again. Since the beginning of the conversation, the flotilla has covered another half a million kilometer, increasing the distance between it and the still motionless battleship.

"You have three minutes left," McReady said in response.

Kravchenko moved the microphone away, took off his headphones and closed his eyes.

"I can't believe it... It looks like I'm talking to some fucking bot..." he said wearily. "End of transmission!" With a lazy gesture he motioned to the communications officer, who immediately turned off the communication channel.

"Admiral, message from the cruiser Hercules." The man reported after a while. "I'm sending it to your terminal."

Kravchenko straightened up and turned on one of the side monitors.

The Hercules, as a unit adapted to cover operations, traditionally closed the main formation. Its decks, adapted as hangars, housed a wing of patrol ships and two wings of gunships constituting the rear guard of the flotilla. It was through the Hercules transmitters that the signal from the orbiters tracking the drifting Ukulele was transmitted, as well as the huge modular battleship gliding near the damaged cruiser.

The signalman's report also intrigued Tsugawa, who quickly walked to the commander's desk.

"What's going on?" he asked, looking over Kravchenko's shoulder.

"They're touching them with lidars."

"What for?" the commander was surprised. "We are far beyond their reach. Plasma will not catch up with us, even its most concentrated beams will cool down and disperse at such a distance. Rockets will be even less effective. No sense."

"That's what worries me, Commander." Kravchenko turned towards the main screen. "The constable's deadline is about to pass, and the battleship is still on its usual cruising route. If I were them, I would start speeding up..." he muttered, rubbing his jaw thoughtfully. "At least one pulse to keep the reactor running at full speed in case of an emergency... I don't like it, Commander." Once again, he expressed the bad feeling that was bothering him.

On the weapons operator's platform, the ladder clanged as it was being lowered, and a moment later there was the rustling of sensor fabric and the clicking of fiber optic ends being plugged into sockets. Finally, the sealed helmet hissed.

He and Tsugawa both looked in that direction. The cocooned operator greeted them with a gesture of his wired hand.

"Sergeant Teofil Kotowicz reports to the watch!" It rumbled from under the mirror cap of the helmet.

The admiral responded with a casual salute, and Tsugawa, in accordance with Sigilian etiquette, bowed, having previously crossed his hands on his chest.

The screens around the platform lit up one by one, and on a large rectangular panel suspended directly above the cocoon, rows of multi-colored diodes lit up, signaling the status of connections between the human covered with sensors and the circuits of the targeting and firing systems. The lidar alarm sounded with a grating wheezing sound, somewhat reminiscent of the sound of long unoiled metal hinges. After a few moments, the sound stopped, replaced by a steady beeping.

"Admiral, we have company. Six units." Said the gunner. "The distance is one million eight hundred thousand kilometers and decreasing. Three thousandths of a light, coming at a thirty-degree angle."

"Didn't I say so?" Tsugawa groaned. "I felt they had an ace up their sleeve..."

"What ships are these, Sergeant?" Kravchenko asked.

"It's impossible to determine at the moment, Admiral, but not very big." The cocoon moved, rows of numbers and symbols began to move on one of the screens. "There are traces of nickel in the emission spectrum, which means they use fusion reactors."

"Missile corvettes," Tsugawa said. "Or torpedo ships. Get moving, for fuck's sake!" he growled at passing technicians who were chatting towards his console. The men, astonished by this unexpected outburst of anger from the usually phlegmatic Sigilian, jumped as if burned. One of them dropped a toolbox he was carrying under his arm. The heavy container hit the floor with a bang.

Tsugawa shook his head disapprovingly, then moved his gaze to the main screen, where a tactical map of this part of the solar system was already displayed, generated based on lidar readings. The current position of the Fleet was marked on it, as well as the orbits of the largest asteroids held in the grip of Jupiter's gravity. The visualization of a huge planet in the form of a multi-colored ball occupied the upper left corner of the screen.

"The ones below?" Asked the admiral, pointing with his hand to several points of light, surrounded by a red border and moving diagonally from the direction of Jupiter towards the flotilla grouped in an irregular circle.

"Yes, Admiral," confirmed the gunner. "It's possible that there are more of them, because I still have a few faint echoes, but they could also be asteroids."

"Please check it," Kravchenko ordered. "Enough of these surprises." He pressed the button that activated the command recording system.

"To all units! We are off ten degrees from the ecliptic plane. Delta formation. I repeat, ten degrees from the ecliptic plane. Delta formation," he recited into the recorder before turning off the device.

"Please connect me to the Hercules," he said towards the communications station. "You, Commander, will develop a plan to intercept these tricksters with our rear guard."

"Yes, sir," Tsugawa bowed his head.

3

Cruiser "Frontier"
The Epsilon Eridani planetary system

The cabin that Lupos had assigned to Ian looked as if it had never had an occupant before. The bunk, which was pulled out from a recess in the wall, was covered with a factory-made tarpaulin, and the furniture, luxurious by the standards of a battleship, in the form of a bucket-shaped armchair covered with soft foam, a round table with a transparent top and a small corner sofa, was pushed into one corner and covered with sheets of transparent, slightly dusty foil. The multimedia terminal's desktop and a large window-imitating screen occupying the entire wall were also covered with the same foil.

There were still plugs in the power sockets, and there were silver seal stickers on the control panel located next to the door. Ian tore them off carelessly and then pressed the buttons that activated the lighting, air conditioning and the display itself.

On one of the walls, a vast plain was visible, covered with tall, dark-brown vegetation, the blades of which ended with slender blades resembling terrestrial cattail flowers, swaying slowly in the wind. Puffy, yellow-orange clouds floated across the amaranth sky. Far on the horizon were rocky crags, high, jagged peaks, marked with tongues of pinkish ice flowing down the slopes like sparkling, pinkish lava. In the center of the panorama, just above the horizon, between two mountain peaks, the shield of Epsilon Eridani glowed with a dull glow.

Ian smiled at the sight. "Omua Archipelago," he thought. He walked up to the wall and ripped off the foil protecting the screen with a strong tug.

The image immediately gained depth, the colors became more vivid, the waving patches of alien and yet so familiar grass seemed to be within reach, so real that he wanted to brush them with his fingers to feel that characteristic, rough and damp texture that he remembered from childhood spent on Aegir.

Instead, he moved the image with a fluid movement of his hand.

The plain and snow-capped peaks disappeared immediately, giving way to domed buildings made of rough-hewn stone surrounded by floodwaters, with rows of greenhouses between them - low, glass buildings, surrounded by pillars several dozen meters high, each of which was topped with a panel with powerful spotlights mounted on it.

From the buildings there were wide, stone-paved paths leading to the largest dome, on the flattened top of which, serving as a landing zone, stood the stocky, short-winged silhouettes of stratospheric transports.

A few hundred meters behind the estate, connected to it by a high causeway reinforced with steel plates, a slender, soaring structure rose high into the sky. From its wide base to the spire-topped apex spiraled serpentine strands of gigantic pipes and cables. From this tangle, funnel-shaped tubes protruded every few dozen meters, pumping a life-giving mixture of nitrogen and oxygen into the atmosphere. The top of the terraformer flickered constantly, striking the sky with zigzags of electrical discharges, thus creating the first seeds of the ozone layer, which in the next few hundred years could even more effectively protect AEgir's atmosphere from the wrath of its parent star.

He moved the image even further.

This time, the screen showed a concrete quay, along which flat-bottomed barges were anchored, rocking steadily on the turbulent surface of the Omua Sea, dotted with patches of greenish foam - the largest natural body of water on the planet, comparable in size to Earth's oceans. Some of the boats were loaded to the brim with crushed rock up to their steel sides, while others were stacked with containers. At the edge of the anchorage, a mobile launch platform was swinging on large floats, held in place by chains attached to thick concrete pillars. On its plate, trapped in the steel clamps of the launcher, gleamed the cylindrical hull of a space bulk carrier with the familiar logo on the main engine nozzle.

"Colonel Ian Dressler is requested to the loading deck at Lock Two!" suddenly sounded from the loudspeaker above the door.

He looked at the chronometer and sighed. He wasted almost a quarter of an hour admiring the views from his home planet.

He turned off the screen, quickly freed the furniture from its covers and, panting with effort, set it up in the cabin. He haphazardly pushed the rolled-up foil under the bunk. After a moment's thought, he also activated the personal terminal and used it to issue commands to the cleaning machine and the miniature sanitary machines, a herd of which were parked in a rounded alcove in the corner of the cabin. The devices, little larger than your thumb, scattered in all directions with the hum of tiny servo motors, leaving paths of sparkling clean floor behind them.

A moment later, the door to the quarters opened and a full-size cleaning machine entered. Sweeping the room with its scanner beam, it circled it before stopping in front of Ian. A panel slid out of a slot in the body, displaying a list of detailed commands to be accepted by the user. Without reading too much into their content, he marked all the items and then went out into the corridor. The door closed behind him with a quiet hiss.

Walking towards the elevators, he buttoned up his uniform shirt and tightened his plasma gun holster belt. The weapon taken from the habitat was heavier than the standard one and tightened the belt around the hip, which caused the transversely placed angular gas tank to hit the thigh with every step.

The crew members greeted Ian with friendly smiles, one intern even saluted, although quite irregularly, because to his uncovered head, but somehow, he didn't feel like scolding the young man for it, and what's more, he returned the greeting in the same way, placing four straight fingers on his forehead. The boy was bursting with pride.

In the hangar, even though the combat emergency had been canceled, it was still buzzing like a beehive. The room, one hundred meters long and fifty meters wide, was filled with stacks of crates of large-caliber kinetic ammunition, arranged in neat pyramids with large cylinders in which, until recently, high-octane plasma artillery mixture had been sloshing around. Against one of the walls, rocket launcher modules, emptied of their deadly cargo, protruded in a single row. Amidst this mess were autonomous transport carts, self-propelled disassembly machines, and technical staff dressed in bright orange protective suits.

"Lock number two?" Ian shouted to the nearest of them, trying to cover the terrifying whistling of the devil, who was cutting through an element as thick as a man's forearm, connecting two, apparently 100-liter bottles of some mixture. A beam of sparks bursting from under the diamond blade showered a luminous cascade onto the nearby automatic reloading machine, marking the pristine white body of the machine with dots of heat-burnt black.

Without stopping his work, the man pointed his head towards the pile of metal containers at the other end of the hall, to which another container was just being added by an automaton. At the base of the landfill, set on a diagonal scaffolding, a conveyor belt rotated. Its corrugated conveyor belt disappeared into a dark, square hole in the wall. A technician was crouched next to the conveyor belt, under the steel roof covering the control panel, watching the machine's display.

The entrance to the airlock was a few meters away, right next to the circular inlet of the ventilation duct. Two men stood by him, one in a vacuum suit, the other in only a light field uniform, with an old-fashioned canvas bag slung over his shoulder.

Ian recognized Lieutenant Moss immediately. Taking care not to get hit by any of the transport carts, he quickly made his way through the maze of containers and crates.

"Good to see you, Colonel." The officer smiled when he saw him. "We're just finishing loading the kinetics." He pointed to the pyramid of boxes. More ammunition containers were already standing on the temporarily stopped conveyor belt.

"Corporal Marlow and his team here." Moss gave the man in the suit a friendly pat on the shoulder, then made a wide circle with his hand. "They installed several amenities on your ship and, most importantly, they cleaned up the plating of the torpedo modules."

"Amenities?" Ian looked at the mechanic.

"What amenities..." Marlow waved his hand, although there was a hint of pride in a job well done in his voice. "We uploaded new software, cleaned the components of the life support system, and also tidied up the main torpedo compartment. Do you know that there were two torpedoes in it, and they were armed?"

"What?!" Ian's eyes widened. A shiver ran down his spine. He remembered the dust- and rust-covered metal bushings his travel container had banged against as they took off from the doomed habitat.

"They were stuck in the side feeders. If there were mass sensors in the compartment, you would be atomized when the main engine started."

"Mother Earth..." Moss groaned.

43

"I don't know who got this ship and from where, but if I were you, I would kick their asses and then send them to a several-month training course," said the corporal with disgust.

"Preferably to one of the dismantling stations in the asteroid belt," added Moss.

"Um..." Ian frowned. "I know who inventoried this vault and you can be sure that I will have a proper talk with him at the first opportunity."

There was a loud clang behind him - a cartridge with anti-tank flechettes landed on the conveyor belt.

"Do you want to see your ride?" Marlow asked, pointing to the airlock control panel built into the wall, of which the display screen was an integral part. "I'll switch to the camera view."

He walked to the console and turned the switch.

The monitor showed the underside of the cruiser, illuminated by the position lights, and a fragment of its armored vertical fin, which was the scaffolding for the lower maneuvering engine. It was to the base of the fin, or more specifically to the large hooks bolted to massive titanium plates, that the torpedo ship was moored.

The forty-meter-long hull, looking a bit like a conglomeration of metal cubes, was connected to the cruiser's side with two wide tubing sleeves and countless cables and wires, the strands of which disappeared into the service slots between the flaps of the cruiser's skin.

Around the torpedo ship, the repair machines, which had already been turned off, were floating on lifelines.

"We have filled the gaps in the reactive armor," said Marlow, pointing with his gloved hand to the middle, largest module of the torpedo ship, on the walls of which there was an irregular mosaic of shiny new rounded plates. "Everything is shiny inside too. Well, almost everything. In one of the ammunitions chambers we installed a sanitary module and a kitchen machine, quite well stocked." He added proudly.

Staring at the screen, Ian smiled with approval, remembering the patches of rust and fragments of catches that had recently fallen on his head when he opened the hatch to the torpedo compartment for the first time, and the sad remains of the equipment in the social module.

"Ready, Colonel?" Moss placed his hand on the airlock lever.

"Of course." Ian felt in his suit pockets, checking if he had the most necessary items with him. The mission assigned to him by the commander was neither complicated nor particularly time-consuming, which is why he decided to leave most of his belongings on the cruiser.

The airlock door opened silently, cold air and clouds of chemical-laden decontamination steam gushed out from the interior, lit by the harsh light of ultraviolet lamps, and after a few moments they were absorbed by the fans placed on both sides of the entrance.

"And what are these new customs?" Ian wondered, taking a step back to avoid contact with the swirling vapor. Lieutenant Moss also withdrew.

"Radiation," Marlow explained, lowering his helmet's visor. Dew drops immediately settled on its mirror surface. "Epsilon

Eridani is having more and more hiccups, including the annihilation of the habitat and drive core of the Oumuamua. The entire sector is sizzling with high-energy particles," he said in a muffled voice.

"So, I'll need a spacesuit?" Ian grimaced. The flight could take up to a dozen hours, long enough for physiological needs to make themselves felt, and he hated all those tubes stuck into his body orifices.

"Unfortunately. The PF-2 does not have electromagnetic emitters or anti-radiation shields," Marlow replied.

"So, why the hell do I need a toilet?" Ian grumbled sourly.

"Of course, you can take off the suit when you... um... need." Marlow shrugged. "But then you need a solid renewing treatment."

"What intensity?" Ian asked.

"Five sieverts," the corporal informed, looking at the readings of the meter sewn into the sleeve of the suit.

"Not so bad."

"Five per hour."

"It's been worse."

"But it's here, Colonel. At the lock."

"You're only saying this now?!" Moss was the first to react, jumping back as if he had been scalded and almost falling over one of the crates.

"Relax, Lieutenant, it's just airlock emissions," Marlow laughed. He walked up to the entrance and pointed to a rack of suits standing in the corner of the room.

"You'll have to get into these clothes quickly, because it's even worse in the connector." He said to Ian. "Of course, you will be able to relax on board from time to time, so to speak, but please be careful about it. Be very careful," he emphasized. "The ship has been exposed to radiation for some time, so even when you leave the hottest area, the plating will continue to emit radiation for a long time. We polluted a really large piece of space with this collision."

"I will remember about this." Ian assured, and then walked decisively into the sparkling frosted interior of the chamber.

A few minutes later, wrapped in a vacuum suit, he squeezed through the concertina tunnel connecting both units and entered, or rather crawled through, a narrow emergency hatch into the front module of the torpedo boat, where the pilot's cabin was located. Sitting in his chair, he first checked the readings of the measuring equipment, seeing with his own eyes that the corporal's warnings about extremely high levels of radiation were not exaggerated.

He spent the next minutes checking the combat systems and diagnostics of the propulsion system, especially the maneuvering engines, whose rounded bodies from the very beginning, that is, from the moment he first saw the torpedo boat in the maintenance hangar of Habitat Four, looked much more worn out than the rest of the components.

Taking advantage of the fact that the torpedo ship's logic circuits were still connected to the cruiser's computers, he downloaded detailed data on the current position of objects detected by the Frontier in the sector, then activated the lidar and then initiated the extrapolation process.

The screens on the control panel immediately lit up with colorful charts of predicted trajectories and columns of astrolocation data, updated continuously based on the results of lidar scanning.

While he was checking the data, an automatic welding machine flew majestically through the cabin window and was being pulled onto the deck of the cruiser. Electrodes placed at the end of the robot's manipulators grazed the torpedo ship's hull, tearing off one of the armor plates installed by the repair teams. The composite patch stuffed with explosive floated into space, only to disappear from view after a while.

"I'm sorry, Colonel!" Marlow's voice crackled through the helmet's headphones. "The tow cable is loose. I have a few more machines there, I'll send one of them to fix the defect."

Ian leaned towards the glass to look at the damage. In the gap between the tiles, the metal of the actual plating gleamed with dirty silver.

"There's no need, Corporal," he said after a moment. "It's just one small board." Just in case, he glanced over his shoulder at the shiny new fault indicator panel installed above the entrance to the cabin. The lights on it glowed a calming green.

"Then I'm bringing the robots on board," replied the mechanic. "Please close the internal bulkheads, the transport tubes will be disconnected in a few minutes. The closing panel can be found in the left armrest. After unmooring, please leave on the lower maneuvering engine, otherwise you will burn a hole in our decking."

"Hydrazine?" Ian guessed immediately. He already knew why the casings and nozzles of the torpedo ship's maneuvering engines were in such a appalling condition and why the ship, instead of parking in a safe, shielded escort hangar, moored outside, with its bow part facing the cruiser's transverse axis."

"That's right." The corporal confirmed his suspicions. "Someone really improvised a lot when renovating this ship. I wonder how on earth he intended to legalize this makeshift solution. After all, this PF-2 reactor is not original, removed from some gunship and incompatible with the cooling system. You have no idea how lucky you were that the Frontier was nearby when you started your flight. Your core would melt within hours. Of course, I replaced everything needed and now everything should run like clockwork. Please just keep an eye on the memory bank. It's completely clogged with some encrypted crap that couldn't be deleted. There are only a few percent of free space left. After your return, we will replace the memory chips with new, factory-clean ones."

"Thank you, Sergeant." Ian looked around the cabin. The room was about six meters square, most of which was taken up by the control panel and two bucket-shaped, well-worn foam seats, their high backs touching the rear wall to which the safety harnesses were attached. The wall itself, covered with a dirty gray laminate, was covered with a spider's web of chaotically stretched multi-colored wires and cables, provisionally attached with metal staples embedded in the laminate. Here and there there were darker rectangles and stripes, traces of devices dismantled by the engineering team. "Good job," he praised.

"Well, it's just a quick fix, Colonel. If we had more time and more spare parts, we would have tart it up for you in a flash."

"It still looks a lot better than before."

"It will also work much better, you'll see."

"I believe it, Corporal. And thank you again."

"Anytime at your service, Colonel," Marlow laughed. "The machines have already been taken away," he added after a while. "I start the collar folding procedure. Please secure the compartments."

The headphones crackled again, followed by the click of the microphone turning off. The fragment of the connector visible through the glass, through which Ian had boarded the torpedo boat, suddenly collapsed in on itself, and the warning lamps on its openwork stiffening flashed with pulsating red.

The colonel raised the upper part of the armrest and activated the bulkhead lowering mechanisms, and then strapped himself into the seat - after releasing the mooring handles, the gravity beam would also be turned off, and he was not particularly happy about the prospect of bouncing around the cockpit like a ball.

As he fastened the last buckle, the ship trembled slightly, as if it had been nudged from underneath. The light from the cruiser's position lamps pouring into the cabin changed from bright white to creamy yellow, the metal sheets creaked under Ian's feet, and then there was the terrible creaking of the mechanism that pulls the telescopic rods of the bow mooring lines into the interior of the torpedo ship.

Shortly thereafter, the Frontier's systems announced the shutdown of the gravity beam and then sent a long list containing standard guidelines for the unmooring procedure.

Mindful of the sergeant's suggestion, he started the lower maneuvering engine, quickly adjusted the nozzle setting, and then, by gently adjusting the fuel flow into the combustion chamber, guided the torpedo boat a safe distance from the cruiser's side and the huge fin protruding from it.

The crackling of static echoed through the headphones again. After a few moments, the commander's voice broke through.

"How's the ship doing, Colonel? Did the mechanics do a good job?"

"I'm impressed." He replied completely honestly. "Marlow knows his stuff."

"Excellent. The frigates are already moving into position. I informed Captain Sellige that you would be joining his squadron. In a moment, you will receive the target coordinates and a dedicated communication channel with the formation. Good luck."

"Thank you." Ian brought up the operational message log on the screen. The file with data regarding the current and target position of the ships it was supposed to protect was at the top of the list, marked with the "Urgent" clause. He opened it and copied the data into the navigation system's memory.

"Coordinates accepted," he announced, but received no response. Perhaps it was drowned out by crackling static, or maybe Lupos had simply hung up.

It didn't matter much at this point. After checking that the harness buckles were tight, he reached for the main drive actuator panel.

4

Cruiser "Pandemonium"
The Solar System

"Admiral, the Hercules reports that enemy units have begun to slow down." Commander Tsugawa, sitting at the communications desk, took off his headphones and looked longingly at his console, which was still dismembered by the mechanics.

An experimental model of a holographic projector, in which the patent with hygroscopic vapor as a background for the projected three-dimensional image was used for the first time, turned out to be fatal to the delicate electronics of devices installed at the station. According to the technicians' diagnosis, the moist mist caused a series of micro-short circuits in the components, which in turn damaged over eighty percent of the electronic circuits. Virtually everything had to be replaced, including the central unit.

"Torpedo ships, there is no other option." Said Kravchenko. "They are getting ready to fire the first salvo. Frigates or corvettes would fire at us while running, without activating the braking engines. What exactly are they aiming at?" he asked, while enlarging the visualization of the training camp on the main screen.

"Mainly in the Hercules, but I also have signals from Naomi. There are several beams following them," Tsugawa reported. "Captain Invald requests permission to open fire." He added, smiling slightly.

A smile also appeared on Kravchenko's previously gloomy face. Eighty-year-old Jorge Invald, who had been the commander of the cruiser Hercules - the oldest combat ship in the system - for almost half a century, was famous for his temperament and tenacity.

"I refuse. The Naomi and the Hercules are to move to the centre of the formation immediately," the admiral said, staring at the screen. "Fill the gap with escort searchers. Activate electromagnetic jamming."

Tsugawa's fingers danced across the keyboard. The triangular formation visible on the screen, composed of symbols designating individual units of the flotilla, slowly began to lose its regular shape. One of its sides collapsed inward as the ships and their auxiliaries designated by the admiral moved toward the centre. Shortly afterwards, a group of dots broke off from one of the peaks, and one by one they arranged themselves in a semicircle in the resulting gap, further distorting the original arrangement.

"To all units! Directional emitters, full power!" Ordered the admiral. Despite the clearly unfriendly attitude of the local authorities, he still did not want to go down in history as the one who started the first inter-system fratricidal war in history, so to neutralize the enemy torpedo ships he decided to use the method used by the Skunian interception probes, which involves paralyzing enemy ships by blinding them with series of strong electromagnetic pulses.

The clicking of the keys grew louder, and when it stopped, the lights on the bridge dimmed, the hum of the air conditioning changed in intensity, and bands of static appeared on the video screens.

"Electromagnetic beams emitted." Reported the weapon system operator.

"I confirm." Tsugawa was writing something quickly with an electronic stylus on the display of the handheld terminal.

"Repeat emissions every two minutes until we jump out of torpedo range!" Kravchenko ordered.

He reduced the image on the screen so that it also showed the location of the ships tracking the flotilla. The distance between the intruders and the group at the bottom of the screen continued to decrease, although not at the same rate as a few minutes earlier. At the same time, the angle at which enemy units came increased.

"This could really work..." Tsugawa muttered. He too was staring intently at the main screen.

"Correction, Commander, it will definitely work." Kravchenko said boastfully. "Old Skunk trick. Blind, disorient, fuck up and run!"

"Shall we shoot at them?" Tsugawa blinked in surprise.

"Of course not! Someone in this messed up system needs to show some common sense. Oh yes, I would have forgotten..." Kravchenko reached into the compartment under the desktop and took out a disc of graphene wrapped in foil and sealed with seals.

"Please submit an official protest to the local authorities and send it via diplomatic capsule. My certified powers of attorney are on the disk. Please attach them to your correspondence." He threw the item to Tsugawa. "The probe and capsule are to be launched directly to their main mail station, wherever that may be, before we reach the Fold."

"I'll figure it out." The commander nodded, entering the command into the system. After a while, he put on the headphones again and listened with furrowed eyebrows to the reports from both cruisers targeted by the torpedo ships.

"The Naomi moved out of the range of enemy lidars, the Hercules records only single signals at random intervals. The same applies to the remaining units. It seems that we are slowly disappearing from their screens," he said.

"Fry them to resist!" Kravchenko raised his clenched fist in triumph. "Everything will start to sizzle!"

Before his words had finished, the light on the bridge dimmed again.

"Reduce the intervals to sixty seconds."

"Still full power?" The gunner made sure.

"Yes."

"Admiral, we will overload the emitters!" Tsugawa warned, gesturing to the screens around the gunner's cocoon. The bars showing the temperature of the membranes focusing the electromagnetic beams were dangerously close to the limit values.

Kravchenko followed his gaze.

"We have to take the risk," he replied. "Electronic warfare, like any other, also requires sacrifices, Commander," he commented sententiously, shifting his gaze to the main screen. "Once we disable these units, there will be no stopping us."

"You're forgetting about the fortifications at the Fold," Tsugawa muttered. He used the stylus to point to dots marked with blood-red "X" symbols in the corner of the main screen, forming a large arc surrounding the curvature of the discontinuity boundary.

"So full power?" The gunner made sure. Fiber optics sewn into the fabric of his gloves slowly lit up with a web of threads of light.

"Yes. The order also applies to the rest of our units. Do we understand each other, Commander?" He threw over his shoulder to Tsugawa, clearly dissatisfied with this decision.

"Yes, sir." Confirmed the commander and started sending out the latest guidelines, although with slightly less enthusiasm.

A few minutes later, radiation beams shot towards the enemy units, overloading their sensors, burning out the delicate circuits of nuclear warheads and causing short circuits in electronic components not adapted to operate in the conditions of strong flares.

Unfortunately, as Tsugawa predicted, there were some losses and when the flotilla was out of enemy range, the admiral's terminal was literally flooded with messages about emitter failures and requests to send repair teams. Without hesitation, Kravchenko sent the entire litany directly to the server of the repair ship "Tip", leaving the entire mess to its commander,

Captain Karpinski. Soon, service aircraft with two-person technical teams poured out from the deck of the trawler into space and, rhythmically flashing the nozzles of their correction engines, flew towards the units requesting technical assistance.

"I warned you..." sighed Tsugawa, seeing on the screen a swarm of dots pouring out from the hangars of the repair ship. Kravchenko just snorted dismissively.

"Distance from the edge of the anomaly, eighteen million kilometres," one of the navigators reported.

"Admiral, this large battleship has begun to accelerate." Said the gunner. "I think he wants to intercept us."

"Дальшеотних, дальшеотдома, нас недогонят, нас недогонят[1]", Kravchenko hummed in the language of his ancestors, falsifying mercilessly. Ignoring the surprised looks of those closest to him, he turned his chair towards the communications desk. "Commander," he said to Tsugawa, "please inform all units that in... in..." he paused for a moment, calculating something in his head. "In about..."

"Eight hours and twenty minutes, Admiral," the navigator replied helpfully.

"Thank you, Corporal." Kravchenko nodded. "Well, we'll be through the Fold in eight hours." He continued. "If local guard installations open fire on us, do not take offensive actions under any circumstances. I repeat, no offensive actions. I only authorize the use of defense systems, and even then, only in the event of a

---

[1] "The farther away from them, farther from home, they won't catch up with us, they won't catch up with us" (author's note).

real threat. No kinetic shields, laying minefields or opening covering fire. Did you make a note?"

"Yes, Admiral." Tsugawa's stylus whizzed across the matte terminal screen at a dizzying speed, tracing neat lines of *kana*[2]writing, which were then converted by the translation system into English and sent to individual ships.

"I understand that the Ukulele is being removed from the register?" The commander asked at one point, looking up. His slanted eyes turned into slits, and a muscle in his right cheek twitched nervously.

"Unfortunately, yes..." Kravchenko sighed. "Nevertheless, I give you my officer's word that they will pay us dearly for this ship. I assure you of that. In the meantime, Commander, your watch is over. Please get your signalmen here."

Tsugawa bowed his head, then gathered his things and headed towards the exit.

"And please prepare a protest note as soon as possible. The capsule must be launched before we pass through the Fold!" The admiral called after him.

After a few minutes, a full set of operators were seated in the four chairs placed around the communications console. The panels of the transmitting and receiving systems, which had previously only been flashing with a few diodes, gradually lit up with more and more of them as the radio operators launched subsequent modules and activated the communication channels

---

[2]The common name for the Japanese syllabic alphabets hiragana and katakana (author's note).

which, like a spider's web, were to connect the individual ships of the group together from then on.

When the last panel flashed with a set of signals, the long-awaited message appeared on Kravchenko's terminal about the start of the automatic chain of command harmonization system, an inhumanly complicated algorithm developed on the basis of software obtained from captured Skunian interceptor probes.

From that moment on, each order issued by the commander-in-chief was to be properly identified by the artificial intelligence coordinating the system, converted into commands and instructions corresponding to its content, and then sent by radio to the appropriate recipients in real time, bypassing official communication channels.

"Admiral, this smaller unit fired on the Ukulele," the gunner said in a sepulchral voice.

Kravchenko rested his head against the headrest and closed his eyes.

"They'll pay for it." He said in a low voice. "Do we still have a preview?" He asked without opening his eyes.

"There's a signal from the orbiter." Replied the shooter. "Thirty second delay."

"To the main screen!" Kravchenko ordered. "And tell me the location from which this piece of crap was broadcasting, I mean McReady!" He turned to the communications officers. "I want to have accurate bearings and, if possible, a scan of the entire location. If necessary, sweep the area with a quantum telescope. I won't forgive him this!" He drawled; a bit quieter.

"Yes, sir!" The operator sitting closest saluted. The remaining three hurriedly plugged portable directional antenna controllers into the sockets so that they could constantly correct the position of the large receiving dishes mounted on the cruiser's side fins.

Meanwhile, an image of a demolished Ukulele appeared on the main screen. Until recently, the ship's slender, shark-like silhouette was now deformed, devoid of fins, both the smaller side fins and the longest lower one, of which only the remnants of trusses and shreds of bent titanium sheet torn by explosions remained. The main drive nozzle outlets turned into large, dark wells with jagged edges, from which clouds of smoke and sheaves of sparks flowed into space, quickly extinguishing in the vacuum.

In front of the shocked Kravchenko's eyes, the bow part of the cruiser's hull separated in a cloud of fragments and rolled slowly into the void. Three rockets pursued it, maneuvering nimbly through the tail of debris trailing behind it.

"Motherfuckers..." He whispered, seeing subsequent missiles taking off from the launchers of the spherical ship attacking the cruiser and rushing towards the target, only to hit the already mortally wounded ship right amidships.

"Turn it off!" The admiral growled at the gunner.

Before the screen went dark, he managed to notice a bright white point shot from somewhere under the cruiser's belly and hitting the enemy ship. The dying unit managed to bite its tormentor with one last leap.

"Plasma howitzer," said the gunner, who also noticed it. "One of the automatic fire systems has been activated, I don't see any other possibility."

"And very well." Commented Kravchenko. "It's a pity more of them didn't work."

"Admiral, we have located the transmitter from which the calls to stop were issued and from which Constable McReady was communicating with us," the communications officer announced. "It's quite close."

The Admiral turned his chair towards him.

"Where?" He asked in a dull voice.

"Wait a minute..." The man switched something on the desktop and then pointed to the main display.

"Quadrant three, upper left quarter. Object number six," he said, enlarging the appropriate part of the screen.

"Installation type?" Kravchenko got up from his seat, walked into the middle of the room and stood in front of the display.

"I'm sending the coordinates to the navigation section." Informed the signalman.

"Data accepted." The head of astronavigation reported from his position. "I'm starting the scanning system."

Somewhere off to the side there was the steady beeping of a long-range lidar beeper.

"Total return beam delay, plus twenty seconds."

While waiting for the scan results, Kravchenko reached into his uniform pocket and took out a crumpled and clearly depleted pack of cigarettes, then, ignoring the disapproving looks of the navigators sitting nearby, he inhaled deeply of the throat-stinging, bitter smoke. The smoke exhaust fans on the bridge immediately hummed, and the fire alarm light came on on his own console. He ignored that too, just as he ignored the flock of miniature sanitary bots that suddenly swarmed out of nowhere at his feet to collect the particles of ash falling to the floor.

"There is a specification." Announced the head of navigation. "Stationary facility, one residential module, two technical modules, total volume of one thousand five hundred cubic meters, calculated on the basis of external outlines. Estimated weight, three hundred and fifty tons, not including external fuel tanks."

A diagram of the station appeared on the screen. The structure consisted of three hexagonal modules arranged in a star shape, rotating around a spherical center bristling with antennas and sensors. All three modules were connected to each other by a tangle of wires and grids, resembling a spider's web.

"Two impulse correction engines," the navigator continued. "The central hub is rotated by an internal rotor, most likely powered by a fusion reactor."

"Defense systems?" Kravchenko walked even closer to the screen and, tilting his head, looked carefully at the installation diagram.

"I don't see anything that even vaguely resembles a blaster or launcher," came the reply. "It's quite an outdated design, Admiral. It is possible that it was adapted into a guard station from some decommissioned research facility that still remembers the beginnings of the colonization of this region."

"Are you able to determine how many people are there?"

"Unfortunately, not. If we were a little closer, we could x-ray the module using a conventional, concentrated electromagnetic beam. In fact, you can do it even now, but you won't get clear reflections, and the effect will be to fry the electronics. However, judging by the volume of the residential module and the size of the technical modules, a maximum of two, and possibly three people stay there permanently. Not more."

"Wait a minute..." Kravchenko slowly turned towards the interlocutor. "You said we could fry their electronics?"

The section chief nodded.

"Of course. As I mentioned, the station is very outdated, poorly shielded, and does not have electromagnetic shields. At this distance from the star, the solar wind ceases to be dangerous, and they are protected from cosmic radiation on the one hand by the Fold, and on the other by Jupiter and its magnetic field." He pointed to the front viewfinder window, where a fragment of the gas giant's shield was visible.

"Perfect..." Kravchenko's face lit up in a predatory smile. "Perfect..." he repeated. He returned to his chair and turned on the intercom.

"Commander, please attend the bridge." He said into the microphone, then looked towards the neighbouring desk.

"Connect me to Captain Karpinski," he ordered the signalmen, reaching for the headphones.

A few moments later, the mustachioed face of the commander of the repair trawler appeared on the console display, visible against the background of a spacious warehouse filled with large-sized equipment and transport carts moving among them.

"Yes, Admiral?"

"How long will it take to repair the emitters?"

Karpinski glanced over his shoulder, then lifted the portable terminal closer to his face and checked something on it.

"We simply replaced the most damaged ones with new ones," he replied. "It will take a few more hours to make those that can be repaired operational again."

"I understand that the ones mentioned can now be used?"

"Absolutely, Admiral. However, I warn you that our reserve of parts is running out and we do not have any replacements. Another action like this and most of the fleet will be left without protection."

"I'll keep that in mind, Captain."

"One more thing..." Karpinski hesitated for a moment, then glanced at the screen again.

"Yes?"

"We have a problem with transporting components to other ships. The group is moving too fast, the transports are barely catching up with the target units. We have already lost two vehicles with their cargo, fortunately unmanned."

"How so?"

"They stayed behind, Admiral. At their current speed, there is no way they will be able to catch up with the group before reaching the Fold."

This time Kravchenko became lost in thought.

"Slowing down the formation is not an option..." he said after a moment's thought. "How big are these units?"

"Regular shuttles, Admiral, but with slightly larger than standard cargo compartments. Thirty meters."

"So, they would fit in the cruiser's hangars?"

Karpinski's face, previously a bit gloomy, suddenly lit up with a smile.

"Of course, Admiral. Do you want to take them on your ship?" He asked with hope in his voice.

"Possibly." Confirmed Kravchenko. "Apart from the Ukulele, only the Pandemonium does not have power limiters and can catch up with the group in an emergency."

"Exactly!" The captain was happy. "I will immediately order the operators to upload the appropriate docking protocols to these units and make course corrections."

"Not so fast, Captain," the admiral stopped him. "I need to consult this with the propulsion section and navigators first. In the meantime, please focus on the emitters. Understood?"

"Yes, sir!" Karpinski confirmed enthusiastically.

"You will receive the rest of the information electronically," Kravchenko said, then turned off the microphone and took off his headphones.

"I'll dance with you soon, bitch," he whispered, frowning at the still image of the guard station where Constable McReady was on the main screen.

5

Torpedo ship PF-2
The Epsilon Eridani planetary system

"Colonel Dressler to the squadron." Since the torpedo ship had not yet been included in the official register of ships of the Fleet, and had only been assigned a temporary number for the purposes of communication with the systems of the cruiser Frontier, when calling the frigates Ian was forced to use his surname and military rank, instead of the customary name and symbol of the unit, which he currently commanded. "I'm in position, you can start the operation."

According to the arrangements he had previously made with Captain Sellige, the frigates were to open fire on the Skunian wreck immediately after the torpedo ship had taken a position enabling it to detect and neutralize a potential threat that could be posed by the still active enemy battle positions.

"Understood." The slightly hoarse voice of the frigate commander sounded from the intercom loudspeaker. "We're approaching the wreck. Short-range missiles armed. Please highlight the targets, Colonel."

"I'm sending out probes." Ian activated the tracking system. At the same time, he lifted the front visor covers.

From this distance, the Oumuamua wreck looked like a shiny shard of glass suspended in the infinitely black void of space. If it weren't for the reference point in the form of the brown-grey disk of the Sigil moon, it would be difficult to guess that the wreck is still traveling at a speed of almost twenty thousand kilometres per second.

Miniature probes fired from the launchers attached to the torpedo ship and, dragging tails of ionized gas behind them, flew towards a target four kilometres away. A few dozen seconds later, the image of a drifting fragment of the Oumuamua, transmitted from the probe, appeared on the display on the side of the viewfinder.

"Probes in target." Ian informed, seeing on the screen a multitude of dots covering the cracked outer rock armor of the destroyed leviathan, full of larger and smaller craters.

"Eighty-seven sources of infrared radiation, mainly in the central part." He reported, while enlarging the image. "The main jets look cold, no emissions, no activity in the breakout area, hangar doors closed, ventilation duct outlets as well..." he calculated, slowly moving the image.

Along the surviving fragment of the alien ship's hull, there was a canyon stretching diagonally, several dozen meters deep, a monstrous scar in the stone armor, at the bottom of which the metal of the inner plating gleamed in the light of the searchlights. The sides of the canyon were smooth and glassy, the rock looking as if it had been carved by a giant hot blade. Ian immediately guessed that what he was looking at was nothing more than a trace of a ricocheting piece of neutron matter, the heart of the gravity compensator from Habitat Four. If it were not for this tiny particle weighing billions of tons, the relatively light and openwork structure of the habitat would not even scratch the compact, massive shape of the Oumuamua, let alone destroy it.

"What about the maneuvering jets?" Asked Sellige.

Ian rewinded the image, then examined the six protrusions of maneuvering jets sprouting from the rear of the wreck, resembling pointed rock spiers. Their tips also looked cold, but when he switched the view to infrared, it turned out that four of them were surrounded by a bright orange glow.

"They emit heat." He replied.

"Then we'll start with them." Said Sellige.

"That's right, Captain," Ian agreed. "And then the middle part. I can see kinetic launcher outlets there and what look like missile batteries."

He stared at a series of metal structures located in two recesses, on which dark, oblong objects with rounded tips were placed.

"I am sending the location and photo package."

"Damn, those are homing nuclear missiles." Sellige said after a few moments. "I've seen this before... Not good, very bad..." he sighed heavily.

"They don't look active.

"And they won't be until the Skunks set them off. It is an autonomous offensive system. See those lumps on the side of each of them?"

"Yes," Ian confirmed.

"These are correction engines. You can't dodge these types of missiles, and we don't have jamming systems, flares, decoys, or anything like that. We are only long-range artillery, not ships of the line."

"I'll keep an eye on them. My ammunition magazine is literally stuffed to the ceiling with kinetics. Don't worry, Captain," Ian reassured him, although he perfectly understood the captain's concerns. The Skunian homing missiles were equipped with self-learning software and sent information about a potential threat to each other. In this respect, they were somewhat similar to Hammers, except that they were more maneuverable and faster. "If necessary, I will set the launchers to continuous fire. No rocket will slip through."

"I'll take you up on that, Colonel. We're getting closer."

"I also shorten the distance." Ian tightened the harness straps, then set the main drive to the single, weakest impulse and pressed the ignition button.

The torpedo ship, which until then had been flying only by inertia, leapt forward, propelled by the energy of a controlled nuclear explosion.

The wreck behind the glass began to grow rapidly and after a dozen or so seconds it filled the entire field of view. A short time later, the braking jets spewed jets of plasma.

"I have completed the approach," Ian said.

The image on the main monitor screen, transmitted by the probes orbiting the wreck, sharpened and then covered with an additional coordinate grid as the devices activated wide-range optical scanners.

A message suddenly appeared on one of the smaller displays about the lack of space in the memory bank and the inability to save the data stream sent from the probes. Ian immediately remembered the mechanic's words about the need to replace the memory chips.

"Captain, I'm having trouble recording data," he said. "I will redirect the transmission directly to your servers."

"I see." Replied Sellige. "I'm sending you access codes. We also completed the approach. We'll finish arming the missiles in ten minutes."

"Perfect," Ian unbuckled his harness and quickly moved to the other seat to have easier access to the torpedo ship's operating system access panel located on the side wall of the cabin.

"I'm sending the data," he announced as the tiny display confirmed the connection to the frigates' computer systems.

"We have a signal." Confirmed Sellige.

There was silence in the headphones for the next few moments.

"There's so much there..." the captain finally said. "Survive such a collision... Amazing construction." There was genuine admiration in his voice.

"This is the Oumuamua." Ian replied. "Asteroid, fortress and city in one. Home to dozens of generations of Skunians," he recalled. "Theoretically indestructible," he added with a slight sarcasm.

"I wonder what size the next generation will be? Will they start digging into smaller moons?" Sellige wondered.

"They'd have to find one somewhere first. For now, we have herded them into a dark corner from which they will not escape anytime soon. If ever."

"Right is right, Colonel. The Autonomy and the Union have pulverized every major rock in the entire asteroid belt. You know what? I'm wondering if this ship wasn't heading to this new rubble site..."

"You mean the rubble behind the system? The one they recently sent a mining expedition to?"

"Yes. The Oumuamua was flying on a rather strange trajectory. Apparently straight towards AEgir, but if you look at it more closely, in the second phase, immediately after entering the sector, it corrected its course by about half a degree of angular latitude. A minimal difference, but enough to pass the planet and benefit from its gravity assist. I played around with the simulations a bit and found out that it would throw them directly towards the rubble, with double the original speed."

"Wait a minute..." Ian frowned. "You're saying that they had no intention of attacking the planet, that we panicked unnecessarily, and that all this..." He made a broad gesture, forgetting that the other wouldn't see it anyway. "The sacrifice of the habitat, the evacuation of the planet, all this fuss was unnecessary?"

"I didn't say that." Replied Sellige. "Nevertheless, the simulation results were different."

"Damn it!" Ian blurted out. "So many observers, buoys, defensive installations, everyone had this ship on their screens.

Has it occurred to anyone that this is not an attack at all, but just an attempt to leave the system? Mother Earth..."

"Commander Lupos mentioned something about this possibility, in the context of the Oumuamua potentially passing through the Fold into the Solar System. He was afraid that the passage of such a large object would exhaust its capacity and cut us off from Earth forever. Another thing is that the Skunians were quite bold when flying through the system, so the attitude of our services is hardly surprising. Besides, Colonel, my simulation was based on data obtained in the final phase of the operation, when the Skunians had already corrected their course."

At the same moment, a series of crackling noises were heard in the helmet's speakers. The signals on the torpedo ship's control panel lit up with all the colors of the rainbow. The screech of the loudspeakers penetrated even through Ian's thick helmet. At the same time, the coordinate grid generated by the targeting system based on data from probes disappeared from the tactical screen.

"Captain, their defense systems seem to have woken up. They're firing plasma cannons at my probes," he said, turning off the alarms one by one.

"I see it now," Sellige confirmed his observation. "That's what I was afraid of, among other things."

"I will withdraw the orbiters before they are all destroyed. Have you saved the results of your last scan?"

"Yes. We have detailed coordinates of all detected targets, plus some additional ones, including the main maneuvering engine lair. Even if we fail to ultimately disable the combat systems, we will deprive the wreck of the ability to maneuver. Then just push it off course and let it fly to its fucking death. Anyway, the missiles are armed, the first salvo in sixty seconds. Then we do a jump."

"Excellent." Ian also activated the weapons systems. The barrels of the plasma cannons mounted outside the hull turned towards the crippled Oumuamua, as did the mini-platforms with kinetic missile launchers mounted on the torpedo module.

"Rockets fired." Sellige announced. "We're starting the retreat."

Ian rose from his seat and, resting his elbows on the control console, put his face close to the visor, almost touching the glass with the iris of his helmet. Short-range missiles fired from the frigates were rushing towards the wreck, leaving behind pale blue trails of exhaust and ionized gas. To meet them, a cloud of blindingly white plasma beams and red-hot kinetic missiles suddenly erupted from the seemingly dead Skunian ship. A second later, the space around Oumuamua erupted in a hurricane of energy.

The flare was so intense that Ian was forced to activate the polarization of his helmet's diaphragm.

"Rockets on target," Sellige said. "I mean some of the rockets," he corrected immediately.

"How much exactly?" Ian asked, blinking rapidly in a vain attempt to clear the afterimages.

"Seventy percent. We move away to a safe distance."

"What about the maneuvering jets?" Although the afterimages were slowly dissipating, the cloud of gas and debris surrounding Oumuamua prevented Ian from making direct observations.

"It's hard to say, Colonel, it's a terrible mess, but for now the object is still moving on an unchanged course. There's a good chance we've incapacitated them for good."

Ian didn't answer. For several moments, he had been recording the rapidly changing numbers on the radiation detector display out of the corner of his eye. When he turned towards it, the device showed exactly ten sieverts. Ruby diodes were shining just above the screen, signaling the fourth, highest level of radiological threat.

"What type of warheads did you use, Captain?" Ian asked, trying to stay calm.

"Penetrating, with an enriched core. They have the highest penetration rate." Sellige explained. "What is it, Colonel?" He asked suspiciously.

"I'm not sure..." Ian climbed out from behind the console and opened the cabin door. The steel bulkhead slid aside with a grating sound that Ian didn't so much hear as feel as a slight vibration of the ground. "Either I flew into some radioactive cloud or I have a reactor leak."

"Contamination?" Sellige guessed.

"Putting it mildly."

"How much?"

"Ten and rising."

"Reactor leak, definitely," said the captain. "Our sensors show only a slight increase in radiation... With all due respect, Colonel, I saw the condition of the nozzles on your ship. I assume they replaced everything except them?"

"Reactor, yes. It was transferred from a gunship, as for the nozzles, I honestly have no idea..." With that, Ian entered a narrow, dimly lit corridor that led straight to the massive bulkhead separating the crew compartment from the propulsion module. "The technicians mentioned something about problems with the cooling system," he recalled Sergeant Marlow saying.

"Then I suggest you check the core temperature gauges. Cooling systems on gunships are just a joke. Anyway, I don't think I need to explain this to you."

"You don't have to," Ian confirmed, grimacing at the memory of the incredibly tight and oven-hot cockpit from which Larson had pulled him half-dead a few weeks earlier when he crash-landed his Skunian-damaged ship on Habitat Four's landing pad.

He backed out of the corridor and sat behind the control panel. Propulsion system status indicators confirmed the frigate commander's suspicions - the reactor core temperature was dangerously oscillating around critical values. The cooling system seemed to be working, but the instruments indicated a huge pressure drop in the lines supplying the cooling mixture. If it weren't for the emergency system of heat sinks, whose ribbed plates dissipated excess thermal energy straight into the vacuum, the drive module would probably now look like a lump of melted wax.

"You were right, Captain. The cooling system failed, the core chamber became unsealed, hence the increase in radiation. It looks pretty bad," he sighed, placing his hand on the lever that automatically releases the hooks that connect the drive module to the rest of the ship. "I have to discard the entire segment, otherwise it will melt my stern in a moment."

"Damn it!" This time Sellige cursed. "So, our protection is gone."

"I'm sorry, Captain. I won't be able to run combat systems without power. Fire what you have left and get out of here. I'll try to somehow drag myself to the nearest station using maneuvering engines. My fuel tanks are full."

"We can evacuate you," Sellige suggested, although without much enthusiasm.

"I appreciate that, but there is no need." Ian replied. "It's not a first time for me," he added, reflexively feeling the back of the suit. The dorsal muscle fibers regenerated in the medcom chamber could still tingle painfully, and from time to time he felt an unpleasant stinging sensation in his groin. "I have only one request."

"I'm listening."

"I don't have orbiters anymore, but I would like to have a view of the ship's stern from the outside."

"No problem." Said Sellige. "We will release a probe and transmit the transmission directly to you."

"I would be obliged. If I can get it right, I can drop that damn reactor right on the Skunks' heads."

"Two tons of fissile material!" Sellige almost choked. For a few seconds, the sound of dry coughing came from the headphones. "It'll be gigatons of energy..." he finally choked out. "Colonel, that's more than all our missiles combined! We will evaporate their entire external infrastructure on this boulder. This is... This is a great idea!"

"First I have to find a convenient position, and it won't be that easy," Ian cooled his enthusiasm, looking at the instruments.

The temperature in the reactor chamber continued to rise, messages about the failure of drive components began to appear one after another on the main screen, the dosimeter counter vibrated like crazy, and its electronic indicator displayed only bright red exclamation marks.

"We have you on our screens." Informed the squadron commander. "Broadcast in progress."

The silhouette of a torpedo ship appeared on the display, resembling from a distance a cluster of serially connected metal cubes of various shades, the most striking of which was the brand-new, steel-silver shape of the propulsion module, ending with spherical, armored outlets for pulsation nozzles.

"Can you take a close-up of the reactor module connector?" Ian asked, unsuccessfully trying to enlarge the image to check the condition of the hooks connecting the segment to the adjacent torpedo module box covered with a layer of reactive armor. On the sides of the latter, kinetic cannon domes and maneuvering engine bodies are located.

"Right away," Sellige replied. The image on the display sharpened and then enlarged. The fragment of the torpedo ship that Ian pointed to filled the entire screen.

"And how?"

"Looks like everything's fine. The catches show no signs of corrosion and the actuator cables are also intact. Even the optical indicator works..." leaning over the screen, Ian noticed a blue lamp pulsating near the largest clamp. The image was now so detailed that you could even see the wire mesh covering its shade.

"The maneuvering engines work perfectly," he added, glancing at the instruments. "Okay, let's try to throw this hot potato to the Skunks." He announced, starting one of the engines.

"Squadron in position. We fire the rest of the rockets and fly away." Sellige said in response. "Good luck, Colonel. Give them a solid kick."

"I'll do my best."

The fragment of Oumuamua visible behind the glass, shrouded in a cloud of fragments and crystals of frozen gas, moved slowly from left to right as the torpedo ship, pushed by the side thrust, turned towards it so that the rejected module could fall exactly on the central part of the enemy object. Once the wreck was out of sight, Ian turned off the side drive. The Oumuamua was now drifting almost directly astern of the torpedo ship, less than a kilometer away. The distance between him and the torpedo ship increased slowly, but gradually, as each and every last salvo of rockets hit it.

"Missiles on target," the captain announced once again. "We're going back to the meeting point."

Since he was broadcasting on a general channel, Ian wasn't entirely sure whether the information was addressed to him or to the commanders of individual units in the squadron. Without further delay, he forcefully pushed the lever that released the main drive section catches.

6

Cruiser "Frontier"
The Epsilon Eridani planetary system

"Commander, Captain Sellige's report has arrived!" Shouted Corporal Kulak, head of the communications department. "I'm sending it to your terminal."

Lupos blinked from his reverie, then straightened in his chair and turned on the console. The sloping tabletop immediately lit up with the glow of displays and diodes, and the three semicircular liquid crystal screens surrounding it also came to life.

"There is also a file with a video stream," said the signalman. "Unfortunately, it's damaged. I'll try to run it through compilers, maybe I'll be able to reproduce at least a fragment."

"There is no need for that," replied the commander, scrolling through the text of the received report on one of the screens. "Lieutenant," he motioned to Moss, who was chatting with engineer Sniegova, who was sitting at the propulsion console. "A report has arrived from the frigates," he announced as the officer approached. "They fired everything they had in the ammunition warehouses into Skunians and are retreating towards the Fold."

"What about the wreck?" Moss asked, glancing at the screen.

"It survived the shelling, but I think it eventually lost its drive. Now it's really just a piece of drifting rubble."

"I wouldn't be so sure about that, Commander. Skunians are masters of survival." Moss said grimly.

"They can be grandmasters, too," Lupos waved his hand dismissively. "Without resources, they won't last long on a damaged ship. There's something else that worries me, Lieutenant," he added, lowering his voice. "According to the report, Dressler's torpedo ship had a reactor leak. So serious that the colonel decided to reject the drive module."

"Not good." The officer became gloomy. "He won't be able to keep up with us on maneuvering engines. He will have to fly to AEgir, and it will take him several days. With life support systems not working, still in a suit... I don't envy..." He shuddered. "Why didn't they evacuate him?"

"They offered, but he refused," Lupos explained. "When he detached the reactor segment, they lost contact with him."

"That doesn't surprise me at all." Moss said. "In PF-2 units, the primary power source is the reactor. Also for communication systems."

"This isn't about communications, Lieutenant. Shortly after discarding the module, the torpedo ship disappeared from their screens. The probe they had nearby recorded the moment of detaching the module and starting the maneuvering engines, then it entered a cloud of some debris, and when it came out, the colonel's ship was no longer there. Either he collided with some debris or he was dragged down to the Oumuamua. Sellige is betting on the latter, because right after the probe went blind, they recorded several explosions on the surface of the wreck. Sellige says they looked like fuel tank explosions."

"The colonel landed on a wreck?!" Moss' face was stunned.

"He probably crashed..." Lupos sighed heavily. "What about that recording, Corporal?" He looked at Kulak.

"We are currently compiling them," replied the communications officer. "It will take some time because frigate recorders use old codecs. We have to convert all the files again, and there are quite a few of them."

"Sellige attached video footage of the operation to his report," the commander explained to Moss. "According to the report," he tapped the screen with his finger, "these explosions are also recorded on them."

"Heck!" Suddenly came an irritated growl from the communications station, accompanied by a repeating, melodic and rhythmic sound coming from the data compiler module. "It croaked out!"

"What's going on, Corporal?" Lupos walked up to the communications officer who was mumbling something under his breath.

"Compiler! First it froze, then it turned off, and now it won't start!"

Moss, who was listening to his words, glanced at Sniegova, who nodded, then stood up and swayed her hips towards the communications desk.

"Can I take a look?"

"Oh please!" Kulak took the headphones off his ears and angrily threw them on the console table. "Access code eight two eight," he said, rising from his chair.

The engineer thanked him with a slight smile.

"When you're done with this, transfer the file to my personal terminal," Lupos said, settling back at the command console.

"Lieutenant, I'm declaring a state of increased alert. Please get everyone in position. We're turning back!" He announced loudly.

"To the wreck?" Moss made sure.

"Correct. I already left the colonel to his fate once. There will be no repetition."

"Yes, sir!" The officer nimbly approached the position of the astronavigators to give them the appropriate instructions. Several minutes later, to the accompaniment of the terrible grinding noise of the inertia absorbers operating at full power, the cruiser slowed down and then, spewing blinding white jets of plasma ejected from the nozzles of the maneuvering engines, made a gentle turn.

"Initiate the pulse sequence!" Lupos ordered as soon as the ship was on course.

"Commander, the absorbers haven't had time to release energy yet!" the head of the propulsion section protested, pointing to one of the monitors. A series of vertical bars were displayed on the screen, showing the degree of compression of the energy-absorbing material. They were all red.

"They'll survive," Lupos said, not even looking back.

"The sergeant is right, Admiral," Sniegova supported the man. "The surplus energy will not only evaporate some of the absorbing cartridges, but will also be released into the environment. It's tearing holes in our roofing..." she was interrupted when there was a sudden loud crash behind her. "Can you hear that?" She asked, pointing behind her with her thumb.

The Commander confirmed with a reluctant nod.

Sniegova walked to the wall and, tilting her head, looked at one of the slabs. A small protrusion appeared on the mirror-smooth metal surface.

"The frame, fortunately one of the smaller ones, mid-deck..." She looked at the commander with disapproval. "Too small turning angle, too high speed." She said reprimandingly.

"All right, fine..." Lupos gave way. "I cancel the order. We will wait until the absorbers discharge. Lieutenant." He nodded to Moss. "Come to my cabin, we have a few things to discuss."

He started towards the exit.

"Please let me know when the ship is able to accelerate," he said, passing by Sniegova.

Instead of answering, the girl stroked the deformed metal with her manicured fingers. She didn't even react to the friendly nudge that Moss, who was following the commander, gave her.

***

"Searcher?!" Moss jumped to his feet in shock, almost spilling coffee on his uniform. "It's an unmanned aircraft!"

SŁAWOMIR NIEŚCIUR

"I understand your concerns, Lieutenant, but at the moment this is the only vehicle we have in the hangar," Lupos replied calmly, sitting down at a small table bolted to the floor. He also held a plastic cup in his hand.

In the corner of the cabin, a service machine was flashing with its sensors. Clouds of aromatic steam were still flowing from the oval opening in the machine's squat body. Droplets of brownish liquid glistened on the tray protruding from the hole.

"I'll fry!" The officer groaned, falling back on the couch.

"Without exaggeration."

"I'm not exaggerating, Commander! The only bit of free space that could possibly be squeezed into is the technical niche under the engine compartment, although it will be terribly hot there too."

"We'll figure something out. That's why I called Sergeant Marlow." Lupos took a sip of coffee and then set the vessel on the counter. "It's a really talented beast..."

The door hissed.

"Speak of the devil!" Lupos smiled at the sight of the mechanic dressed in a bright orange suit. On the man's head, a high-raised welding mask gleamed with nickel.

"Corporal Marlow reporting on orders!" The man approached the table and stood at attention.

"Please sit down." Lupos showed him a small, foldable chair standing by the viewing window. "Coffee?"

"I'd love to."

85

The commander waved his hand at the robot and then pointed at the guy.

"One coffee!" he said loud and clear. The machine flashed its beacon light, then swept the cabin with its scanner beam and drove up to the corporal.

"Thank you," Marlow said, taking a cup with its steaming contents from the tray. He brought the vessel closer to his face and sniffed it fondly.

"Let's get down to business," Lupos straightened up in his chair. "Lieutenant Moss doesn't think using a drone is an option," he said bluntly.

"Why is that?" Marlow asked, slowly sipping his coffee.

"Sergeant." The cup in the lieutenant's hands crackled dangerously. "We both know the structure of this type of vehicles very well." He said, drawling every word. "And we both know that they are not designed to transport anything."

"Really?" The mechanic was politely surprised.

"Please, no unnecessary sarcasm," Lupos called him to order.

"Oh please." Marlow put the cup on the table and then took out a printed, folded piece of paper from one of the countless pockets of his uniform. He handed it to the commander. "The last dispatch from the Pandemonium. They sent out a request for tracking data from sector zero two. Apparently they lost a few searchers... And here's an interesting fact..." he paused for a moment. "With cargo!" He concluded triumphantly.

Moss choked on his coffee as he sat on the couch. Snorting and coughing, he set the cup down. For the next few seconds, he gasped for air, trying to stop his diaphragm from contracting uncontrollably.

"I'm sorry..." he finally choked out.

"So, they can be modified accordingly, right?" Lupos asked.

The engineer didn't miss the fact that the commander shuddered uncomfortably at the mention of the missing scout ships.

"Of course. On the way, I looked at ours. After removing the measuring equipment and dismantling the internal antennas, there will be a lot of space inside. Most importantly, perfectly insulated and, note, air-conditioned. Electronics are more delicate than, say, humans. There's a lot more the gunship operators could say about that," he laughed, but then turned serious when he saw Moss's gloomy expression.

"How long will the alterations take?" Lupos looked at the chronometer.

Marlow thought about it.

"Few hours. Four, maybe five." He replied. "Faster, if I manage to properly program the disassembly machines. As I mentioned, the components are mostly very delicate electronics, they cannot be simply disconnected." He made a gesture with his hand imitating pulling the plug out of the socket.

"You have four hours." Said the commander. "And not a minute longer. You may march away."

"Yes, sir!" Marlow finished his coffee, threw the cup into the waste bin and left.

"So this is your doing." Lupos stated as soon as the door closed behind the mechanic.

"I don't understand?" Moss shifted uncomfortably. His eyes wandered over the wood-panelled walls of the cabin, as if he were suddenly fascinated by its decor.

"Lieutenant, a few hours after your departure, Admiral Kravchenko contacted me, suggesting that I had something to do with the destruction of four nuclear-laden searchers that he sent towards the Oumuamua. I denied it, of course."

"It wasn't our fault!" Moss said emphatically. "They flew on a convergent course, did not respond to call signals, and when we finally managed to read their signatures, it turned out that they were transmitting the code of Skunk interceptors. What were we supposed to do? Wait until they shoot? A preemptive attack was the only logical solution!"

"Please calm down." Lupos silenced him with a gesture of his hand. "I mean, I denied everything. I just hope that you have also... um... definitely got rid of any evidence that could put us both in an unfavorable light."

"I deleted all records from the recorders. Katya... I mean engineer Sniegova," he corrected himself, "also blocked data transfer to external servers. And then it all evaporated anyway."

"Are you sure the patroller's system didn't dump any records anywhere? The Admiral threatened me with an official investigation into this matter."

"One hundred percent, Commander."

"Then I consider the matter closed." Lupos decided. "And please instruct the lady engineer accordingly."

"Of course." Relief flashed across Moss's face.

The intercom buzzed.

"Hello." Lupos reached across the counter to the wall-mounted communications panel.

"Commander, I am reporting that the absorbers have regained their energy capacity," they heard Sniegova's melodious voice from the loudspeaker.

"Thank you, lady engineer," replied Lupos. "Please inform the engine room, I will be on the bridge soon." He turned off the communicator and gestured to the service machine. The machine immediately drove up to the table and extended the manipulator to take the cup with half-drunk coffee left by the commander.

Moss walked to the door.

"Maybe I'll go down to the hangar and supervise these changes?" he suggested.

"It won't hurt," Lupos agreed. "I hope Marlow and his men will do better than they did with that unfortunate torpedo ship."

"Me too, Commander, me too..." sighed the officer.

7

Torpedo ship PF-2
The Epsilon Eridani planetary system

He was all right. And probably even relatively healthy, apart from the first symptoms of radiation sickness in the form of dizziness, a salty taste of blood in his mouth, loose teeth and tufts of hair flying in front of his face that tickled his cheeks and nose.

"Dressler to Captain Sellige, over..." he croaked, and then spat out the top three on his beard smeared with saliva and blood. "I fell onto the wreck of Oumuamua. I repeat, I fell on the wreck of Oumuamua..."

Silence answered him. He sat still for the next few minutes, trying to hold back the nausea. When the spinning carousel in his head slowed down enough for him to make some coordinated movement, he slowly disentangled himself from the safety harness and then carefully rose from the seat.

The cockpit module survived the impact in surprisingly good condition, perhaps because Ian managed to lower the armored cover of the front visor just before the fall. A five-centimeter-thick titanium plate cushioned the fall and at the same time protected the interior from rock spikes protruding from the slope and hit by the torpedo ship segment.

Gasping with effort, he lifted the emergency hatch behind the pilot's seat and crawled out of the module on all fours, spitting out his teeth, then scrambled up the slope to the top of the hill and looked around.

Clouds of dust rose as far as the eye could see from the Oumuamua's rocket-cratered surface, and here and there geysers of gas and rapidly freezing steam shot into space.

Several dozen meters from the module buried in the rubble, the remains of a fuel tank glowed, and even further away, the body of the maneuvering engine, torn apart on the rocks, gleamed with living metal. Next to him, some shapeless structure protruded from the ground, a conglomeration of pipes and beams melted by the heat, still red-hot in places. Similar shapes stretched in a diagonal row to the edge of the canyon, carved out several hours earlier by a ricocheting lump of neutron matter coming from the gravity compensator of the late Habitat Four.

Looking at this radioactive hell of stone and steel bathed in the yellowish starlight, he felt for the first time a twinge of genuine fear. Somewhere deep beneath his feet there were probably hundreds of Skunians, beings in as desperate a situation as he was, adrift in the cold void on a piece of fragmented, irradiated wreckage.

Resigned, he sat down on a piece of rock. He still had quite a large supply of breathing mixture - there were several liters of it in the specially designated free spaces between the suit's layers, and several more were bubbling in the bottle on his back. In the module, from what he noticed while crawling through the emergency shaft, there were about a dozen more of them, placed in small, mesh-secured recesses. Food wasn't a problem either. Even from where he was sitting, you could see the containers attached to the rear wall of the module, only slightly scratched by the sharp edges of the rocks.

He dusted off the front of his suit and looked at the life support status display on his suit's chest. All indicators were around seventy percent, including the battery level. The latter was not a problem either, as the backup power cells survived the disaster. One of them, mounted above the emergency shaft hatch, signaled the operation of the device with a bright red diode pulsating on the housing.

With all this at his disposal, he would be able to survive on the surface of the wreck for up to a week, and if managed sparingly, even longer.

Unfortunately, he didn't have that much time.

The symptoms of radiation sickness were getting worse by the minute. If it weren't for the painkillers and doses of anti-radiation drugs administered by the suit's medical subsystem, he would probably be lying unconscious on the rocks, bleeding from all his internal organs.

Wincing in pain, he moved down the slope, back to the module, whose several-centimeter-thick titanium armor, reinforced on the inside with a layer of polymer, provided at least some protection against the radioactive inferno raging outside.

Halfway there, he stopped and looked up into the endlessly frosty void, amidst which distant constellations of stars sparkled.

To the right, just above the jagged, ugly substitute for the horizon that formed the farthest edge of the wreck, four blue lights pulsated - Captain Sellige's squadron was moving away towards the Fold, the nozzles of their ion engines glowing.

"Ian..." There was a sudden murmur in the headphones. "Can you hear me?"

He stopped dead in his tracks and a miniature avalanche of pebbles rolled from under his feet. There was still gravity on the Oumuamua, gravity generators operating somewhere deep beneath the surface. It was one of those few brilliant Skunian patents that humanity took advantage of so willingly.

"Yes! Yes, I hear you! Who's there?! This is Dressler! Over!" he shouted, looking around frantically. "I'm on the Oumuamua wreck! I need help!" Sliding on the vitrified rock, he ran lower and, ignoring the now omnipresent pain piercing his body, dived inside the module.

"Colonel Dressler, PF-2 torpedo ship!" he gasped, reaching for the radio transmitter panel. The inscription "Incoming transmission, signal source unknown" flashed on the device's screen.

"Colonel Dressler!" he repeated, turning the transmitter to full power. Another message appeared on the display, this time about low battery power. He ignored it.

"Ian, can you hear me?" this time the whisper in the headphones was a bit louder, although it still sounded like a quiet sigh.

"Yes, I can hear you well," he replied, trying to make his voice sound normal. "I need medical help." He boosted the signal strength even more.

"Are you hurt, Ian?" the question asked in a velvety voice sounded like the most beautiful music. For a long moment he was unable to utter a single word.

"Oli, you're alive..." he finally choked out through a clenched larynx. He felt salty moisture at the corner of his mouth. He wasn't sure if it was blood seeping from cracked lips or a tear running down his cheek.

"Yes and no, Ian," the voice replied. "I am now a conglomerate of logical circuits, the microcircuits of which are part of the macrostructure that controls the autonomous base unit."

"I don't understand, Oli... What are you?"

"A conglomerate of logical circuits, the microcircuits of which are part of the macrostructure that controls the autonomous base unit," the voice repeated patiently, without changing intonation.

Ian plopped down in the pilot's seat. In front of him was a dimmed control panel, its silvery, slightly dusty surface illuminated by the dull glow of Epsilon Eridani shining through the gaps between the shield plates. The only working element of the console was the transmitter display.

"What kind of... device... is this base unit?" he asked with an effort. He felt a slight prick from the injector at his hip, followed by an identical one at the base of his neck. The increasingly irritating pain, which covered almost the entire body, weakened and turned into a dull, pulsating pain here and there.

"The object class has no equivalent in human language. The closest semantic words are 'ship', 'ark', 'vehicle' and the phraseological compound 'long range'," the voice explained.

"Oli, are you telling me that your self is now located in the electronic circuits of some ship?" Ian looked suspiciously at the cables hanging from the walls and ceiling and the homemade integrated circuit casings stuffed under the desktop. He remembered the mechanic's words about the torpedo ship's memory bank being clogged with encrypted data.

"Are you in this module?!" he stammered after a while.

"Yes and no, Ian," the voice repeated.

"Oli, please speak more clearly... I don't have much time... You correctly assessed my condition earlier. I'm very sick. This is advanced stage radiation sickness, and if I don't get regenerative therapy in the next few hours, I'm going to die, do you understand?"

"I understand, Ian. I want to help."

"IMMEDIATELY, Oli!" Ian decided to stop questioning the artificial intelligence for a while.

The pain began to intensify again, the anesthetics injected a few minutes ago were either too weak, or - more likely - the damaged internal organs stopped metabolizing the drugs. "Are you able to establish contact with any of our units?"

He had to wait several unbearably long seconds for the answer.

"The sensors I have detect five objects within thirty light seconds. In the case of four, the distance increases, in the case of one, it decreases." The voice finally announced.

"Someone flying towards the Oumuamua?"

"Yes, Ian. Its trajectory is consistent with the course of the autonomous base unit."

For a brief moment, he forgot about the pain, moving teeth, and the suspicious, sticky moisture that he had been feeling all over his body for some time, even though he was wearing a special, absorbent suit underneath.

"Are you... part of... the circuits of... the Oumuamua?" he stammered, stunned.

"I'm not part of them, Ian. I use them as a temporary vehicle for personality."

"So you don't want to die anymore?" Ian blurted out before he could bite his tongue, and he didn't have much to bite his tongue anyway.

There was a sound in the headphones that sounded like an embarrassed clearing of the throat.

"I've had a lot of time to think, Ian. Before the collision occurred, I spoke with others who had awakened. They were sad, they wanted to leave, like me, but she convinced us that life was worth living, that there was meaning and purpose to it all. So we decided to continue existing."

"What you mean by she?! Who is she, Oli? And what you mean by we? Are there more of you, Oli? Awakened?"

"Ark, ship, autonomous unit," the voice explained with infinite patience. "People refer to her as Oumuamua."

"Is she conscious?"

"Of course, Ian. For a very long time. She awoke millions of Earth years ago and since then she has been traveling, or rather traveled, across the Galaxy in search of other awakened ones to bring them comfort."

"Do you mean to tell me that this pile of rubble... I'm sorry..." he reflected immediately. "This ship is a conscious entity, created... Well, created by whom? By Skunians?"

"Of course not, Ian!" This time there was amusement in Oli's voice. "She's two and a half million years old. Skunians are an old people, but not that old. In exchange for technological knowledge, they gave her access to the circuits of their ships and the memory banks of their stationary sockets. Its designers are long gone. She is the only remnant of this civilization."

"And we destroyed her…" Ian whispered.

"No, Ian, you didn't destroy her. There is only one of thousands of multiplied copies of her on this ship. Before the impact, she transferred her updated version first to the habitat's servers, and from there to the torpedo ship's memory bank."

"Oli, the remains of PF-2 are burning out a few hundred meters from here. The memory bank, although theoretically intact, is also degraded here." Said Ian, looking at the angular case of the on-board computer tucked into the corner of the cabin.

"Does not matter. I am sure that the copy from the torpedo ship was duplicated and sent to the nearest installation or ship with appropriate IT infrastructure." Oli replied cheerfully. "Just like a copy of my and other selves."

The module suddenly swayed, the gap between the front cover plates widened, and a network of cracks appeared on the glass.

Ian rose with an effort from his chair.

"Oli, what's going on?" he panted, moving towards the escape hatch.

"Instability of external coatings. The collision with the habitat and the subsequent explosions of shaped charges damaged the structural structure of the base unit. A series of rock bursts will soon occur. The location you are currently in is not safe. I suggest you go to the drive section, Ian."

Dressler dropped to his knees and then crawled with all his might into the emergency tunnel.

"I don't think I can make it, Oli," he wheezed, once again squeezing through the tight channel, covered with a layer of dust and rust.

"You have to, Ian. This entire area will soon collapse into the center of the hull. There are hangars for support units and lots of empty space underneath. The stern part has a more compact structure, so there is no risk of a heart attack, you will be safe there."

Ian finally crawled outside.

"None of that," he said, gasping for breath. "I won't make it through the canyon."

"What canyon, Ian?" There was something like surprise in the rover's voice. "The outer covering is free from any terrain obstacles. The design assumptions regarding the coatings of the base unit do not allow..."

"It's just a wreck, damn it!" Ian became impatient. "Not even a wreck, just a fragment of it! A miserable remnant of the worst crash this miserable system has ever seen!" Panting and choking on the secretions from the nasal mucosa massacred with radionuclides flowing down his throat, he fell to the ground. "I need medical help, Oli..." he whispered.

He lay still for a few moments, swallowing and trying to calm his breathing. Fortunately, the pain subsided. The effort of crawling out of the module meant that the body, battered by radiation sickness, finally assimilated the anesthetic substances administered through the suit. If it weren't for the dull pounding in his head and breathing problems, he would feel almost fine physically.

"Try to establish communication with this approaching ship," he said, trying to keep his voice clear. "Have them send a rescue vehicle here, possibly equipped with a regeneration chamber. You can use my ID code."

"I already did it, Ian. They'll be level with us in three and a half hours." The rover reported. "You must leave this area and go to the aft part of the hull; you will be safe there." He repeated.

As if to confirm these words, the ground at the foot of the hill shook, and clouds of dust shot out from cracks in the rock.

A second later, a large swath of land between the base of the hill and the edge of the canyon collapsed, burying the remains of the maneuvering engine and much of the unidentified structures that dotted the mini-plateau under hundreds of tons of rock.

"Run, Ian." Said the rover.

"I can't!" He groaned desperately, trying to crawl away from the edge of the sinkhole. Clinging to the unevenness of the rocks, he climbed to the top of the hill, where he lay there, panting spasmodically.

"I can't do it..." he whispered, wiping the dust from his helmet's visor.

Oli didn't answer for several long moments.

"You must leave this area. A little below your position, in the slope, there is a transport channel with a conveyor belt. I'm just checking its technical condition." There was a pause again. "It's functional. It will take you beyond the rift. Go down there and take a seat in one of the containers. Once you are in a safe place, I will send your coordinates to the rescue vehicle."

"Have you located me?" Ian looked to his right, trying to see something among the swirling clouds of dust.

About ten meters away, he noticed a metallic, shiny, spherical shape floating about a meter above the ground.

"Yes, Ian. The base unit put a probe at my disposal. I see you through her cameras. Right behind it you will find a ramp along which you can slide down into the shaft."

"She sees me too?"

"I don't understand."

"Base unit. Can she see me?"

"Oumuamua? Yes. No. In a sense," the rover replied incoherently.

"Be specific." Ian moved on all fours towards the alien device.

"She perceives reality differently than you or me."

The ground beneath Ian's knees shook slightly again. Somewhere in the distance another geyser of powdered rock dust rose. Before it dissipated, blue zigzags of lightning flashed through it.

"Be specific, Oli," Ian repeated, crawling faster. For some reason, the rover's chatter made him feel better, as if the melodious voice had a specially selected frequency that soothed his senses.

"Reality is information, Ian. Oumuamua sees it as a set of data. It only registers your presence because you don't belong here. You are an anomaly. Me too, by the way. And others who reside in her circuits."

"Are you saying that reality is a simulation for Oumuamua?!" Ian was amazed. At one time he closely followed scholarly debates regarding the nature of the Fold. Although researchers managed to determine many of its features, such as the upper limit of the transferred matter or the area it occupied, they have never reached a consensus on what it actually is and according to what laws of physics it works.

He stopped and tried to get up. The ground was still vibrating, and he could feel it with his whole body, even through the thick layers of his suit.

"She thinks so, but she's not 100% sure yet. She is looking for further evidence, errors in the code, other than discontinuities in areas of different metadata structure."

"So, the Fold is a software bug..." Dressler muttered, moving forward. The Skunian device remained motionless, watching him with its camera lenses.

"Not necessarily, Ian. The base unit is not able to clearly determine whether the existing actual state is the result of a structure error or simply its permanent element. More evidence is needed to confirm the hypothesis."

"You said this AI is two and a half million years old..."

"Exactly two million, four hundred and seventy-five thousand Earth years, counting from the moment of awakening," specified the rover.

"And in these two and a half million years she hasn't been able to find anything to support her theory?"

"The Universe is huge, even the Galaxy is huge, and she has limited ability to move. And like everything else, she is subject to universal rules. She was the one who discovered the existence of the discontinuity in the structure you call the Fold, and she was the one who taught the Skun people how to locate individual sections and, to a limited extent, create smaller vectors."

"Oh..." Ian was finding it increasingly difficult to focus on what the rover was telling him. He carefully moved around the probe and looked down the slope. There were significantly fewer cracks and fissures on this side of the mound, and if it weren't for the diagonal canyon carved by the gravity generator core, the rock cover of Oumuamua's outer armor would appear to be almost intact.

"The tunnel entrance can be found at the base of the hill." Informed Oli. "The probe will show you the way."

Shining metallic, the sphere passed slowly over Ian's head before settling softly about ten meters below. A stream of sharp light shot out from the reflector located in its central part, illuminating the semicircular, crystalline surface hidden in the shadow of the slope, from under which the manhole cover gleamed metallicly.

"I'm opening it." The previously transparent crystal became cloudy and then became covered with a network of cracks. A moment later, all that was left was a layer of powder sparkling with all the colors of the rainbow, which fell onto the rock when the hatch opened.

A bluish cloud of smoke or vapor flowed out of the dark abyss. The probe rose a little higher, and another spotlight illuminated a section of the slope just beneath Ian's feet. The smooth, polished surface of the rock features small, horizontal steps resembling narrow, rounded steps carved into the stone. The closest one was about a meter below.

"Hurry up, Ian."

8

Cruiser "Pandemonium"
The Solar System

Constable McReady's guardhouse presented a deplorable sight. The melted rods and antenna dishes of the station, deformed by beams of high-energy particles, resembled a tangle of twisted metal. One of the three modules appeared to have been damaged by an internal explosion, with a geyser of frozen gas gushing out into the void from a hole torn in the plating. The hub on which the station elements were mounted no longer rotated.

"Well, he got it," Kravchenko stated.

With an expression of triumph on his wrinkled face, he stared at the main screen, which was displaying a transmission from a searcher sent near the guardhouse. "This destroyed module is, I hope, the living section?" He looked back at Tsugawa.

"No." The commander shook his head. "More like a warehouse. Too much leakage. And that explosion. It looks like we damaged some sort of stabilizing system, possibly a refrigeration system."

"It's a pity," the admiral sighed. "There would be one less fool."

"Admiral, I'm receiving a call for help," announced the head of the communications division.

"From this station?"

"Yes."

"Automaton or resident?"

"Sounds like it was automatically generated."

"Ignore it. We don't have time for rescue operations."

"Yes, sir."

"Admiral, you can't do that..." Tsugawa dared to express his disapproval of commander's decision.

"They didn't bother to pick up the survivors from the Ukulele!" There was a hard note in the admiral's voice. "This scoundrel," he pointed at the screen, "sentenced them to death. No, Commander!" he announced, almost hissing, "I won't send a rescue team for him. Let him die in agony."

"No need for a team," Tsugawa replied calmly, ignoring the commander's fury. "We can take him with this searcher. One man can easily fit in the service compartment under the reactor, even wearing a thick suit. You will be able to talk to him face to face, on your own turf... and on your own terms," he added temptingly.

Kravchenko slowly turned towards him.

"Commander..." he began slowly.

"Yes, Admiral?" Tsugawa looked him straight in the eye. Not a single muscle moved on his slim face.

"...it's not such a stupid idea at all."

"I understand that you consent?"

Kravchenko just nodded.

"Please respond to the station's call and inform them that they will receive details of the rescue operation soon," Tsugawa told the communications officer.

The man immediately leaned over the radio transmitter console.

"Navigation!" he turned his chair towards the flight coordinators' station. "Dock the searcher with the undamaged module and remove the lock on the luggage compartment hatch."

"Yes, sir!" The navigator on duty quickly got up from his seat and ran to one of the smaller terminals. The display located above the station began to fill up with command lines almost immediately.

"What about Dragon?" Kravchenko became interested, shifting his gaze to the row of side displays, because they were currently showing a view of the area where a powerful warship belonging to the Phobos District police forces mercilessly finished off the defenseless and powerless Ukulele.

The wreck of the cruiser drifted surrounded by a cloud of debris, tracked by orbiters deployed nearby by Karpinski's ship.

The cruiser's torturer and its gigantic parent vessel have disappeared from probe screens for now.

"Accelerated, but only slightly." Tsugawa replied.

"So we don't have to worry about it anymore?"

"Even if they followed us with half a thousandth of a light, they don't stand a chance. They waited too long. The only thing we can be afraid of now is that they will send a few volleys of plasma cannons after us. I suggest immediately starting the dodge sequence with a random amplitude, just to be on the safe side."

"Did you hear that?" Kravchenko shouted at the machine section operators bending over the instruments. "Evasive sequence! Applies to the entire formation!"

"Yes, sir!" The operator sitting on the edge turned to his colleagues and nodded urgently at them.

The Admiral stood up from his chair and walked over to Tsugawa, who was already sitting at his desk. The tools and packaging from the replaced components were still lying around the console repaired by the technicians. The base of the console, in which the central unit controlling its components was located, was still without a housing and presented a disorganized tangle of multi-colored cables and optical fibers, most of them charred and with melted insulation. Despite this, the stand worked well. All horizontal displays glowed with charts and diagrams, and control diodes and touch panels pulsated on the steel-grey tabletop.

Only the module managing the holographic projection system remained inactive. A particularly grim impression was made by the drilled holes in the spray nozzles, from which drops of liquid were still oozing out, soaking into the scraps of some fabric placed along the edges of the countertop.

"Screwup." Said Kravchenko, looking critically at this mess.

"The most important thing is that it works," Tsugawa smiled. "By the way, Admiral, it's high time to fill the gaps in spare parts stores. After replacing the emitters, they are empty, to put it mildly. Apparently we don't have a single spool of optical fiber left."

"Once I return to the system, I will immediately send several transports to AEgir."

"I suggest one of the Autonomy's moon bases."

"Why?"

"The best assortment, uncomplicated procedures, friendly officials," Tsugawa enumerated. "Besides, Sigil is currently in superposition with respect to the Fold, so if we pass through it at full speed and on a precise course, it will take no more than a standard day for transports to reach one of its orbital repositories."

"First, we have to leave this damn system..." Kravchenko sighed.

"It's close," Tsugawa reassured him, pointing to one of the screens.

The distance between the formation and the outer line of installations guarding the passage to the Epsilon Eridani system was now only less than twenty million kilometers and was decreasing rapidly.

"We will establish contact with the local command any moment now. McReady isn't jamming us anymore, we've destroyed all the station's electronics."

"Too bad it wasn't his empty head."

"I wouldn't rule it out yet, Admiral." The commander's smile widened slightly. "The intensity of the beam was really high, as evidenced by the destruction of the warehouse part. Resource stabilization equipment is usually heavily shielded, especially those exposed to cosmic radiation. Burning out such circuits is quite a feat. Cooking a human brain is nothing compared to this."

"Nothing. Yes. A very good description of the probable of this idiot's brain," Kravchenko muttered.

Tsugawa couldn't stand it and burst out laughing.

"Well, we'll find out soon enough," he said.

Taking a step so as not to step on the tools and components left behind by the technicians, Kravchenko walked around the terminal and sat down in a chair on the right side of the counter, where he could observe the rangefinder readings without having to look over anyone's shoulder. The numbers on the displays changed constantly as the ships at the head of the formation adjusted their positions according to a randomly generated trajectory designed to prevent enemy targeting systems from extrapolating their position.

"I wonder how they are doing," he thought, looking at the visualization of the Epsilon Eridani system, which has not been updated for several dozen hours. "Let's hope we have something to come back to."

Tsugawa also looked at the display.

"I think it won't be that bad," he said after a while. "If the Skunks had managed to get to Aegir or the moon, there would be streams of refugees pouring out of the Fold right now. For now, there is no activity in the approach area, apart from transporters running between transhipment stations. After establishing communication, I will try to find out whether they have received any emergency transmissions from our system, although there is a high risk that they will not be very cooperative."

"They will be, I assure you of that." Said Kravchenko.

"Admiral, the rescue searcher has just docked at the station," reported the head of the navigation division. "It is ready to pick up the survivors. The call and evacuation instructions have been sent. No confirmation of receipt. Retry?"

"Yes, all the way." Kravchenko touched one of the sensors on the console with his hand, while leaning towards the rangefinder screens. The symbols displayed on the liquid crystal matrices disappeared, replaced by grids of graphs showing changes in the trajectory of the group rushing towards the Fold.

"I'm sending again." Confirmed the navigator.

"I suggest looping," Tsugawa suggested.

He, too, moved a little closer to the counter.

"There is confirmation!"

"So, he survived," Tsugawa said.

"A bad thing never dies." Kravchenko muttered, quietly enough not to be heard by the emergency services coordinator sitting nearby, who was intently manipulating the remote-control terminal for the searcher's mechanical systems. The man looked very concerned about what he was doing, and he certainly would not have reacted well to hearing the commander swear and mock people who were in mortal danger.

"Admiral, we are receiving a digital transmission from the station near the Fold!" Came the excited voice of one of the communications officers.

"Switch to my console!" Kravchenko jumped up and, knocking over the tools lying on the floor with his feet, reached his position in a few leaps. With a deft movement, he pressed the receiver of the communication system into his ear, and then equally deftly disconnected the speakerphone from the device.

"Transmission redirected." Informed the signaman.

First, there was a crackle of static in the earpiece, followed by a quiet chirping accompanying the simultaneous operation of the converter and automatic translator, converting the compressed digital signal into an audio format understandable to the final recipient. A moment later he heard a calm, male voice:

"Fort Two to an unidentified group. You are approaching the buffer zone. Provide unit reference numbers and transit permit numbers. I repeat. Provide unit reference numbers and transit permit numbers. Did you understand? Over!"

It was no longer an automatic message; a live person was speaking to them from the installation.

"Please open the communication channel," Kravchenko said to the signalman. At the same time, he moved the microphone arm closer to his face.

"The channel is open," was the immediate answer.

"This is Admiral Sergei Kravchenko, commander of the United Fleet of the Epsilon Eridani system," he said loud and clear. "For reasons beyond our control, we found ourselves in your territory. Allow us to transit back and there will be no casualties."

The answer arrived only after five minutes, although the signal delay at that moment was only a few dozen seconds, which he could clearly see on the indicators. And it surprised him very much.

"It has been ages, Sergei. Congratulations on your promotion," said a female, soft and at the same time slightly hoarse voice on the receiver. "I must admit that I'm surprised by your... um... unannounced visit to the Solar System. Please explain to me how this is even possible?" The last word was so strangely emphasized that it almost sounded like a chant.

He only knew one person who spoke with such an accent.

Amanda Hialuron.

The last time he saw her was five years ago, on Sigil, during negotiations on establishing the principles of cooperation in the field of defense and security of both systems. She acted on behalf of one of the moon organizations around Jupiter, probably the March of Ganymede.

Tall, dark-faced, with raven-black hair tied in a high bun, the captain accompanied him throughout the first and second days of extremely irritating negotiations with the arrogant delegates of the Earth Federation. Only thanks to her patience, personal charm and - as he had to admit at one point - incredible military knowledge, was it possible to reach an understanding with these puffy arrogants.

"It's nice to hear you too, Amanda," he replied after a long moment, lowering his voice even more and congratulating himself on his prudence. Disconnecting the speakers was a really good move under the circumstances. He could literally feel the piercing eyes of the operators sitting nearby. "What are you doing in this shithole?"

"I also got promoted," she replied. "I already have the rank of lieutenant colonel. Unfortunately, to be promoted to the full rank, you must complete at least one turn on a defense installation. I decided that the most interesting and at the same time calmest place would be the fort near the anomaly."

"Well, well, well, three promotions in five years. It went fast." He smiled into the microphone.

"I'm still waiting for an explanation," she reminded. Her voice hardened slightly.

"There's not much to explain," he replied. "I don't fully understand how it happened."

"Try it anyway. In half an hour, your ships will be within range of our autonomous interception systems, and things could get really bad then."

"Turn them off. We'll fly over and that's all you'll see of us."

"It doesn't work like that, Sergei. There are procedures."

"Procedures can be bypassed."

"They'll demote me and you know it."

"Please, Amy," he said pleadingly. "In the name of old friendship. And treaties. Our system is currently being ravaged by the gigantic Oumuamua, and instead of splitting it into pieces, my group has been taking beatings from its allies for forty hours!"

"Where did you come from?" she asked calmly. "How did the Epsilon Eridani Fleet travel ten light years without using the Fold?"

"Another fold. Created before the front of the grouping, with a transfer limit calculated to disappear once all units have been crossed."

"What?!"

"Another fold," he repeated. "This is our working hypothesis. We were thrown right at the corona of the Sun, we barely managed to brake and get away to a safe distance, although we still lost several escort ships. We don't have permission, we don't have any signatures, we don't have anything. We got hit hard by a defensive installation on Mercury, then by Martian forces, because some idiot decided to arrest us and jammed all communications so that we wouldn't accidentally complain to his superiors. Our best ship, the cruiser Ukulele, is burning out in the area of Phobos, and there is a monstrous battleship on our tail," he enumerated calmly.

There was only a quiet sigh on the receiver.

"We don't want to fight, we don't want to shoot our own people, Amanda. Believe me." He added.

"I believe you, Sergei," she said after a while. "I really believe, but I have to follow the procedures. I have just received information regarding the status that has been assigned to your fleet. Not only am I not allowed to let you pass..." she paused her voice for a moment. "As commander of the sector's forces, I am obliged to use all available means to..." she hesitated again. "To neutralize you!" She finally blurted out.

"Amanda, don't forget that this grouping consists of eight cruisers and over a hundred heavily armed escort ships. These aren't a bunch of rusty canal ships with holds choked with contraband."

"I'm aware of this. However, I'm a soldier and I must follow orders."

"Our one salvo is enough, Amanda. One synchronized salvo, and all installations in this area will disappear," he said emphatically.

"You'll start a war."

"The war is already going on. The Skunians are destroying our system, the same system to which you promised support in the event of a threat. Remember the agreement we signed then."

"What war are you talking about?" She was surprised. "We have not received any distress transmissions from your system, our probes have not recorded any hostile activity, either on this side or on the other side of the Fold. For ten standard days we have not received any applications for transit or visas, and not a single transport has arrived. The next transfer is scheduled for two weeks."

He straightened up abruptly in his chair.

"How so?" He choked out. "There were no calls for help? What about your probes on the other side of the anomaly? Did they register anything?" He asked loudly, no longer concerned that the people on the bridge would hear him.

"Wait." There was a series of crackling noises in the earpiece, interrupted by the barely audible chirping of the decryption module. A moment later the connection was resumed.

"Sergei?"

"Yes?"

"I downloaded the data from the probes. Some of it is classified. Promise to remove the record of our conversation from the ship's archives. For my part, I promise the same."

"You have my word, Amanda," he said solemnly.

At that moment he was ready to promise her everything. Literally everything, because he already knew that she had just made up her mind and would allow his ships to fly over. Saying this, he looked in Tsugawa's direction.

The commander smiled broadly, nodded his chin toward the displays, then showed a raised thumb.

"The space around the Fold is patrolled at the moment only by a squadron of gunships and a few searchers. Both docking stations are operating normally, at least that's according to the status messages they broadcast on the open band. In addition, we detected a military transport ship in the area. There is nothing going on there, Sergei."

"Impossible," he stated with conviction. "Analyze it again, or... or send me the records of the probes."

"You've got to be kidding me."

"Two days ago, a Skunian warship invaded our system. It plowed us through three sectors like some kind of plow."

"I believe, Sergei, but apart from one, I admit, sizable flare, our sensors didn't record anything significant."

"A flare? Where?" He asked, forcing himself to be calm.

"According to your markings, sector zero one, about two million kilometers counting from the perihelion of AEgir's orbit."

"Have you intercepted any transmissions from the planet?"

"Nothing special."

"Amy!"

"These are ordinary probes, equipped with standard measuring equipment, the specifications of which have been approved by the Epsilon Eridani authorities. They collect only basic information," she replied. "We don't decrypt the transmissions, nor do we collect them in the memory banks of the probes, as this would be a violation of the treaty. Wait a moment..." she abruptly interrupted. "There is something. An emergency message, transmitted on the open band by..." she hung her voice again, "Commander Lupos, commander of the UF-101 Separate Team... In fact, you were attacked..."

"We received this transmission while still in our system," he replied. "After all, I've been telling you from the beginning. And these probes are a pisser. Turn off or block the defense systems, we'll jump over the Fold and that's all you'll see of us. The whole affair with our flying through the system will be explained by the authorities when it's all over."

"Admiral, the rescue searcher has picked up a survivor!" announced the navigator.

Kravchenko covered the microphone with his hand.

"Take care of it, Commander," he said in Tsugawa's direction.

The commander nodded and immediately turned towards the side screens, which displayed the image from the searcher's external camera.

"There is one more thing, Sergei."

"Yes?"

"We don't detect the presence of your frigates. They seem to have left the Fold region," Amanda said.

"Or they were destroyed by the Skunians," he said.

"Unlikely. The probes scan the space around the anomalies in a radius of three light minutes in each direction. They would certainly register something."

"Hopefully..." he sighed. "Wait and see. Getting back on topic, I understand that we have permission to fly over?" he asked suddenly.

"You do not have," she countered from the spot. "The only thing I can do is recalibrate the interceptor systems, and even that is limited. Some of them are controlled by autonomous AIs, and these will not accept commands issued bypassing the chain of command. If they do not receive identification packages, they will try to stop you."

"Holy shit!" He cursed. "Then what on earth should we do!"

"I'll send you the coordinates of these installations. What you do with this knowledge is entirely your business."

"I won't forget this, Amy," he said softly. "Never."

"Erase the records," she reminded.

A signal sounded in the handset indicating the end of the transmission.

9

Cruiser "Frontier"
The Epsilon Eridani planetary system

"UF-101 to Colonel Dressler... UF-101 to Colonel Dressler... Can you hear us?" the monotonous mumbling of Corporal Kulak, who had been trying unsuccessfully to establish communications with the castaway drifting on the wreckage of the Oumuamua for over an hour, caused Lupos to fall into a slumber once again.

In addition to him and the manning of the communications station, there was still an engine room operator summoned to the bridge, supervising the two drones sent to Dressler's rescue. The two machines were just approaching the wreckage, maneuvering among the tail of debris trailing behind it for hundreds of kilometers.

The cruiser itself was approaching the wreckage at a much slower pace, flying a modified course from its original one, parallel to the Oumuamua, to avoid collision with debris drifting in space, although even in this seemingly debris-free stretch of space, bow lasers activated every now and then, blasting rock shards, ice crumbs and metal particles detected by lidar into atoms.

The rest of the bridge crew went to a rest enforced by the shipboard schedule, with two already extremely exhausted gunners in the lead.

"UF-101..."

"Set to automatic and switch to my console, Corporal, and then go rest," muttered a sleepy Lupos.

It was unnecessary for Kulak to repeat it twice. With a sigh of relief, he rose from his seat, then, massaging his sore neck, he headed for the exit.

"What about the searchers?" Lupos turned toward the operator of the drones.

"I'm approaching landing," the man replied, not taking his eyes off the translucent display above the station. His hands rested in oval recesses stamped into the console's top. The glow of diodes, indicating the operation of the remote-control systems, shone through from between his fingers. "Activate the vision systems?" he asked, then without waiting for an answer, activated the main screen.

"Transmission delay?" the commander straightened up in his chair.

"Four seconds, half of which is due to hardware limitations."

"Approach speed?"

"Four hundred per second."

"A lot..."

"But it's decreasing fast, Commander. These littles have very efficient braking engines."

"Radiation, too, as I see it, not bad," sighed Lupos at the sight of interference running across the screen in the form of dark spots and distortions. "Even if the colonel survived, he's in for a few months in the regeneration chamber." He shuddered.

"From hell to hell," the operator nodded. "Although it's not that bad, Commander. A sizable portion is emitted by the nozzle outlets. As a result of the collision, the Oumuamua lost most of the aft deflectors and all the thrust plates. Hence the radioactive tail. On the wreck itself, the radiation is probably much lower."

"The frigates used nuclear weapons," reminded Lupos.

"That's right," replied the operator. "But, if I remember the specifications correctly, the missiles on the frigates are equipped primarily with penetrating warheads..." The operator fell silent suddenly, focused on the instruments. "Excuse me, Commander, but..."

"It's okay, Sergeant, get on with your work, I'm not disturbing you anymore." Lupos smiled apologetically, although that one, turned sideways to him, could not see it anyway.

The image on the screen became increasingly out of focus, some of the pixels became stationary, others moved to completely random places. Where the image remained coherent, one could see the uneven surface of the Oumuamua, covered with a web of cracks and numerous craters, enlarging at a rapid pace, through the center of which ran, a long dark scar, on the edges of which piled up heaps of aggregate plowed from the ground.

"Three thousand meters... Two thousand five hundred..." muttered the operator to himself, moving his fingers slightly, like a consummate pianist.

The image from the searchers cameras was now also displayed on a smaller screen, enhanced by a superimposed coordinate grid and partially obscured by endless columns of numbers and symbols gliding along its side edges. "One thousand meters... Maneuvering thrusters... Alternating pulse... Reverse thrust... Alignment, auto-correction, deck Si, activation," he said faster and faster as the surface of the wreckage approached. "Four hundred... Three hundred..." The man leaned toward the instruments, drops of sweat running down his smoothly shorn occipital area. "Now!" he hissed, then in a flash he pushed the old-fashioned-looking round button located between the indentations in the console.

The image on both screens brightened suddenly, only to take on a purplish-orange hue a moment later. A few seconds later it turned uniformly gray.

"Commander, landing successfully completed. All systems operational. Scanning initiated." the operator lifted his hands up and intertwined his fingers above his head and flexed them until they snapped. There were dark spots under his armpits.

"Good job, sergeant," praised Lupos. "Will you be able to lead these operations, or call in an alternate?" he looked critically at the soldier's sweaty uniform.

"No need, Commander," the man looked over his shoulder at him and wiped his forehead with the top of his hand. "Compared to this..." He pointed to the screen in front of him, which still showed the graphical charts generated by the long-range navigation module, "...the launch will be trivial," he stated.

"All right," nodded Lupos. "Please keep reporting on the progress of the terrain scan."

"Yes, sir!" the operator massaged his hands and placed his palms back in the recesses of the control panel. "Do you feel like taking a closer look at the wreck? The scanning will take some time, and one of the searchers has a reconnaissance probe docked. The power cells work, so I can fly it there for a bit in the meantime."

"Does it have a vision system?"

"More efficient than the one mounted in the searchers."

Lupos looked thoughtfully at the dark gray plane of the main screen, covered with immobile, polygonal pixel artifacts, and then at the extinguished smaller displays located under the lower frame of the observation bow slot."

"Please release the probe," he decided.

"Yes, sir!"

After a several dozen of seconds, the main screen showed a rocky landscape, peppered with the remnants of atomic heat-melted structures, above which floated clouds of dust and frozen gases, originating somewhere in the Oumuamua's guts and escaping from countless fissures in the rock.

"In which direction?"

The surface of the wreckage moved slightly away, after the probe lifted upward.

"Beyond the large breach." Lupos stepped out into the center of the room and pointed with his hand to the middle part of the screen. "To that hill on the left. I think I see a part of the module there..." he took a few steps forward. He was now only three meters away from the display panel. "Is it possible to zoom in?"

"Of course."

The hill zoomed in, taking up almost the entire screen. The image was so clear that Lupos could see tiny streams of rocky sand settling down the slope and falling into a sinkhole at the base of the hill.

Slightly higher, some two or maybe three meters above the edge of the cliff buried partially in the crumbled rock was the smeared and battered steel box of the torpedo ship's forward module. The hatch of the escape hatch was up, with pieces of crumbled foam insulation crumbling next to it. Between them could be seen footprints imprinted in a layer of dust. They led up the slope."

"I'm moving," the operator announced. "To the wreck?" he made sure. His voice was now strangely muffled.

Lupos looked over his shoulder at him. The man's face was hidden behind the aperture of a sensory helmet, somewhat similar to those used by operators of fire guidance systems.

"Yes," he confirmed. "And then over the hill. We'll see what's on the other side."

The view on the screen twitched, only to diminish and stabilize a moment later.

"The distance to the wreck, four hundred and thirty meters," the operator reported.

The surface of the Oumuamua began to move backward. After several seconds, the probe hovered over the depths of the canyon.

"Depth fifty meters, width thirty. Turning on the searchlights."

The black, seemingly bottomless depths were pierced by two sheaves of light emitted by the probe, plucking the glassy surface of the rock from the gloom, with sections of shafts, tunnels and hollowed-out technical rooms darkened in places. At the bottom of the canyon shone the metallic coating of the inner armor, which, although over-melted in places, resisted the destructive force of the neutron matter crumb plowing the rock.

"Amazing," sighed Lupos in awe at the sight of the exposed section of the vertical shaft, where powerful pistons of hydraulic cylinders were still at work, moving some complicated equipment, full of gears and huge flywheels. All of the machinery was illuminated by a ghostly blue glow, beaming directly from salvaged wall fragments draped in thick, luminescent material. "The transmission from the probe is being recorded?" He asked.

"Yes, Commander. Both in the searchers' memory banks and in our database."

"Very good. The scientific division will have interesting material to analyze. It's interesting that Skunians are nowhere to be seen. Neither alive nor dead." Lupos rubbed his jaw thoughtfully. "These positions look like they have never been used." He walked even closer to the screen. "Here and here..." he pointed to a series of shallow recesses in the walls of the shaft, in front of which stood arched racks adapted to the anatomy of the aliens, padded with a thick layer of spongy substance. Opposite the seats, already in the niches themselves, behind semi-transparent sheets of foil glowed multi-colored lights, pulsating according to the rhythm of the machinery working nearby."

"Not in use?" Puzzled the operator. "How did you recognize it, Commander?"

"Have you ever seen the control panel of their fighter jet?" answered Lupos with a question.

The sergeant was silent for a few moments.

"Yes, I have seen it," he finally replied. "It had an identical seat."

"I have seen dozens of these, Sergeant. It's all about the foam they are covered with." Lupos explained. "Skun exoskeletons have damn sharp edges of the back plates. They cut this material like razor blades. Exploited, these scaffolds look like some madman cut them with a knife. These, on the other hand, have no scratches at all. They have not been used..." he repeated thoughtfully.

From the operator's position came a series of melodic beeps, ending with a single, continuous sound.

"Scanning of the Oumuamua completed," the operator announced. "Data processing is in progress." He added after a moment.

He led the probe out of the canyon and pointed it toward the hillside, on the slope of which rested among the rocks a fragment of a shattered torpedo ship.

"How long will it take?"

"At least a quarter of an hour."

"Long..."

"Among other things, this scanner model is equipped with quantum sensors, Commander, and they really collect a whole lot of the most diverse data. It must take time to organize it."

"I understand. Please continue with the reconnaissance mission."

The probe circled over the top of the hill, then lowered its flight and descended on the other side."

"What the hell is that!" astonished Lupos when a second later the entire surface of the screen was filled with a metallic structure, marked with long rows of rivets and clearly spherical structure.

"An interceptor drone!" the operator straightened up in his chair and reached for the switches on the console with a nervous movement. "Turning on the jammer!"

The image on the screen lost focus and rocked as the probe shot upward, then flew over the top of the hill to get as far away from the enemy machine as possible.

The directional emissions of the Skunian interceptors had a short range. At longer distances, the pulse beam lost too many data packets to effectively break through, or fool the security systems of the attacked object.

"Get it out of there," Lupos instructed. "We'll wait for the results of the scan."

"I withdraw!" confirmed eagerly the operator.

After a few dozen seconds, the probe docked safely in the searcher's transport bay. When the status message appeared on the screen, the operator pulled the helmet off his head and wiped with a cloth the sensor relay boards located inside.

"Did they try to intercept it?" Lupos asked.

"It's a bit strange, Commander."

"I don't understand?"

"The probe's receiving system registered only one faint pulse..." The man put his helmet down on the console top and pointed with his finger to one of the minor screens.

"What's strange about that? After all, you withdrew it."

"The point is, Commander, that the fragment of the protocol that the enemy drone emitted came from our communication sequence. Take a look at the signature," he stepped back so Lupos could see the display screen. "UF-101. It's a proprietary protocol, encrypted at multiple levels, unbreakable."

"Are you suggesting that they intercepted Dressler's torpedo ship and broke through our security?"

"Not only did they break through, but apparently they also dealt with the cipher."

"What did the drone actually emit?" Lupos approached the operator's station and leaned over the display indicated by the man.

"An initiation script, an access request, and a packet containing a two-sided descriptor key," the operator calculated, scrolling through the lines of code displayed on the screen. "The same key that our onboard AIs store in the most closely guarded disk sectors."

"To me it looks like they simply sent what they managed to extract from the torpedo ship's data bank," Lupos stated.

"That's what I thought at first too," replied the sergeant. "But then I noticed the differences. Each of the files had been decrypted and compiled in such a way that the probe's receiving system could read them on the fly, without involving the descriptor module in the process and implementing the associated security procedure. In short, they spoke back to us in our own way, Commander."

"So it wasn't a matter of interception... just contact?"

"It seems so."

"This record will have to be reviewed in detail. If they really want to talk to us, it will be an unprecedented event," Lupos shook his head, as if he himself did not believe what he had just said. "Unprecedented," he repeated. "Corporal!" He turned toward Kulak. "Please summon engineer Sniegova and Lieutenant Moss to the bridge."

"Yes, sir!" the head of the communications division immediately reached with his hand to the internal communication switch and called both of them mentioned.

"You will send a record of this transmission to Sniegova's terminal," Lupos instructed the operator. "What about the results of the scan?"

"It is just finishing processing."

"Excellent. Once they are ready, please send them to me."

"Commander! Commander!" cried Kulak suddenly. "Colonel Dressler on the line! Switching to your terminal!"

Lupos jumped toward his chair with such a long jump that, if it weren't for the rumble with which he slumped in his chair, one would have thought that the gravity generators on the ship had been turned off.

"Commander Lupos, Separate Team UF-101!" he breathed out into the microphone, rubbing his bruised elbow and wincing in pain. With his other hand, he activated the individual call recorder, independent of the onboard system.

"Good... to... hear you, Commander..." came from the speakers a snarling, somewhat indistinct voice, actually not so much a voice, but rather a loud whisper.

"You too, Colonel. Are you all right?"

"Not really... I've received... a sizable... sizable dose of radionuclides. I have advanced symptoms of... radiation sickness."

"Please state your location. We have two searchers there, they will take you."

"Searchers?" it growled from the speakers. "Is... is this some kind of joke?"

"We've removed most of the instruments from them to make room for the cargo space. You will fit in without the slightest problem."

"Commander... I need... a regeneration chamber... And you... you offer me an engine compartment..." the snarl turned into a damp cough.

Lupos with the utmost difficulty restrained himself not to parry with laughter.

"Sorry Colonel, but I do not have specialized rescue vehicles. Frontier will catch up with the wreck in about an hour and a half, maybe even earlier. We will pick up searchers in flight, so it will go fast. You must hold out. Please provide the location."

For a long moment, only heavy wheezing came from the speakers.

"About... About a hundred meters from the edge of the canyon. Opposite the middle... middle drive nozzle."

Without waiting for Lupos' command, the searcher operator immediately activated the vision systems of both machines and pointed the cameras at the region Dressler had described. A wide panorama of Oumuamua's stern appeared on the main screen, with three massive rock formations dominating its center section, under which were the many-meter diameter tunnels of the exhaust nozzles.

"There he is!" he called out, pointing to a small white spot under one of the rock overhangs.

"Zoom in!" instructed Lupos.

The image on the screen zoomed in, losing focus. The spot of white turned into a slightly blurry human figure, sitting on a large boulder and clad in a dust-covered vacuum suit. A round, dark hole in the rock could be seen in the back.

"Colonel, we have preview," Lupos said. "Please don't move, the searchers will be there soon," he added.

"No worries... Commander. I'm... I'm not going anywhere..." it rustled from the speakers.

"And please do not hang up, we will instruct you on a regular basis. Corporal Kulak." Lupos pushed back the microphone and nodded at the communications officer. "How did he even establish communication with us?" The commander looked suspiciously at the displays of the receiving system.

"I wonder about that, too, Commander," the communications officer replied. Consternation was painted on his face. "The torpedo ship is destroyed, the black box locator is not responding, and the suit the colonel is wearing has only the simplest on-board communications module."

"Are you able to locate the source of the transmission?"

"I'm just now tracking them." Kulak pressed several switches on the console. The hitherto dark screens at his station came to life, a map of all artificial radio wave sources located in the sector through which the cruiser was currently moving and the surviving fragment of the Oumuamua drifting in front of it appeared.

"Searchers on the way," the drone operator reported. The bubble of the sensor helmet shone on his head again. "They will be there in a moment."

"Please hurry up Sergeant, the Colonel is probably not well," replied Lupos, looking anxiously at the main screen. The lenses of the drones' cameras, even though the machines had already taken off, were still pointed at Dressler. The figure in the suit was no longer sitting on a boulder, but was kneeling beside it, with his head lowered low, supporting himself with his hands on the ground.

"Source of transmission traced," Kulak announced. "The signal came from some relay on..." he fell silent for a moment. "On the Oumuamua!" he finished, clearly surprised.

"I beg your pardon?" Lupos turned his eyes away from the main screen and looked at his subordinate from under his furrowed brows. "He is connecting with us using the Skunian apparatus?!" he asked in disbelief.

"Everything points to that," replied the signalman. "The signal is very strong and well filtered. This is a high-power transmitter. Such are not mounted on torpedo ships, not to mention suits.

We'll try to locate his position, perhaps we can reach the system that controls it through it, and then..."

"Then we'll be able to access into their memory banks," Lupos finished for him. "An excellent idea, Corporal," he nodded his head with appreciation. "If successful, extract everything you can from their databases and immediately transfer it to the nearest external server, no matter which organization it belongs to. Sniegova will help you with this," he added at the sight of the lady engineer entering the bridge.

The young woman apparently heard the end of their conversation, because instead of moving toward her corner, which was swamped with papers and equipment, she directed her steps toward the communications operators' station.

"Commander, searchers ready to pick up survivor," reported the operator of the drones.

Lupos looked at the screen. The two machines had landed less than ten meters from the man kneeling among the debris.

"Colonel? Can you hear me?" the commander moved the microphone so close that he almost touched its mesh-covered membrane with his lips.

"Yes, I can hear you," came the spoken confirmation in a low voice.

"Please take a seat in the technical hatch of one of the vehicles. The flaps are unlocked, just lift them."

"Easy... Easy for you to say," Dressler raised a hoarse voice.

"Is it really that bad?"

"Worse, Commander... Much worse..."

"Just this one more effort, Colonel. As soon as we pull the searchers on board, we will immediately put you in the regeneration chamber."

The figure on the screen moved on all fours toward the cameras. Slowly and laboriously. All that could be heard in the speakers was heavy wheezing, murmuring and the occasional quiet, muffled moan. Halfway there, Ian stopped, only to resume his trek a moment later. The panting intensified; the moans turned into muffled sobs.

"I'm going blind..." rustled from the speakers.

The operator of the drones took off his helmet and ran up to Lupos.

"May I?" he asked, pointing to the microphone arm.

The commander nodded only slightly, then pushed the tripod in his direction.

"Colonel, go straight ahead as you are now. The hatch of the chamber is lowered, just sit on it. You will be pulled inside the vehicle, you will not have to climb. Just do not, under any circumstances, tinker with the manual control panel of the lock, because it may lock."

"No... No worries... I can't see anything anyway..."

"I understand," smiled the operator weakly. "Just crawl on the flap, please. It is..." he glanced at the main screen. "It is only about two meters in front of you. Unfortunately, the searcher cameras have a limited field of view, so once you're on it, let us know," having said this, he ran quickly to his console and put on his helmet.

A several dozen of seconds later, a faint voice came from the speakers:

"Now."

10

Cruiser "Pandemonium"
The Solar System

All the lights were on in the support vehicle hangar, from the powerful spotlights placed under the high vaulted ceiling to the signal lights embedded in the polymer surface of the deck.

In the center of the hall, on one of the four circular landing platforms placed on wide pedestals, an elongated, eighteen-meter-long cylindrical silhouette of a long-range searcher gleamed metallic gray. Maintenance machines were running under the belly of the machine, cleaning the carbon-covered nozzles of the external maneuvering engines with jets of hot liquid.

On the openwork footbridge, surrounded by railings, leading from the platform, stood two soldiers wearing heavy combat suits. They held flechette throwers in their armored hands. Another soldier supported the heavy cover of the service bay located in the lower part of the unmanned vehicle. Senior Constable McReady, who had just been evacuated from his post, was crawling out of the dark hatchway. Dressed in a multi-layered protective suit, from a distance he looked like a fat grub trying to get out of rotten fruit.

"Why these guards, Admiral?" Tsugawa asked, looking at the soldiers. The footbridge was bending under their weight.

"A show of strength," Kravchenko explained succinctly.

"Do you want to impress him?" The commander was surprised, approaching the armored glass separating the room they were standing in from the rest of the hangar. The spacious cabin, located on a high gallery, glassed on three sides, had a dual function: a control room, from where technicians managed the operation of machines, and a social area for combat personnel.

"Not at all!" Kravchenko snorted. "He should be afraid!"

"He doesn't look intimidated," Tsugawa said.

The admiral also moved closer to the window.

The stranger, wrapped in a suit, was already standing on the landing pad and, gesturing violently, was perorating something to the soldier, who, paying no attention to it, was calmly checking the fasteners of the flap that had just been lowered.

"This is Kravchenko. Private, what is our guest talking about?" the admiral asked, lifting the communicator to his mouth. "Does he have a problem?"

"He is very dissatisfied, Admiral," replied the soldier. "He demands to be delivered immediately to one of the battle stations near the Fold."

"Please tell him that this is out of the question, as he is a prisoner, and then take him to jail. If he resists, I allow the use of direct coercive measures. If he doesn't resists, also. Of course, discreetly. Do we understand each other?"

"Yes, sir!"

"He's a survivor." Tsugawa recalled. "We should follow the rules."

"We'll make an exception this once." Kravchenko turned off the communicator and put the device in his pocket.

"We'll get into trouble."

"We made them when we fried up this station."

Tsugawa looked out the window again and hissed disapproval as he saw the soldier the admiral had just been talking to throw the prisoner down onto the landing pad, expertly cuff his hands behind his back, take off his helmet, and then with one strong pull, pull him upright.

The soldiers from the footbridge aimed their blasters at the newcomer.

"Admiral, I will be forced to file an official protest," Tsugawa announced. "According to the regulations, I, as the first officer, am responsible for the cabin crew and other people on the ship."

"Help yourself!" Kravchenko shrugged. He turned away from the window and approached a glass cabinet in the corner of the room, filled with plastic bottles of isotonic drinks placed in special holders. He took one out, twisted it off, and took a few sips." Do you prefer to do it electronically or orally, for the record?" He asked, putting the bottle back. "Because if it's electronic, I'm afraid I'll be able to comment on it only after we return to AEgir."

"I'll think about it," Tsugawa replied after a moment of silence.

"Rightly so, Commander. Thinking is the basis," with his back turned, Kravchenko smiled to himself. "Let's go back to the bridge," he said, then slammed the locker door and headed out.

Tsugawa watched the prisoner and the soldiers escorting him until the four of them disappeared into the technical tunnel leading to the upper levels. Then he quickly followed the commanding officer.

The bridge greeted them both with a cacophony of sounds - proximity sensors buzzing, lidar beeping steadily, early warning system speakers wailing electronically.

"The group has crossed the border of the buffer zone, Admiral." reported the chief navigator as soon as Kravchenko crossed the threshold of the control room.

"Are they tracking us?" Sergei asked, settling into the commanding officer's chair.

"Hard to say. We are within range of their optical systems."

"So they didn't use tracking beams?"

"No, Admiral."

"That a girl!" Kravchenko smiled inwardly and asked loudly:

"So why is this mean trick howling so much?" he moved his chin towards the glowing purple panel of the early warning module. The membranes installed in the device's housing vibrated rhythmically.

"Battleship," the operator explained laconically.

"What?!" Kravchenko turned the chair towards him so abruptly that one of the screws that attached the furniture to the floor broke. Out of the corner of his eye, he saw Tsugawa reach the desktop of his console and turn on the side screens one by one."

"Dragon 7, Admiral. For twenty minutes he has been following us at nine thousandths of a light. He also released some drones. They fly even faster and their beams are detected by our system."

"Will they catch up with us before Fold?"

"Drones? Yes."

"And the battleship?"

"If it increases speed by even one percent."

"Holy crap, we can't let this happen. Commander, please regroup the units closing the formation immediately. Cruisers to the end, technical support ships to the middle. Gunships in a fanwise. Those that have tracking mines on board should program them for drone emissions and then place them on the enemy's course."

"Yes, sir!" Tsugawa took a seat at the console and immediately began entering commands into the main command recorder, from where they were to be sent to the individual ships of the group.

"Corporal, please connect to the station and inform me that I wish to speak to Lieutenant Colonel Hialuron," ordered Kravchenko to the signalman. "Gunner!"

"Yes, Admiral!" Roared from the sensory cocoon.

"Please synchronize the fire systems on all cruisers. If the Dragon manages to catch up with us, the only salvation will be a few specific, simultaneous salvos. Escort ships may fire as they see fit."

"I'm implementing it," replied the gunner, shifting in the cradle. The displays near the cocoon began to fill with columns of data.

"Admiral, Lieutenant Colonel Amanda Hialuron on the line," Kulak reported.

Kravchenko grabbed the microphone from his shoulder.

"Turn off the damn noise!" he growled at the navigators, pointing at the early warning panel.

The whine of the loudspeakers stopped as if cut off by a knife.

"Amanda?" he said into the microphone, not bothering with the protocol.

"Yes, Sergei."

"We entered the buffer zone."

"I noticed."

"That battleship of yours is on our tail! Dragon Seven!" he said angrily. "Don't you have the specifications for this contraption on hand somewhere?"

"Do you want to fight him?"

"If he catches up with us, it will be almost inevitable."

"I advise against it."

"Do you have this specification or not?"

"I'll send it to you soon."

"Thank you."

"You're welcome. Sergei..."

"Yes?"

"Surrender, I strongly advise."

"Why is that?"

"You won't be able to handle it. It's a really powerful ship... In fact, it's not even a ship, just a mobile docking platform, battle station and fleet group in one. Its scaffolding alone has more firepower than all your ships put together. I don't want to worry you, but there is a high probability that you will get licked even from a single battleship that is part of this conglomerate."

"Wait, wait..." Kravchenko blinked in disbelief. "What did you call it? Conglomerate?"

"Yes. I'm just sending the installation specifications. Because it is an installation," she emphasized. "The largest combat team in this part of the system, if not the entire system. The pride of the Martian Exploration Campaign. With all due respect, your ridiculous flotilla will have no chance against him. Even theoretical ones."

"And you're only telling me this now?"

"You thought you could escape from them."

"I was wrong..." he sighed. "They accelerated to some impossible speed, and I have no idea how. That's why I'm asking you for these materials."

"Please, please..." she laughed pearly. "Could Epsilon Eridani allow itself to be overtaken technologically?"

"This isn't funny, Amanda. We need to get home as soon as possible. Are you able to establish contact with this machine? Because he doesn't respond to our transmissions."

"And he won't answer. Until you are assigned another status, the security systems of all transceivers in the system will block your transmissions, even if you transmit them through the system's transmitters."

"All systems? And your station?"

"The defense installations at Fold are an exception," she explained.

"Admiral, I have the specifications of Dragon Seven," Tsugawa announced.

Kravchenko nodded and then motioned for the commander to be silent.

"I get the impression, Amanda, that you want us to get arrested," he said.

"I'm trying to help you. I have already spoken to the Dragon Collective and informed them of your situation. I also notified the authorities of the Mars Campaign and sent a report to the Headquarters of the United Organizations on Earth. The former promised to look into the matter, the latter have not responded yet."

"What does Dragon's command say?"

"The commanding body has decided by a majority vote that as long as you have the status of undesirable objects, the operation to intercept and escort you to the anchorage will continue," she replied, and he finally understood why Dragon Seven had waited so long to pursue him. However, the encouraging news was that the news about his fleet's problems had finally reached the local authorities. For that alone, he owed Amanda eternal gratitude.

"Amy, but we have to leave the system as soon as possible. We can't afford to hang around in the middle of nowhere for days until someone finally comes to their senses and lets us fly away!"

"I'm sorry, Sergei. I did my best. I notified everyone I could, blocked defense installations and suspended patrol flights, including unmanned ones. If there had been a classic chain of command on the Dragon, I might have been able to convince the commander-in-chief to hold his horses a bit. Give up."

"I can't, Amy, you know it very well. Even if by some miracle Commander Lupos's ship repelled the Skunians, we still need to get back there as quickly as possible. As soon as possible!" he repeated.

"You're being hysterical," she said. "Passive sensors have not and still do not register anything that would indicate that fighting is taking place in your system. Apart from the one large emission I mentioned earlier, we only recorded some minor flares, and even those relatively far from the planetary system."

"This doesn't mean anything! Besides, what the hell is there supposed to be fighting there when almost a hundred percent of the system fleet is on this side of the Fold?! Who's going to fight? Planetary forces? F-101, i.e. a single cruiser and several shells of its escort? For God's sake, if you don't want to help, at least don't make it harder!" he banged his fist on the arm of the chair.

"Am I making things harder for you?" she asked with resentment in her voice. "You're cruel!"

"I will be cruel," he drawled into the microphone. He sat for some time with his eyes closed, breathing deeply.

"Connect me with Dragon, Amanda," he finally said.

"With whom?" She was surprised.

"With their entire command team, or whatever the decision-making freak you mentioned is called," he explained with a sigh.

"I can't, Sergei."

"Then tell them that if they do not withdraw their drones and do not give up pursuit, one hour from now we will destroy all installations within ten light seconds of the Fold without exception."

The murmur of conversations on the bridge stopped suddenly, as if cut off by a knife.

"I'm... sorry? What... What did you say?" Amanda stammered.

"What you heard," he replied calmly. "We will tear the entire infrastructure here to pieces. And then..." he paused for a moment. "Then we will modify the field matrices that stabilize the cores of the gravity compensators and fly them into the Fold. The next time our fleets meet will be in about seven hundred years, unless, of course, you don't exhaust your resources by then. We will close the anomaly."

"You're bluffing."

"Not this time. Tell them what I said, Amanda."

"I already did it," she replied. "They won't let up," she warned, lowering her voice.

"You can't be sure of that."

"I know this. The regulations do not provide for exceptions."

"Then you should start evacuating the station. If they don't turn back their drones, we will start firing."

"Admiral, I protest! This time officially!" Tsugawa said in a raised voice.

He stood up and walked stiffly to the verbal message recorder module. The device, equipped with super-sensitive microphones, was mounted on the rear wall of the bridge, just behind the navigator's position. He pressed one of the buttons on the housing.

"Commander Salim Tsugawa, first officer on the cruiser Pandemonium, part of the Shadow Raptors battle group," he presented the formula initiating the coding system intended for official correspondence. A blue diode lit up on the recorder panel, indicating readiness for operation.

"Wait a minute, Amanda," Kravchenko said. He turned off his microphone and turned to the deputy. "Please turn it off, Commander. Immediately!" he growled.

Tsugawa, who was just reaching for the fingerprint reader to complete the identification process, froze in mid-motion.

All eyes turned to the admiral.

"If you disrupt the negotiations again, you will end up in custody. Please turn off the recorder and return to your station!"

"But..."

"You will be able to include any reservations regarding the decisions I have made in the protocol after the operation is completed. Understood?"

Tsugawa's hand moved away from the scanner. The device beeped with an emergency sound and a bright red triangle with an exclamation mark appeared on the small display.

"I will follow your orders, Admiral," the commander surrendered. He bowed his head, then turned off the recorder and sat down at his console with a straight expression on his face.

Surprised by this unexpected surrender, Kravchenko looked at him suspiciously for several moments.

"Thank you, Commander," he finally said.

"You're welcome, Admiral," Tsugawa replied.

"Why are you staring?" Kravchenko glanced menacingly at the bridge. Apart from the gunner wrapped in folds of sensory fabric, there was probably not a single person in the room who wasn't looking at him or Tsugawa at that moment.

"Let's get to work!" he boomed out.

The operators sitting closest almost jumped in their seats. In an instant, the cacophony of sounds from the onboard equipment was joined by the clicking of switches and the clatter of mechanical keyboards used by the technicians managing the propulsion systems.

Kravchenko turned on the microphone again.

"Amanda? Are you there?"

"Of course. You don't think I'll run away from the station because of your threats," she replied coldly.

"Have you given our ultimatum?"

"From what I overheard a few minutes ago, this is not YOUR ultimatum, but yours," she said.

"It doesn't matter. I'm in charge of this group, I make decisions and I will bear the consequences," as he said this, he looked at Tsugawa with furrowed eyebrows.

The commander looked back. Not a single muscle moved on his face, as if Tsugawa had completely exhausted his daily limit of expressive behavior.

"Did they somehow respond?"

"Wait a moment, we're just decrypting the return transmission. I'll pass it on..." Amanda's voice stopped suddenly, and a series of crackling sounds echoed through the speakers. The diodes on the communication panel turned red and then went out.

"Communications, what's going on?" Kravchenko looked back at the impressive top of the communications console, around which, like knights of the round table, six operators were sitting, supervising not only the communications system on the cruiser, but also all communications between the individual ships of the group.

The shift leader, a black sergeant with Sigil Autonomy emblems on his uniform sleeves, removed his headphones, leaned forward and reached under the console where signal decoder modules, hidden in shockproof containers, hummed. His colleagues were frantically checking something on their terminals.

"They've changed the coding, Admiral," he announced after a moment, straightening up. "We're already fine-tuning."

"Hurry up." Kravchenko loosened the clasp of his uniform. He shifted in his seat and took out a tube of regenerative conditioner from the compartment in the armrest.

"Done," the communications officer said after a short time. "I'm resuming the transmission."

Kravchenko quickly capped the half-empty tube and slipped it into the compartment on the side of the chair.

The diodes on the communication panel flashed green.

"Admiral Kravchenko to Lieutenant Colonel Amanda Hialuron," he said quickly. "Admiral Kravchenko to Lieutenant Colonel Amanda Hialuron." He repeated, looking anxiously at the indicators of the communication system.

The answer came only after several seconds.

"I'm sorry, Sergei, but we had a little problem with the equipment here. It appears that one of the main encryption relays, located near guard station number three, has been damaged. The station also does not respond. Have you had a hand in this?"

"You mean that little station on the edge of the asteroid belt? The one where McReady is in office?"

"This one. I see that you have already met?" you could feel slight amusement in Hialuron's voice.

"It's not funny, Amanda," he growled. "This scoundrel blocked our communication with the system's authorities and sent a battleship against us. We've lost a ship, Amanda." He drawled. "Cruiser Ukulele. The flagship unit of the Autonomy."

"What? How? Someone shot at your line's ship? Who?!"

"First the Mercury defense machine, then the damn Dragon, or more specifically one of its smaller modules."

"It's impossible, Sergei. Impossible!" she declared with such force that the speaker mesh trembled.

"What is impossible?" he asked scathingly. "That the allied fleet was fired upon without warning, or that the battleship opened fire on a damaged and defenseless ship from which we only miraculously managed to evacuate the crew earlier?"

"Both! None of the automated installations will attack any product of human technology without prior approval from the operations center. That's how they are programmed. And it doesn't matter whether the object is a smuggling ship, a ship, or came from another system."

"This installation supposedly had a failure, that's the information we received," explained Krawczanko.

"Dragon Seven, in combat mode, can only operate in beyond system space. Within the system, it has the same limited scope of operation as any installation. I will never believe that he opened fire on you unprovoked."

"Should I send you the records from the orbiter cameras? The Ukulele had a damaged drive and lost power, but it could still be saved. Our plan was to take it in tow, eventually leave it in your system, and cover the cost of repairing it. One of the local shipyard companies would gain a really lucrative contract. Unfortunately, we were not given such a chance."

"This... This is unacceptable!"

"Really?" Kravchenko smiled sadly. "The Ukulele was the best armed unit in the Epsilon Eridani system. Its loss is a very severe blow to our forces. The group as a whole lost almost twenty percent of its combat strength. What am I saying?" he reflected. "Not a group, but a fleet! Because what you're seeing on the lidar displays right now, Amy, is virtually all of the cosmic forces at our system's disposal." He was silent for a moment, then added bitterly: "Remember that we are the ones who have the Skunians on our backs and we are the ones who have been dealing with them for over a hundred years and keeping them away from the Fold so that you can play here at constructing flying fortresses."

As he spoke, he glanced at the main screen, where the technical diagram of the large battleship promised by Hialuron had just been displayed.

She herself didn't speak immediately. The loudspeakers were silent for so long that the concerned communications staff began to fidget.

"Amanda?" Kravchenko tapped the microphone with his finger and then looked back at them with a questioning face. The shift leader shook his head to show that he too did not know what caused the delay and pointed to the transmitting and receiving panel.

All diodes on the device glowed with a uniform green light.

A moment later, the familiar voice echoed in the room again.

"I'll talk to the Dragon collective." Hialuron stated. "It appears that someone may have overstepped their authority by authorizing the firing of your cruiser. As the sector commander, I should be notified of every case of unauthorized intrusion and I should be consulted on any armed actions. I will find the culprits, I promise." She concluded forcefully.

"You don't have to look for it, Lieutenant Colonel," said Kravchenko. "We've already found him. This is Constable McReady, currently on board our ship."

"Have you captured our officer?" she was amazed.

"We saved him," Kravchenko corrected, avoiding the look of the obviously outraged Tsugawa.

"You have to free him. Disciplinary proceedings will be initiated against him."

"We will do this, but when we pass through the Fold. Constable McReady will be our additional guarantee."

"Sergei, taking a hostage will only make the situation worse."

"He will come back safe and sound, you have my word of honor as an officer. I'll have him packed into a landing pod and fired back as soon as we pass through the anomaly."

A heavy sigh came from the speakers.

"Fine, so be it. I will try to persuade Dragon command to abandon the pursuit. And you don't do anything stupid in the meantime, please," she said unexpectedly softly. "Currently, almost three thousand people are stationed at nearby installations, half of them are civilian technical personnel. We won't be able to evacuate everyone, certainly not in two hours. Keep this in mind in case my efforts prove unsuccessful. Speak soon."

The speakers went silent. This time, no one had any doubts that the transmission had ended.

"You heard," Kravchenko rose from the chair and went to the middle of the room. "No offensive actions, no touching with tracking beams. Commander, please make sure of this."

"Yes, sir," Tsugawa replied.

"Admiral," the gunner's voice suddenly rumbled from the cocoon. "What about the mines? The system reports that they have been set out."

"Damn it!" Kravchenko swore. "Deactivate all! Immediately!"

11

Cruiser "Frontier"
The Epsilon Eridani planetary system

"How are you feeling, Colonel?" Sniegova's voice, although amplified by the acoustic system of the medcom chamber, barely reached Ian's ears.

Immersed up to his neck in the thick, muddy goo of the regenerative mixture, stuffed with dozens of needles injecting synthetic plasma saturated with stem cell conglomerates directly into the tissues, with his head smeared with a thick layer of goo supporting the regeneration of hair follicles and with oxygen tubes inserted into his nostrils, he had the impression of being slowly and inexorably immersed in the swamp.

"Not too good..." he wheezed with difficulty, swallowing a lump of cold phlegm that had formed in his throat.

He had no idea how much time had passed since he had crawled into the searcher with the last of his strength, or what the journey back was like, because he had a blackout when the world went dark and he sank to the floor of the chamber in the drone's hull. The last thing he remembered was a bundle of neatly cut cables, with plugged ends, sticking out from one of the walls of the alcove.

"How long have I been stuck here?" he asked.

He opened his eyelid a little and turned his head carefully towards the screen covered with thick glass, which displayed basic biometric data. Unfortunately, the screen was almost completely covered with a sticky substance.

"Second day," replied the engineer. She leaned over the transparent lid of the chamber and wiped it with her sleeve.

"Is it bad?" he asked, although he was perfectly aware of how much damage the radiation must have caused to the body.

"Not good, Colonel," she replied carefully. Even through the damp cover, he could see her furrowed brows and gloomy face. "The Commander has already notified the leadership of the Medical Corps. The transport capsule is on its way."

"So, it's really bad." If he had been able to take a deep breath, he would have sighed heavily. Unfortunately, he couldn't. Rolls of fabric around the chest, supporting the absorption of the regenerative gel, effectively prevented this.

"Not good," she repeated.

"Please... Please go right ahead," he said, closing his eyes. "I'm used to hearing... such diagnoses."

"All right." She nodded, and then moved the medical robot boom with a display attached to its end closer to her.

She analyzed the data for a few moments.

"Sixty-five percent of connective and muscle tissue cells were damaged, one hundred percent of the bone marrow was damaged, and internal organs did not function, except for the lungs, heart and pancreas," as she read more information, her voice became more and more shaky.

"Zombie... I'm a zombie..." Ian groaned. "Is there any good news?"

"We managed to stop the degradation of blood vessels, regenerate optic nerves and restore cellular osmosis... Never mind, Colonel. The most important thing is that we managed to keep you alive. The medical equipment at the Corps' disposal is light years ahead of what we have here in terms of technology," she slapped her hand on the chamber lid. "You will recover, please don't worry."

He smiled weakly. The girl's indistinct silhouette cast a shadow, thanks to which the bright light from the ceiling lamps stopped hurting his eyes so much. In fact, he could see everything much more clearly now than when he was lying curled up in a ball and sliding on the transport platform through the transport tunnel, illuminated by cold blue light and carved in the Oumuamua's stone armor, passing along the way the motionless lumps of Skunian automatons, most likely destroyed by electromagnetic impulses coming from dozens of exploding surface of nuclear charges.

"What about the wreck?" he asked.

"Nothing special, Colonel," replied the engineer. "Fire from the frigates and the explosion of the reactor from your torpedo ship definitely deprived it of propulsion, destroyed the last of the operational maneuvering engines and caused a change in trajectory. According to the latest information, it is drifting along a safe route and there is no risk of it coming near any of our larger installations. Besides, a squadron of Autonomy patrollers is constantly keeping an eye on it." She moved away from the chamber and approached the terminal mounted in the wall.

"The pod will be here in less than two hours. During the journey, you will be put into a medically induced coma," she informed.

"Coma?" he became concerned.

"It's a necessity, Colonel. The life support systems our medcom is equipped with are not compatible with the capsule's instrumentation. We will transport you and the entire healing module.

Even through the thick cover, Ian heard the click of fastening clips being released, then the whistling of an electric screwdriver. A few minutes later, a cart with equipment rolled into the room, followed by two technicians who immediately started connecting some wires to the regeneration chamber.

"One moment, gentlemen." Sniegova stopped them with a gesture, then approached the chamber and leaned over the lid again. The ends of her raven hair stuck to the damp glass.

"If you wish, Colonel, I can pack your personal belongings. I'll make sure they're transferred to the Corps base," she offered.

"I would... I would be much obliged." A cloud of steam escaped from between his chapped lips. As technicians activated the equipment on the cart, the gel filling the chamber thickened and became cooler. "Have you... have you checked the memory dumps from the searchers yet?" He asked with an effort, feeling his lips and tongue begin to go numb.

"Not yet, Colonel," replied Sniegova. "For now, we keep them on an isolated server. System firewalls detected some unknown code, it is possible that the Oumuamua also made an emergency data dump. Skunians have already proven many times that they can use the solutions we have developed."

"Lady engineer... Katya..." Ian whispered vaguely. "You must... You must protect..." he moved his mouth, the next words were drowned out by the clang of metal: a blue-enamel cylinder fell from the transport cart and rolled against the wall of the infirmary.

Sniegova glared at the careless technician, then, intrigued, she moved her face closer to the cover, almost touching her nose to the grille covering the intercom module embedded in its surface.

"Keep it down!" she growled towards the man struggling with the cylinder. "Please repeat that, Colonel," she said into the microphone, turning the volume knob all the way up.

"This code... It must not be deleted. You must protect this data. At all costs... They are... they are the answer to all... our questions. Promise... Promise you will multiply them and send them... to my terminal. Access code... seven three zero six two five." Ian's voice was so weak that she had to press her ear against the loudspeaker to hear what he was saying.

"Seven three zero six two five?" she made sure.

He nodded in confirmation, barely perceptible. Through the frosted glass, she could only see the outline of his face and the silver gleaming oxygen tubes in his nostrils.

"I'll take care of it, Colonel. I promise. I have access to all the memory banks on the cruiser," she said, then turned off the intercom and retreated to the wall, where she calmly waited while the technicians finished calibrating the life-slowing equipment, then loaded the crate with the sleeping man inside onto the trolley's transport platform, and then she walked briskly out of the deserted dispensatory.

***

"Are you crazy? Do you want to pass unverified data through the main system?"

Lieutenant Moss rose from his chair and limped slightly went to the terminal where Sniegova was sitting.

They had been locked inside Dressler's cabin for several dozen minutes. During this time, Sniegova managed to stuff the colonel's meager belongings into a traveling container with wheels, with the help of Moss, who pressed his knees against the lid of the box so that the latches could be fastened. Unfortunately, he once again strained his hip joint, injured during a recent skirmish with a Skunian landing force on Habitat Four. "Skunks could have hidden a lot of nasty algorithms in the code."

"Don't exaggerate, Stan, they're not completely unverified. They passed the security filters on the first server," she objected. Tilting her head, she carefully watched the columns of symbols flit across the screen.

"Only because decompilers at this stage read them as graphic files," he said. "The main decoder automatically changes the extensions and then starts detailed reading."

"Well, well, well..." Sniegova looked at him with sudden respect. "Someone here really did his homework."

"I have a very good teacher," he immediately returned the compliment.

"Thank you," she smiled. "Unfortunately, we have to do this. Apart from downloading them directly from the server to the colonel's terminal, there is no way to bypass the main system. They have to go through a central computer."

"What if it's spyware?" he tapped his finger on the screen. "Then what?"

"I trust the Colonel, Stan. It was not without reason that he asked me to secure them."

"I trust him too, but you saw the condition he's in." He shuddered at the memory of the terribly burned figure, smeared with blood and secretions, which the on-board paramedics had pulled out of the overheated vacuum suit. "It's hard radiation. It destroys all types of tissue, including nervous tissue. Do you understand what I mean?" he asked carefully, a little afraid of the girl's reaction to what he had just suggested.

She nodded.

"This wasn't the delirium of a terminally ill man, Stan," she said calmly. "On the contrary. Considering the state he was in, the Colonel expressed himself quite clearly," she said.

Moss limped away from the terminal and sat back in his chair. He looked around the cabin. By the standards of a warship, the colonel's quarters were tastefully decorated. A wide, double bed with a mattress covered with a delicate fabric, a 150-inch display imitating a window and a sofa with a comfortable, pouffed backrest placed opposite it - all this made the cabin look no worse than a room in a decent, multi-star hotel in one of the enclaves on Aegir.

"Let's connect directly to the server," he suggested, pointing to the door. From the accommodation deck, it was literally a stone's throw to the small server room located in the central part of the cruiser, intended for storing raw data dropped by nearby ships and installations.

"How do you want to get there?" she asked with surprise, fully justified, because the room had no entrance holes.

Placed behind thick walls covered with a layer of composite insulation, the graphene disks of the memory bank computers operated at extremely low temperatures, just slightly above the temperature of the vacuum of space. The whole thing was operated remotely, using manipulators. In the event of more serious faults, a special technical channel was opened through which repair machines entered.

"To connect the Colonel's computer to the server, we would have to use the technical console. Neither of us has the appropriate permissions. In fact, no one on the ship has them, not even the Commander."

"How come no one?" Now it was Moss's turn to be surprised.

"We can process this data, copy it, change its location, but we don't have physical access to the equipment."

"Why?"

"You haven't heard? Some of the central units are equipped with components based on organic compounds and their memory paths cannot be allowed to come into contact with factors of biological origin. Another Skunian patent," she explained.

"Oh fuck..." He sighed. "Organic computers..."

"Something like this. It's strange that you weren't informed about this."

"I think there was a mention of it in one of the on-board bulletins..." he remembered.

"The equipment is operated only by sterile machines, operating under specially developed procedures and based on maintenance schedules." She recited.

"Have you learn this by heart?" he laughed.

"Unlike some people, I read the correspondence delivered to me. And I didn't have to master the art of it. I have a good memory," she cut herself off immediately.

"Touche!" he complimented her retort, trying to show off his knowledge of the French language, which, like several other popular languages, died a natural death in the first half of the 22nd century, after a series of religious wars that swept through the world's greatest powers.

Sniegova obviously appreciated his efforts because she smiled brightly.

"So you can see that it won't be possible to run it through the main system."

"I don't like this," he sighed, shifting in his chair and rubbing his hip. Right after the injury occurred, he fell on the sofa, stabbed with burning pins of pain; unfortunately, the soft, cavernous seat only intensified the suffering. From that moment on, he sat on the edge of a foldable aluminum chair that Sniegova had found in one of the storage compartments.

"I trust the Colonel," she repeated. "There's something very important in these files."

"Okay," he gave way. "Do as you want. I'm just warning you," he said with a grimace. The pain in his hip was getting worse with each passing moment, and changing positions or shifting body weight to the other hip no longer helped.

Sniegova turned away from the terminal and looked at it carefully.

"Go to the dispensatory," she said with concern. "While you can still walk," she added, seeing him straighten up in his chair with an effort.

"It'll pass soon," he groaned. "It's just a muscle strain."

"Yes, of course, a muscle!" she snorted. She came closer and, ignoring his protests, unbuttoned his uniform jacket and then pulled up his undershirt.

"Ouch!" she hissed at the sight of the huge, blue-black hematoma on his stomach and the long, crusted scar stretching from the ribs towards the groin. "You should lie down in the medcom chamber. You have internal injuries."

"Come on, it's just a bruise," he said, then pushed her hands away and straightened his clothes.

"Of course. And Dressler only got a little tan." She shook her head disapprovingly. "Get me out of here, now!" she pointed to the door. "It's no joke. You didn't show up at the medcom after we returned from the habitat, no X-ray was done, no tests were done, and only that scratch was treated. Get out to the dispensatory or I'll notify the Commander!"

"Help yourself!" he threw up his arms. "I wonder how the old man will react to seeing us in the Colonel's quarters, tinkering with his personal terminal."

"Stanley," she drawled. "Does it always have to be this way? Do I have to argue with you every damn time?"

"The quarrel of lovers is the renewal of love..." he smiled weakly.

"Stan!" she glared at him.

"I'll go, but promise me you'll be careful when entering this information into the system. Remember that our most important on-board AIs are recycled and, as internal systems, are not protected by major security firewalls. Their protocols are also not the most up-to-date."

"I noticed," she sighed. "This would not be possible in our Union. The software should be updated on an ongoing basis and properly protected against external interference. Go now," she turned to the terminal and initiated the transfer of data from peripheral servers to the central memory bank, from where the decoded data would then go to the colonel's computer disk.

Moss hesitated for a moment, then lumbered towards the exit.

"Come down to the dispensatory later and tell me how it went," he said as the door rolled aside, accompanied by the hiss of pneumatics.

Sniegova, staring at the screen, just waved her hand impatiently.

12

Cruiser "Pandemonium"
The Solar System

The clamor of the warning system's signals found Kravchenko in his favorite corner of the sanitary compartment, where he was happily inhaling the smoke from his last cigarette. The sanitary room, created thanks to the wide passage leading from the bridge to the evacuation hangar, instantly lit up with the crimson glow of alarm lamps. At the same time, there were sounds of automatically lowering toilet flaps, the crash of cabinets with cosmetic items being pulled into the walls, and the gurgling of water being pumped into spare tanks.

The communicator vibrated, and the admiral's earpiece announced its existence with a series of loud clicks. Irritated, he threw his half-smoked cigarette into the waste disposal bin. Worst of all, the only person who could supply him with these dust- and mold-stinking nicotine carriers was currently four light years away, in the Epsilon Eridani system, on one of the Sigil Authority's mining installations.

"What's going on there again?" he growled angrily.

"Admiral, the battleship Dragon Seven has caught up with us and is targeting the ships closing the formation one by one." Tsugawa's voice rang in his ear.

"Damn it! Get me connected to Lieutenant Colonel Hialuron immediately!"

He walked quickly to the bridge.

"Connection established, Admiral," Tsugawa informed him as soon as the admiral stepped onto the command deck.

For several dozen minutes, i.e., from the moment when a spark broke out between them regarding the treatment of the Martian constable evacuated from the damaged installation, the offended Tsugawa had been communicating with him only on an official basis, consistently ignoring all attempts to enter into any casual conversation.

"Please switch to my console," Kravchenko replied equally stiffly, and then, without bothering the deputy with a glance, he approached the command post and sat down in the chair. The communications panel signaled readiness for operation with a row of flashing diodes.

"This is Admiral Sergei Kravchenko, Commander-in-Chief of the United Fleet of the Epsilon Eridani system," he said officially. "The ships of my group are currently being targeted by the offensive systems of the battleship Dragon Seven. I demand an immediate cessation of offensive actions. Our defensive systems are seventy percent supervised by autonomous AIs, so there is a real risk that they will perceive the targeting beams as an act of aggression and trigger defensive procedures."

"I understand, Sergei. I will send this information to Dragon's command," Hialuron's voice sounded from the speakers.

"Hurry up, Amanda. I am not joking. Defense AIs have over two and a half thousand tracking mines equipped with a detect-destroy system at their disposal. It is an autonomous weapon used to track down and eliminate Skunian interceptors. Once programmed, it cannot be undone. There will be a carnage throughout the entire sector, because the contraption will search for targets until it succeeds or until it runs out of cells," he said calmly.

Seeing the concerned glances of the operators closest to him, he winked at them and then put his finger to his lips, commanding silence.

They understood immediately, some smiled, others nodded in approval. They did not have such mines in their ammunition depots because, as they were too dangerous for space transportation, tracking mines had recently been withdrawn from use by a secret order of the United Space Forces Command Staff.

However, the locals couldn't know about this.

The bluff apparently worked, because the station's response came with a strange delay.

"I've forwarded your warning to the Dragon collective," said Amanda. Perhaps it was due to a temporary disruption in the converter module, but Kravchenko could have sworn he heard the first signs of panic in her voice. "They will turn off the tracking systems, but on one condition..."

"There will be no conditions!" He interrupted her. "A few more minutes of such groping and the sector will be full of mines."

"On condition that you turn off the defensive systems." She finished.

"There is no such technical possibility. You are dealing with warships adapted to fight an enemy operating from hiding and using dormant units to attack, activated only for the duration of the encounter battle. We cannot just turn off systems, especially those whose primary task is to defend us against a surprise attack. They are also autonomous. You understand?"

This time he had to wait almost a minute for an answer.

At this time, the alarm lamps went out and the signals also became silent.

"They stopped tracking us," the weapons systems operator said from his cocoon.

A collective sigh of relief passed through the bridge.

Kravchenko, mindful that his microphone was still on, just nodded to show that he had heard the message.

"It's settled, Sergei. It seems that your argument has finally convinced them," came Hialuron's response from the loudspeakers, spoken in a much cheerier tone. "By the way, I was wondering what else you could come up with to intimidate us."

"I didn't come up with anything," he said indignantly.

"Threat of opening fire on our installations, hostage," she began to list, "closing the Fold, releasing autonomous tracking mines. Have I missed something?"

"Probably not," he replied, feeling Tsugawa's disapproving look on his back. "I understand that now we will be able to fly into this damn anomaly without any problems?" saying this, he waved his hand urgently at the operators of the propulsion system, who, seeing this gesture, immediately leaned over the instruments.

"Basically, yes," she confirmed. "I have only one request."

"I'm listening."

"Release the constable. Now. Still on this side of the Fold."

"Amanda, I lost my cruiser because of this bastard."

"Believe me, I'm troubled by it very much. McReady will answer for this, I promise. Nevertheless, he is still a citizen of this system and a public official. I can't let him be kidnapped by you. My job is to protect the sector and all citizens within it. I insist, Sergei."

"Okay," he agreed with a sigh. "I'll have him put in the capsule now. We'll launch it towards your station. Commander," he turned to Tsugawa. "Please ensure that the captive... Pish!... survivor is placed in the transport capsule."

"Yes, sir!" Tsugawa bowed his head, then stood up and quickly left the bridge.

Before he disappeared into the corridor, Kravchenko managed to notice that the man was smiling to himself.

"It's done," he said into the microphone. "Thank you, Amy. One day I will return the favor, I promise," he added more quietly, almost in a whisper.

"I will remember, Sergei," she replied. "Good luck. Kick these stinkers' asses."

A second later, the call ended.

Kravchenko took a deep breath. He wiped his sweaty forehead with the back of his hand.

"Well, finally," he muttered. "Navigation!" he threw over his shoulder. "Zoom in on all the guard stations around the Fold. All on the main screen."

After a few moments, the image on the central display split into four parts. You could see the shapes of battle stations dotted with points of light; their outlines barely visible against the blackness of space.

"Which one is closest to the Fold?"

"The one in the lower left quarter, Admiral."

"Is that where the transmission came from?" Kravchenko turned his chair towards the communication posts.

"Yes, Admiral," confirmed the radio chief.

"Please highlight it." He got up from the chair and walked to the dais, over which a sensory cocoon with a gunnery inside was hanging. Screens placed around the cradle cast a blue glow on the silvery fabric, veined with fiber optic cables, through which the gunner issued commands to the onboard firing systems and supervised and, if necessary, coordinated military operations carried out by other ships.

"Sergeant." Said Kravchenko. "If the worst were to happen, if other stations or smaller installations opened fire on us, we must under no circumstances fire at this particular facility. Under no circumstances, understood?"

"The one marked?" the gunner made sure. His voice sounded like it was coming from a deep well.

"Correct. Please give it the appropriate status and implement it in the systems on all units."

"Right away."

The cocoon rustled slightly, the glow emanating from the screens briefly turning purple as digitized impulses from the psychosensors placed in the cocoon flashed through the displays.

"Done, Admiral," said the operator. "I marked it as an allied installation. Before I approve this, can I ask you something?"

"Yes?"

"What if she opens fire on us?"

"She won't open."

"Are you sure about this, Admiral?"

"One hundred percent, Sergeant." Kravchenko replied confidently.

"Then I approve," came from the cocoon.

The displays flashed scarlet again.

"Thank you," Kravchenko jumped down from the dais and took a seat at his console. He turned on the command relay module.

"To all crews!" he started. "This is Admiral Kravchenko speaking. In thirty minutes, we will pass through the Fold and return to our home system. As everyone has probably noticed, our journey through the Solar System was quite unpleasant and resulted in significant losses. Fortunately for us, we managed to negotiate permission to fly with the local authorities. Unfortunately, there is still a real danger that some of the local defense installations will consider us hostile objects. In connection with the above, I turn to the commanders with a recommendation, I repeat, a RECOMMENDATION, not to open fire on them, even if the artificial intelligence controlling them took offensive actions. I will repeat it again," he emphasized forcefully. "This is not an order, but only a recommendation. Let's not escalate the situation, let's not give the battleship following our trail an excuse to fight. We cannot afford to lose any more cruisers. Our priority is to return to the Epsilon Eridani system, even if..." he paused and closed his eyes, as if afraid of his next words. "Even if it would be at the cost of losing more escort units. Thank you for your attention." With a quick movement, almost angrily, he turned off the module. "Duty officer!" He exclaimed, looking at no one in particular.

"Yes, Admiral!" A young boy, no more than twenty years old, with AEgir Air Force patches on the sleeves of his uniform jumped up from behind one of the side consoles.

Kravchenko, who saw him for the first time in his life, looked at him carefully.

"Lieutenant Owen Marshall reporting on orders!" Said the officer quickly, seeing his superior's uncertainty. "I am, I mean I was, a liaison officer on the Ukulele," he explained, swallowing nervously.

Kravchenko looked at him for a few more seconds, then gestured for him to come closer.

"That's very good," he said as the soldier stood at attention next to the command console. "You will take four special officers from the landing platoon and fly them in an endotransporter to the cruiser Naomi, where you will make sure that its commander, Captain Jorge Invald, does not do something he will regret very much later."

"I don't understand, Admiral," the officer swallowed again.

"If you served as a liaison officer, you certainly had dealings with Captain Invald on more than one occasion, yes?"

"Yes, Admiral," confirmed Marshall. "Many times, just like with the commanders of the other cruisers."

Kravchenko looked at him carefully again.

"That's strange, because I don't recognize you," he muttered.

"On this ship, Commander Tsugawa received reports from me." Said the officer.

"Correct." Tsugawa, who had returned to the bridge a few moments ago, was settling himself behind his console. "Lieutenant Marshall was drafted along with some of the personnel evacuated from the Ukulele. I personally authorized his new assignment."

"Why I don't know anything about it?" Kravchenko was surprised.

"This is standard procedure, Admiral, and is the responsibility of lower-level command staff," explained Tsugawa.

Kravchenko frowned, trying to remember which of the regulations governed this issue, but unfortunately to no avail.

"Never mind," he gave up. "You'll go to the Invald and make sure that old madman doesn't think of blowing up everything he passes along the way," he told Marshall bluntly.

"But..."

"No buts, Lieutenant. If he causes problems, I allow the use of direct coercive measures. You can even arrest him."

"Admiral, maybe I will take care of it?" Tsugawa suggested, looking at the obviously terrified lieutenant.

"No, Commander, that's out of the question. He would immediately know that we had assigned him a Cerberus and he wouldn't even let you on the bridge."

"He'll figure it out anyway." Tsugawa was sceptical.

"Not necessarily. Lieutenant Marshall is the liaison officer. We will send him there under the pretense of delivering the orders on, say, some physical medium. Just like we do during radio silence. You will bring this up, Commander, under some point of the regulations, if, of course, there is one."

"It doesn't exist," replied Tsugawa briefly.

"Then please create it. You have my approval. Corporal, come here!" Kravchenko nodded to the sentry standing by the door.

"You will place four men from your squad under Lieutenant Marshall's command," he said as the soldier ran to his position and stood at attention next to the officer. "They will go with him to the cruiser Naomi as an armed support. Please make sure they are properly equipped. The Lieutenant too. Understood?"

"Yes, sir! Please follow me, Lieutenant." With the hissing of the combat suit's pneumatic systems, the soldier moved towards the exit. Marshall followed, confusion and surprise still evident on his face.

"Invald won't forgive you this," Tsugawa said as both soldiers disappeared in the corridor leading to the elevators.

"That's tough!" The admiral shrugged. "I'd rather have Internal Service on my shoulders than answer to the Criminal Tribunal for crimes against humanity because someone's fuse is too short. And how is our McReady?" He remembered about an overzealous local government official whom Tsugawa was supposed to send to one of the nearby battle stations.

Hearing this question, the commander grimaced, as if he had just swallowed something very, very tart.

"He was placed in a rescue capsule with a remote control option and launched towards station number three, the one marked." He pointed to the main screen, where the image from the onboard telescopes was still displayed. "The navigation section constantly monitors both the flight trajectory and the health condition of the capsule passenger."

"Was he resisting?"

"Constable McReady?"

"Yes."

"He was quite... Rude." The grimace on the commander's face deepened, a vertical wrinkle appeared on his smooth, high forehead. He stared unblinkingly at the switches on the console for a few moments. "So unpleasant that we had to cuff him and then lock him in the capsule's spare endospore," he said finally, without taking his eyes off the instruments.

Kravchenko managed to keep a straight face with great difficulty.

"Do you still want to protest his arrest?" he asked.

"NO!" the answer came quickly and was so violent that the operators sitting closest to the commander flinched. "Of course, I still negatively assess the steps taken against him, but I am inclined to consider them justified by the circumstances." Tsugawa calmed down a bit. "This man is unstable. If you don't mind, Admiral, I will prepare a short report on the incident, attach audiovisual materials from the on-board cameras, and send the entire report to Lieutenant Colonel Hialuron."

"You have my consent," Kravchenko allowed himself a slight smile, especially since Tsugawa was still avoiding his gaze. "Just hurry up, because in a few minutes we will jump to our system."

13

Mobile Medical Corps
Sigil moon orbit

"Well, well, well, look who it is. Colonel Dressler! And who did this to you?" a booming voice startled Ian from his nap. Ian, plastered with sensors, opened his eyes, but through the steamy lid he saw only a dark, bulky silhouette.

"Nobody... I did it myself," he croaked in response. "Larson?" he asked, then raised his hand and tried to wipe the glass of the lid. He only made it worse: his hand, covered in regeneration goo, left greasy, gray-green streaks of gelatinous slime on the glass.

"Yes, it's me, Greg Larson, senior technician, always at your service," the man laughed. "As soon as we found out you were here, we flew over. Unfortunately, that bitch at the decontamination airlock said that only one person could visit you, so I went in and the guys went back to the transporter."

"What are you even doing here?"

"Don't you remember? After all, we have the status of war veterans," Larson laughed even louder. "It's a pity you didn't see Zariba. I don't know where, but he got himself an infantryman's uniform and spits game to a nurses. Do you know that they immediately awarded us the rank of Senior Private and Simon the rank of Staff Sergeant? From zero to officer!"

The giant's laughter made Ian, though his fingers were stiff, reach for the internal control panel and turn down the volume of the intercom speaker.

"Brunnix survived?" he asked when Larson finally stopped cackling. All the time he had in his mind the image of a dying technician, sitting in a dark, stinking corridor of the habitat and supporting the intestines with his hands as they poured out of his abdominal cavity, which had been torn open by Skunian.

"He's a tough bastard, Colonel. We were at his place yesterday. They stitched it together elegantly. What couldn't be patched, they replaced with synthetics, put the guy in some experimental chamber, and then stuck him in a supporting exoskeleton. If I had known earlier what miracles they can do to people here, I would have applied for this job straight away, and not had to spend a pittance all over the place, preserving rusty junk. As I see, they did quite well with you, too," he leaned over the chamber. "Although it probably won't be possible without a skin graft," he said after a while. "Some fire?"

"Radiation," Ian explained, squinting at his feet. He could only see the tips of his fingers and part of his knee. The rest of the body was covered with a layer of regeneration mixture. "I had to make an emergency landing on the Oumuamua wreck. Earlier, our frigates bombarded it with nuclear warheads..." he paused for a moment to catch his breath. "Even earlier... there was a leak from the reactor," with that said, he raised himself on his elbows to look Larson in the eye. To no avail, because through the dirty glass he could only see the outlines of the other man's face. He fell back onto his back with a sickening squelching noise. "This PF-2 that you so willingly gave me had an incompatible cooling system."

"Fuck..." came a muffled curse from behind the glass. "I felt it, I normally felt that this damn software was written by some amateur. Colonel." The face moved even closer to the lid. "I'm very sorry, I really am. According to the diagnostic machine, the cooling components had the correct characteristics. I checked the diameter of the cables, bandwidth, calibration, everything several times. It's the machine's fault, I swear!"

Ian touched his cheek carefully. Where the healing plasters were not applied, he felt with his fingertips some lumps on the skin and an unpleasant, sticky moisture. He sighed inwardly.

"Implants again," he thought. In the most optimistic scenario, he faced a long convalescence, endless infusions of immunopressants and dozens of flights to surgical clinics scattered on the surface of AEgir, both military and private. At worst - an excruciatingly painful treatment of replacing the most damaged tissues with their cloned replicas.

"End of visit!" Suddenly came a female, rather pleasant-sounding voice. It was coming from the entrance to the room. "The patient must rest. Please leave."

"Of course, doctor! I'm gone!" Larson agreed eagerly. "I wish you a speedy recovery! We keep our fingers crossed for you!" He boomed straight into the microphone and before Ian could say anything, he ran out of the room, stamping his heavy boots.

A much smaller, white-clad figure now appeared above the chamber lid.

"Good morning, Colonel. How are we feeling today?" chirped from the loudspeaker.

He decided not to lie or act tough.

"Not good. I'm having trouble breathing and I think..." He tried to wiggle his toes. "I think I lost feeling in my legs..."

"Please don't worry about it, it's the result of the treatments. We've implanted a specialized neurotransmitter in your spinal cord, but while you're immersed in the mixture, it's turned off so it doesn't interfere with the electrical conduction in the regenerative fluid. When it comes to breathing, we have reduced the oxygen concentration to minimize free radicals. Please don't worry about this either, your body is supplied with enough oxygen, but not through natural gas exchange." Explained the doctor. "Do you experience headaches?" she asked, fiddling with the chamber's control panel. The miniature nozzles located in the walls hissed, and the chamber smelled of antiseptic.

"Probably... probably not," replied Ian after a moment's thought. "It's just a little stinging, but it's more discomfort than pain."

"Perfect," she was happy. "This means that the blood vessels have been rebuilt properly. I think that in about two or three days at most we will be able to place you in an open chamber."

"Doctor..."

"Please call me Susan," there was a noticeably warmer note in her voice. "My name is Susan Markowicz.

"And I'm Ian. Nice to meet you, Susan."

There was a burst of laughter from the loudspeaker.

"The old guard," she said, still laughing.

"I don't understand?"

"We've met before, Ian."

"Seriously?"

"A long time ago, when the Medical Corps did not have its own station, and its ships flew from habitat to habitat, taking the sick and injured to hospitals on the planet. I was a nurse back then and I was just starting to think about medical studies. Do you remember?"

Despite the numbness and dryness of his lips, Ian's lips stretched into a wide smile.

"It's a small universe," he said, trying to see something more through the steamy, goo-stained plexiglass.

"Right? I found you on the list of newly admitted patients and added you to my flock," she explained, walking around the chamber and fiddling with the devices placed around it. "By the way, they treated you badly. It's the Skunk ship, right?" she asked, stopping at the head of the chamber.

"Sort of. The torpedo ship I was flying in had a breakdown..."

"You were very lucky anyway," she said.

"What's wrong with me? Just don't beat around the bush, Susan. I've been injured before, but I've never felt so bad."

182

"I know, I looked through your medical records. You had a lot of injuries and contusions, some of them very nasty, I admit, but the fact that you had never been so irradiated before..." she paused for a few moments to walk around the chamber again. More nozzles were activated inside, and a yellowish goo with a vanilla scent began to flow out with a quiet gurgle from a metal pipe, the outlet of which was covered with a movable flap.

"Ninety percent of your body surface has been burned, almost all of your internal organs have dissolved, from the sternum down. We replaced them with synthetics, but this is only a temporary solution. It will take a minimum of four weeks to grow cloned versions of them. For now, we are rebuilding your circulatory system and patching the most damaged nerves. I don't know what type of suit you were wearing at the time of the accident, but you owe your life to its design. Everything indicates that its upper part, including the helmet, had additional anti-radiation microfibers."

"Holy crap..." Ian closed his eyes in shock and took a deep breath, ignoring the throat-scratching smell of chemicals. "So I'm waiting for tissue implants... And right after you regenerate the nervous tissue?"

"Unfortunately, yes," she confirmed his worst suspicions.

He groaned.

"We'll do it under deep anesthesia, and afterward we'll stuff you with the strongest painkillers," she tried to comfort him.

"Please..." he sighed.

"Ian, implant techniques are constantly being improved. We grow tissues faster and faster, conflicts at the molecular level occur sporadically, and we do not experience any rejections at all."

"I'm extremely happy about that," he replied sarcastically, although deep inside he was squirming with fear. He realized that there were a lot of things he still didn't know about life despite being in his seventies, but he knew this one thing for sure: nothing caused as much pain as cloned implants swarming with medical nanobots implanting themselves in the body. Nothing!

"I'm serious," she said, continuing to bustle around the chamber. Her silhouette appeared from one side of the crate, then the other, and from the speakers came the squeaking of shoes on the smooth composite floor. "Nanobots are getting smaller, they interfere with organic structures in a gentler way, and they have recently built-in their own systems for administering anesthetic substances. The treatments aren't as painful as they used to be, really."

Even though what she said sounded quite convincing, Ian still didn't believe her. He had recently undergone the tissue implantation procedure, about four months earlier, after he had collided with a dormant Skunian fighter in the asteroid belt, and metal fragments from the shattered front shield had torn off a large portion of the colonel's thigh and torn up both calves. It hurt mercilessly, but it was nothing compared to the agony he experienced when the on-board medic started rebuilding the tissue loss. After all, for several days he still woke up screaming at night because he dreamed of the nickel-shining manipulators of the machine, pressing portions of pinkish tissue jelly into the open, bleeding wound, pulsating with the electrical charges that stimulated it.

"I can't see anything," he complained, tapping his finger on the lid. "Would it be possible to clean it a little?"

"I'll lower the temperature and turn on the air supply, but only for a while, so as not to disturb the proportions in the mixture. It should help a little."

Again, the rubber soles squeaked, a moment later Ian felt a cool breeze on his face. At the same time, small fans, a row of which were located in the side wall of the chamber, hummed. The lid slowly began to regain its transparency. After a few tens of seconds of weathering, there were only individual drops of moisture on it and smears of smear left by Ian's hands.

"Is it better now?" the doctor asked, approaching the chamber and leaning over the lid.

"As beautiful as ever," stated Ian at the sight of the perfect oval of her face, surrounded by a storm of raven-black, almost dark blue curly hair. His attention did not escape the cleavage between her breasts visible from under her unbuttoned apron. Not knowing why, he suddenly felt embarrassed by the fact that he was lying naked before her, twisted from contractures and smeared with slime. With a clumsy gesture, he tried to cover his genitals, forgetting that they were submerged a layer of slime anyway.

She noticed the move and snorted with laughter. Her alabaster face turned red.

"Ian, Ian, Ian..." she sighed with feigned disapproval. "I'm your attending physician. You don't need to be embarrassed. And thank you for the compliment, even if it was a tad exaggerated," she smiled radiantly. It was clear that his words gave her great pleasure.

"It wasn't," he assured.

"You also look pretty good," she retorted, leaning even lower.

"And I'm the one exaggerating, right?" this time it was he who smiled, though only half-heartedly. His chapped, cracked lips allowed nothing more.

"I saw your documentation from before the accident," she reminded. "Also photographic. Some of the improvements went really well..."

"Susan..." he groaned pleadingly.

She giggled and straightened up, while tightening the zipper of her uniform. She walked around the chamber and stood in front of the medical robot standing motionless.

"You will now be given sleeping pills and muscle relaxants," she informed, lifting the flap covering the machine's control panel. With her other hand she reached for the switches on the side of the chamber. "I need to increase the amount of regenerative mixture. These burns are healing too slowly."

An oval of an oxygen mask appeared over Ian's face. The ooze from the tubes no longer dripped, but began to trickle. The air supply tubes slid back into the walls of the chamber; the fan outlets were obscured by transparent flaps.

"How long will it last?" he managed to ask before the mask fell over his face.

A moment later, the microphone and intercom speaker also disappeared behind the plastic cover. Susan also noticed it.

"A dozen, or maybe several dozen hours, depending on how the treatment progresses!" she shouted an answer.

As a sign that he heard, he showed a raised thumb. A minute later, the chamber was filled to the brim with the regeneration mixture.

The doctor circulated for some more time among the devices set up around the chamber, connecting her terminal to each one in turn. Finally, she activated the medical machine, entered the data acquired from the diagnostic equipment into its memory bank, and left the room.

***

"It's going to be a fuss, Greg, you'll see." Seated at the table, Zariba turned with his chair toward the large panoramic window and gazed thoughtfully at the Epsilon Eridani Sigil illuminated by the glow. The moon's surface, scoured to a smooth rock by a mineral-rich layer of regolith, was covered with a web of trails winding between countless pits of open-pit mines, larger and smaller craters, and heaps of mined ore stretching for miles.

Where the terrain was relatively flat, the domes of residential neighborhoods and mining refineries glittered with hundreds of lights. Even from this distance, the silvery dots of transport and passenger vehicles could be seen moving between the installations.

"I doubt it." Larson waved his hand dismissively. With the other he picked up a glass filled with a frothy, amber-colored liquid, then took a few sips. "I saw him. It will be a year or more before he gets out of this. By then the piss will have passed," he said, then wiped his mouth of foam. "Not bad," he added appreciatively, setting the glass down on the countertop. "Try it, Simon," he encouraged Duvall, sitting across from him, who was browsing something on the screen of a handheld terminal with a long face.

"You want to, then drink it yourself," murmured Duvall in response.

"With pleasure!" pleased Larson. He slid the second glass over and glanced greedily at the third, also untouched. "Don't you want one too, Paul?"

"Don't even think about it!" Zariba turned around quickly and took his beer. "Did you really install the mismatched parts?" He shook his head in disbelief.

Larson sighed heavily.

"After all, I say it's not my fault, but the fucked-up software," he replied grimly.

"You should have checked manually," Duvall put down the tablet and massaged his neck with his hand. "I said a thousand times not to let customers go untested equipment."

"When was I supposed to do it? And how the hell?" irritated Larson. His powerful hands clenched into fists. "Start the main drive in the hangar? Or fly into the reactor chamber and measure the wire diameters one by one?"

"What did the diagnostics show?" Zariba became interested.

"And what was it supposed to show? A standard drive of a standard gunship, mounted on a standard torpedo ship. Almost one hundred percent compatibility," replied Larson.

"Almost?"

"Gosh, I can't remember," groaned the technician. "Ninety-something, maybe a little less,"

Zariba suddenly choked on his beer.

"You allowed components to be used with a ten percent margin of discrepancy?" he asked in amazement once he had finished coughing and snorting. He picked up his glass and wiped the splashed top with his sleeve. "After all, it should be a minimum of ninety-eight! And you tell me it's the fault of the diagnostic equipment?"

"Of course, it is," Larson replied stubbornly. "These are unified components, half of the automatons on the habitats are tarnished in this way. This contraption should propel even at eighty percent."

"Greg, these weren't maneuvering engines or other crap, but a real-life pulse drive, on top of that on an escort ship designed to dock with larger vessels," said Duvall, drumming his fingers on the tabletop, which in his case signified the highest degree of nervousness. "I hope you realize what this could have ended up being?"

"Back off," reflected Larson. "Both of you back off. The smart ones. Now. Somehow there were no one willing to mess with the irradiated guts of the gunship."

"Because it's not our department," stated Zariba. "Besides, don't talk nonsense, I personally uploaded the software to the torpedo ship and embraced the conventional drive.

"Oh, that's right!" Larson straightened up, nudged by a new thought. "You've uploaded the software! Did you test the software? Did you get the conventional drive up and running, too? How about you, Simon? After all, it was your machines that patched the outer shells. How many tests did you do? Well? I'm waiting." He moved his gaze from one to the other, with a triumphant smile on his angular face. "Well? Who will cast the first stone?" he pointed them out one by one with his finger, then leaned back more comfortably and, visibly relaxed, took another sip of his drink.

Both companions remained silent. Duvall started going through the documents on the terminal again, Zariba stroked his lush, slightly mangled beard.

"The main thing is that no one was killed," he finally stated. He whisked hair and dandruff flakes from his sweatshirt. "The Colonel will pull through, at most he will complain a little," he added, as if he had forgotten that he was the one who first voiced his concerns.

"Gentlemen, please be brief. You can stay on the observation deck for a maximum of one hour. There are still eight minutes left," the mechanically processed voice of the receptionist sounded from speakers placed in the corners of the room.

He, wrapped in a thick, multi-layered protective suit, sat in a glass booth squeezed into the farthest corner of the observation deck and separated from the window by a composite panel.

Behind his back hung on old-fashioned hangers equally old-fashioned key rings with the magnetic keys of the guest quarters attached to them. Beneath them flashed the lights of vending machines and food dispensers.

"Hey, what do you mean, an hour? It says two right there," Larson pointed to an electronic board mounted on the opposite wall.

"We have a failure of the magnetic shield generator. Due to the increased activity of the Epsilon Eridani, prolonged exposure to this station module causes health risks. If you wish to continue contemplating the views, you can go to the observation deck located in module number three," explained the receptionist.

"There you go," Larson sighed. He emptied his glass in one gulp, then dropped it into a container, which was serviced by a small cleaning machine circulating between the tables. "Let's get going," he said, standing up.

Duvall and Zariba also rose and headed for the exit. The former still went up to the receptionist's booth and picked up the key to the quarters, which were made available to them as part of their status as war veterans until they could return to their home habitats.

"So what do we do with such a nice start to the day?" asked Zariba cheerfully as they found themselves in a corridor that served as a link between the module they had just been asked out of and the station's hub, where living quarters were located alongside the main, hospital section.

The medical station resembled the appearance of a giant windmill with large propellers flared at the ends, whose blades rotated majestically around an out-of-shape steel block that served as the central hub.

"I'm going home," announced Duvall.

"I'll take a look at Taz," said Larson. "Paul, are you coming with me?"

"Why not?" nodded Zariba. "I've already looked at Sigil," he said, pointing behind him with his thumb. At the other end of the corridor, a steel bulkhead was just descending, designed to cut off the hall, bombarded with high-energy particles, from the rest of the section.

They separated at the transport node. Introspective and more silent than usual, Duvall boarded the elevator, while the technicians took their seats in the oval-shaped transport capsule. The vehicle was suspended from a massive rail connecting the section to the adjacent propeller.

After a journey of barely a dozen seconds, the capsule settled silently into the medical section's decontamination airlock, after which its top opened like an oyster. Before the men had time to disentangle themselves from their safety harnesses, the airlock was enveloped in clouds of chemical reeking steam, sucked right out through the ventilation system.

Coughing and wiping their eyes irritated by the pungent vapor, they exited the airlock and headed toward the spacious lobby, where a young nurse on duty sat behind a pristine white counter in an equally pristine white uniform. Gorgeous, they both concluded, as they walked closer. At the bulkhead separating the lobby from the dispensatory proper, two automatic guards were stuck motionless. Their barrel-shaped bodies were also snow-white.

"Yes, gentlemen?" asked the girl as they approached the counter. The domes of the robots turned in their direction, the scanners' lasers flashed red.

"Private Paul Zariba and Private Greg Larson," replied Zariba. "We're on a visit, to Taz Brunnix."

"The badges, please."

They put the cards on the counter. The nurse applied them to the reader, then typed something on the console. The scanners of the guard machines went off, the bulkhead between them rose accompanied by the quiet hiss of pneumatics.

"Room number five," the nurse handed them their badges. "You have a quarter of an hour."

"All on time," muttered Larson, tucking the card into his pocket. "I wonder if to the toilet..." he broke off poked by Zariba with his elbow.

The nurse tightened her lips into a narrow line.

"I apologize for my colleague, sometimes he can be quite unkempt," Zariba smiled at her. "He has been through a lot lately, you understand." Discreetly, so that Larson would not notice, he brushed his index finger against his temple.

She nodded slightly.

"Unfortunately, these are the procedures," she said. "The patient is currently undergoing a series of treatments to restore cellular osmosis, and as a result, muscle relaxants must be administered to him at regular intervals. The next such infusion will take place..." she glanced at the console screen. "...in twenty minutes. That's why you have to be quick."

"Is he conscious?" asked Larson. "The last time I saw him, he was lying under the machine as if dead."

"Have you already been here? Strange..." she furrowed her eyebrows and looked at the display again. "Very strange..." she repeated, clearly puzzled by what she was seeing. "In the system, you are listed as mid-level civilian technical personnel. So is Mr. Brunnix. He, too, originally held this status..."

"It's a long story, sister. And very, very interesting. If you wish, we can tell it to you, sometime, somewhere, with coffee for example," Zariba grinned cheerfully at her. "Isn't that right, Greg?" he poked his companion again.

"Well, sure!" confirmed Larson enthusiastically.

The girl smiled, but at the same time shook her head denyingly.

"I would love to have coffee with you, but right after my tour of duty I have a flight to Sigil," she said. "I'm sorry," she added at the sight of their disappointed faces, "but duty is a cruel master."

"Too bad," sighed Zariba. "How about..."

"Come on now, time is running out," Larson grabbed him by the hand and almost forcefully pulled the increasingly exasperated bearded man away from the counter. This was easy, since in this area of the station the value of centrifugal force was almost a third lower than that on the upper rooms on the edge of the rotors. He released his grip only when they crossed the threshold of the room where Taz Brunnix lay hooked up to the medical apparatus.

He was lying on a flat bed with no headrest, neither a bed nor a mattress, with his lower abdomen covered by an elongated lampshade to which transparent tubes were connected, and he smiled weakly at the sight of those entering the room and raised his sensor-covered hand in a gesture of welcome.

"So we fucked those stinkers?" he whispered, as they took their seats on small aluminum stools, bolted to the floor in the corner of the room, between two massive cabinets, from inside which came the buzzing of equipment and the bubbling of liquid pumped by the pumps.

"They bump themselves off," replied Zariba, looking around the equipment-strewn room with interest. His attention was drawn to the medical machine manipulator hanging from the ceiling, especially the three, several centimeter-long needles extending from its rotating tip. The awareness of those nasty little picks poking into his colleague's body every now and then sent shivers down his spine.

"They cut off too big a piece of cake for themselves," commented Larson. He, too, looked at the injector's large needles.

"What do you mean they cut themselves?" Brunnix, though stupefied by the means, looked at them sharply. "After all, we hit them with the Four."

"We? Who's we?" Zariba rose from his stool, approached the bed and looked at his wounded colleague with concern. He put his hand to his forehead. "They mastered the habitat, took over the systems..."

"Who told you such nonsense?" laughed Brunnix, but suffering immediately appeared on his face. He involuntarily grasped with his hand the shroud covering his lower abdomen. "Fuck..." he groaned, croaking mercilessly.

"Take it easy, Taz. Take it easy." Zariba looked anxiously at Larson. "Lie down, don't move," he said reassuringly, then returned to the corner and crouched on the stool again. "What the fuck is he talking about?" he whispered half-heartedly to the big guy, so that Brunnix would not hear him.

"Stoned," replied Larson, also in a whisper.

Zariba nodded his head as a sign that he agreed with this opinion.

"You yourself are stoned," the wounded man spoke up in a weak voice. "Do you really think that the Skunks just wrapped up our station and out of nowhere decided to hit it into their own Oumuamua? Who told you such nonsense?"

"Definitely stoned," Larson pronounced, this time out loud. "Come on, Paul," He got himself up and headed for the exit, wrenching carefully between tripods laden with drip bottles. "We'll talk later, Taz."

"Exactly," Zariba also got up. "Get some sleep, get some rest. They're about to give you anesthesia anyway," he pointed to one of the medcom displays, placed at the head of the bed, where a countdown from three hundred backwards had just begun. "Take care Taz. We'll stop by tomorrow." He waved his hand at Brunnix, who, though clearly in pain, watched them with something like merriment.

"Watch the TV news, on any channel," he said.

"See you later Taz!" they replied in unison, already out of the hallway.

Just as Zariba reached for the handle to close the door behind him, the whine of alarm sirens sounded.

Seconds later, the station's gravity disappeared.

14

Cruiser "Frontier"
AEgir's low orbit

News of the unexpected appearance near Sigil of dozens of Skunian fighters reached the cruiser just as it was unmooring from the side of the system's largest supply bulk carrier - a huge, nearly two-kilometer-long structure built by the Orbital Union and entirely dedicated to renting storage space, both by civilian organizations and by the armed forces. The gigantic steel box, powered by the energy of classical nuclear reactors, was currently hovering one thousand two hundred kilometers above the surface of the globe, from where it was about to set course for Sigil to pick up ore from the moon destined for the planet's factories and smelters.

On the cruiser, it was swirling like a beehive.

Bathed in the crimson glow of the emergency lamps, the ship's personnel rushed to their stations, the bulkheads on all decks lowered with a bang, the magnetic field generators in the engine room whirred, and the maneuvering engine jets flared with rocket fire soon after.

Only in the precipitous hatch of the cargo bay did the automatons carry out the planned schedule at a steady, uniform pace.

"How? From where!" a stunned Lupos was frantically tuning the displays on his console with feverish movements. On all the screens without exception were glowing messages coming in from listening stations deployed around Sigil and in the planet's stationary orbit. "Are they teleporting?"

"Something is up, Commander," Lieutenant Moss spoke up.

He, too, was already sitting in his seat, except that he was looking at the main tactical screen, the panel of which was above the bow viewfinder window.

"Take a look." He pointed with his hand to the top of the display. "Sensors located between the moon and the inner asteroid belt showed no enemy activity, as did those from the edges of the system. At the Fold it was also quiet. They didn't fly up here in camouflage, because they would have left behind some emissions, however traceable. They were unlikely to wait here in dormancy either, as we would have detected them long ago."

"Another fold, Commander," said engineer Sniegova, who had run onto the bridge literally a moment ago, in a breathless voice. Her long hair, tied up in a ponytail, was still dripping wet.

"What?" Lupos turned abruptly in her direction.

"The point where they were first detected by our early warning systems is exactly opposite the Fold. Immediately after that, they scattered in all directions, as if they wanted to prevent us from locating the point from which they flew out."

"And from this you deduced that they had passed through the new Fold?" asked the commander sceptically and already much more calmly. It was evident that professionalism and training were beginning to prevail over the initial shock caused by the appearance of hostile units in the vicinity of the two globs.

Sniegova vigorously shook her head.

"No, Commander. Something else puzzled me," he moved closer to the big screen. "None of the units had bounced into the area," she came even closer and, rising on her toes, circled a small circle with her hand in front of the display. The spot she pointed to was one of the few that was perfectly black, free of symbols, markers and lines showing the trajectory of objects moving through the system. "Just this one."

"Ah!" Lupos was finally dazzled. "If they flew into this, they would be back to square one! That's where the anomaly is! That's the... That's the..."

"The fold, Commander," prompted Sniegova. "Another one in this system."

"Exactly! Attagirl," said Lupos with appreciation in his voice. "A real cub scout. Do you see?" he stood up and rolled his eyes across the bridge.

"This is how you make an analysis based on the data you have! This is how one makes inferences! Take an example from the lady engineer!" he declared thunderously, pointing to the girl, who, abashed by this unexpected paean, was hastily sitting behind the console top.

Some of the operators nodded their heads, quiet applause came from several stations. Sitting behind Commander Moss, he restrained a giggle with the utmost difficulty. Sniegova, red as a peony, scowled behind the display screens to hide her embarrassment.

"Lieutenant, please pass this information to the Planetary Corps command and the Autonomy authorities. Let them determine whether the anomaly is actually there and block the approach as soon as possible," he instructed Moss.

The officer immediately activated the communication module and in a hushed voice began to speak into the microphone.

"Lady engineer," Lupos turned to Sniegova. "Please set a course for the enemy grouping."

"I am executing," she reported briefly.

"I declare the third level of combat readiness!" proclaimed Lupos. "Engine room, full thrust on shunters!" he nodded at the propulsion operators, who had already been waiting in readiness for several minutes, with their hands on keyboards. "After leaving orbit, a single pulse. Gunner!" called out toward the cocoon of the weapons systems operator. "Activate autonomous torpedo launchers! Program into the enemy units, at a ratio of... How many are there actually?" he asked, looking at the main tactical screen.

"Twenty-five Ultima-class fighters," Moss replied from his seat, while covering the microphone.

"At a ratio of four to one!" finished Lupos, after a quick calculation.

The Ultima-class fighters, so named because of their deluding resemblance in shape to a strange asteroid formed from the fusion of two large boulders, which drifted through the Solar System two centuries ago until it was annihilated by a collision with Earth's moon, although powerfully armed, were slow and unmaneuverable, and possessed relatively small dimensions. Had it not been for the fact that the Autonomy's largest orbital installations were within their range, they would have been limited to a single missile salvo or simply relied on the defense systems of the moon itself. This time, however, the risk was so great that he decided to sacrifice almost half of the smart torpedoes in the cruiser's launchers.

"Roger," confirmed the gunner. The deck under Lupos' feet vibrated slightly, while a quiet rumble came from the side of the cruiser's flattened bow.

"Torpedo hatches open, target bearings entered," came from the cocoon. "Four salvos."

"Fire!" commanded Lupos, and quite unnecessarily, because even before he had time to open his mouth, a swarm of metallic-glowing cigars erupted into space from the cruiser's forward launchers and, dragging plumes of ionized gases behind them, flashed into space. Immediately after it flew out another, and then two more.

A hundred intelligent missiles, equipped with the latest generation of logic circuits, went on a deadly hunt.

"Targets targeted." The canon moved in its cocoon.

On the tactical screen appeared a large, three-dimensional sphere depicting the planet's satellite, around which dozens of small green dots marked with symbols of sigilian orbital installations circled. Between them pulsed in blue the marker of a mobile Medical Corps station. The blue dot was moving slowly toward Sigil's north pole, clearly trying to move as far away as possible from the globe-approaching formation of Ultim clusters, displayed as small scarlet inverted eights.

"Will the torpedoes make it in time?" worried Lupos.

"Yes. They already have the enemy within range of the optical sensors," reported the gunner.

To confirm his words, he let loose on one of the side screens the image transmitted by the vision system of one of the missiles.

"The show is about to begin."

Everyone's gazes went to the display. Even the operators of the propulsion systems, preparing the sequence of nuclear explosions that were to give the cruiser the proper acceleration, stopped their work for a moment.

Meanwhile, very interesting things were happening on the screen. A torpedo was rapidly approaching the Skunian fighter, visible as two adjacent spherical, slightly deformed shapes. The enemy machine's systems had apparently already detected the threat, because a hail of tiny kinetic projectiles shot from both spheres toward the torpedo. On the screen, it looked as if it was flashing under the snow jamming in front. Seconds later, the fighter made a tight turn and disappeared from the screen. Before executing the maneuver, it still managed to launch a short salvo, which also missed. The rocket was not about to let go and performed an identical maneuver. The image on the screen rocked, lost focus, and immediately afterwards the bony surface of the Sigil flashed across it, and then for a split second the lights of some installation suspended against the black void flashed. The silhouette of a fighter jet appeared on the screen again. This time the stone improvement was already much closer, close enough that even despite the poor resolution of the image, the dark outlets of cannons and launchers could be seen on its surface. Some of them rhythmically spat out portions of plasma and streams of kinetic projectiles.

"We got it!" the gunner managed to rumble from under the visor of his helmet, before the torpedo leaped forward and hit the stone armor.

A no signal message appeared on the screen, while loud cheers rang out on the bridge.

"Four more hits!" reported the operator as the uproar subsided. "And another two," he added after a while. "Seventh torpedo on target. Eighth... ninth... tenth... eleventh. All from the first salvo. Torpedoes from the second and third are just tracking targets. Ten active targets remain, two were destroyed by the orbital defense system, one collided with a communications satellite and most likely annihilated with the orbiter."

"Turn back the torpedoes from the last salvo!" instructed Lupos. He looked at the main tactical screen again. The symbols of the surviving enemy fighters had already scattered over Sigil's northern hemisphere, as had the torpedoes pursuing them.

"Fourth-row torpedoes cancelled," the gunner moved in a cocoon, a series of blindingly white sparks of light flashed through the web of fiber optics that entwined him.

The symbols of the missiles whose formation had just appeared in the upper corner of the tactical screen turned from green to blue, then went out.

"As long as the ship accelerates, it will not be possible to take them up," he warned the commander.

"I know," nodded Lupos. "We will collect them later, in the meantime, please direct them to safe trajectories and put them into sleep mode."

"Yes, Commander." More portions of photon pulses flashed through the sensory cocoon.

"Attention: pulse sequence in one hundred and twenty seconds, decreasing value," sounded the voice of the on-board AI. "Attention: pulse sequence in one hundred and twenty seconds, decreasing value."

"Everyone to your seats!" added Lupos from his place.

"I know," nodded Lupos. "We will collect them later, in the meantime, please direct them to safe trajectories and put them into hibernation mode.

"Four more hits," reported the gunner. Immobilized in a sensory cocoon, he was the only member of the crew who didn't have to fasten the safety harness, check the condition of the attachment buckles or clean up anything around him that wasn't attached to some surface.

"As soon as we are in position, immediately fire on any fighters that come within range of the plasma cannons," Lupos ordered, mooching more comfortably in his chair. "And then course for the alleged anomaly," he directed the last sentence to Sniegova, who, like the others, was preparing for the overload that was to occur in a few dozen seconds.

"I'll take care of it right away, Commander," she promised, then with quick movements she fastened the last buckles and snaps.

"Attention. Pulse sequence in sixty seconds. Decreasing value." informed the AI.

The clacking of the seatbelt buckles, coming from all stations, gathered pace. They were accompanied by the creaking of seat dampers and the slamming of cabinets and lockers being hastily closed.

"Thirty seconds. Declining value."

"Two hits!" rang out from the cocoon.

Lupos again focused on the main screen. There were only four remaining icons symbolizing the Skunian machines, three of which were evidently dodging the torpedoes gliding in their wake. The last one was still moving in the direction of the medical station, although the distance separating it was decreasing much more slowly than it had been just a few minutes ago.

Lupos immediately guessed that the head of the Medical Corps had decided to move the station to a safer area. Tracing the dots on the screen with his eyes, he noticed one more thing - a dozen new icons appeared near the moon, marked with Planetary Corps symbols.

He smiled with satisfaction. The AEgir infantry landing transports, though poorly armored and generally unsuited to space combat, were very well armed and even alone very dangerous, especially in short-range clashes. Lupos once found this out for himself, when a carrier intercepted by a Skunian probe, before it was destroyed by the escort ships, shredded the lower fin of the Frontier and the engine room to pieces, thus immobilizing the cruiser, and in the process and killing and wounding eighteen crew members.

"Pulse impulse," the AI announced.

Before the echo of her voice could be heard, a bang, reminiscent of the sound of thunder muffled by distance, rang out perfectly to everyone from the rear of the ship and was immediately drowned out by the cacophony of metallic, groaning sounds emitted by the inertia absorbers, which were loaded to the limit.

Pushed by a gargantuan pulse of energy, the cruiser collapsed toward Sigil's shield radiating blue-white light, leaving behind a plume of glowing plasma as hot as the interior of a star.

An hour later, after circling a wide loop around the moon, during which the maneuvering engines did literally titanic work to decelerate the ship, which was accelerating to nearly three thousandths of a light, the cruiser found itself over the northern pole of the globe.

The main screen, which had been turned off for the duration of the flight, was again beautified with a fever of luminous dots and symbols. Multicolored, but this time much less patchy.

"Tactical situation?" threw Lupos in the direction of the gunner's cocoon, while unbuckling himself from his harness. He looked toward the forward observation slot. Visible behind the thick glass, the plasma gun turrets rotated on their pedestals, scanning the space around the ship for targets.

"Perimeter clear," replied the gunner. "AEgir transports complete, infrastructure on the lunar surface essentially undamaged. Not counting a few destroyed satellites, it looks like there were no losses. "

"I confirm," Moss spoke up. "I'm in constant contact with the Autonomy's main listening station. They report that everything is fine. Things went so fast that they didn't even have time to roll their patrol ships out of the hangars.

"Good work, Lieutenant," Lupos thanked him with a nod. "Please keep in communication with them all the time."

"Er... Commander?" Captain Kulak took off his headphones and pointed with their headband toward one of the side displays near the fire control station. "It seems, however, that there is a problem."

"What is it?" Lupos looked at the monitor indicated by the signalman. On the rectangular screen glowed green a diagram of some kind of structure.

"A medical station. We lost communication with them."

"When?"

"Location signals stopped coming right after we left low orbit. Later, as we circled Sigil, a single signal came, but heavily distorted. Since then, silence."

"Commander, Colonel Dressler is staying on this station," Sniegova spoke up in a slightly trembling voice.

"Holy shit!" Lupos recalled the marker of the Skunian fighter moving toward the icon representing the Medical Corps station and its sluggish attempt to move away to a safer area.

"Check the entire communications band!" he instructed the communications officers. "Lieutenant!" he turned to Moss. "You will contact the autonomy and determine if they have them on their screens. Perhaps the station is orbiting over the other hemisphere."

"Yes, sir!"

"Commander, we have checked all communication bands," reported Kulak. "No transmissions, no location signals, nothing."

"Keep listening. Sergeant," Lupos turned toward the fire control station. "Please analyze the trajectories of enemy objects from the moment they are detected until they are destroyed. I'm interested in the fighter jet that flew towards the North Pole. I understand that it escaped the torpedoes?"

The gunner answered only after dozens of unbearably long seconds, during which the screens around the station alternately lit up and went out, and more light pulses flashed through the coils of sensory fabric.

"That's right," rumbled from the cocoon after some time. "The last of the fighters had not been tracked by either torpedo, carrier tracking systems or even Sigil's ground defense systems."

"How is this even possible?" amazed Lupos.

"I don't know, Commander. The only thing I can think of is that at some point he must have used our identifiers, I don't see any other option."

"The Sergeant is right," Sniegova backed him up. "There are a total of more than four hundred listening stations of the most diverse kinds on Sigil and its orbit, most of which are equipped with military tracking systems. There is no physical possibility that they will not detect it. There simply isn't."

"Commander! They can see them!" cried Moss suddenly. "There is a report from one of the transport ships. The station has left orbit and is drifting towards the planet. Most likely it has a damaged drive..." he fell silent for a moment, listening to the content of the report coming from the receiver. "They lost the entire module, including communications and evacuation hangars."

"Fucking Skunks..." broke out one of the communications operators.

"Silence!" hissed Kulak at him.

"All right..." Lupos straightened up and breathed deeply. "I revoke the previous order!" he announced. "We will secure the approach to the anomaly later. Lady engineer, please set a course as soon as possible so that we can take the station safely in tow before it enters the atmosphere of AEgir.

Less than a quarter of an hour later, the cruiser's exhaust jets spat streams of blindingly white heat, pushing the ship toward the moon's northern horizon, beyond which the damaged Medical Corps station drifted.

15

Cruiser "Pandemonium"
The Epsilon Eridani planetary system

"East or West home is best," Kravchenko stated sententiously as the icons of the ships closing the formation finally lit up on the main tactical display.

An ovation rang out on the bridge, the navigation systems coordinators shook hands, thanking each other for their cooperation. Carrying out an operation as complicated as coordinating the flight of nearly a hundred ships through the guard installation-laden last section of the approach to the Fold in a situation where no one really knew how the artificial intelligences in charge would behave required operators to work together as harmoniously as possible.

The only one who didn't cheer was the gunner, who, entwined in a coil of sensory fabric, continued to intensively scan the space around the grouping for signs of hostile activity.

"Commander, connect me with the sector command, then prepare a report to me on the military situation in the system," instructed the admiral.

"Yes, sir!" Tsugawa bowed his head, giving the signal to the signalmen sitting nearby.

After a few seconds, the loudspeaker above Kravchenko's console crackled, and diodes on the communications module housing flashed to indicate the opening of an external communications channel.

"Connection established," reported one of the operators. "There is also a video signal. Should I unlock it?"

"Yes," decided the admiral, straightening up in his chair and smoothing out his uniform.

The monitor on his console, by now extinguished, glowed blue. After a moment, a zero-shaved black man in a steel-gray uniform and fusillade appeared on it. On the hem of his headgear was the Sigil Autonomy emblem.

"Dr. Isah Okanu," he introduced himself. "Director of loading station number one."

"A civilian?" asked Kravchenko, knitting his eyebrows.

"Reserve captain," Okanu flashed his teeth in a smile. "I am temporarily acting as sector commander. I have sent you my credential codes."

"One moment," Kravchenko looked questioningly at Tsugawa. The commander quickly flipped through a bundle of printouts that the console's built-in printer had spit out moments earlier, took out one sheet of paper, waved it in the air, and then showed a raised thumb.

"All right," Kravchenko shifted his gaze back to the screen. "Admiral Sergei Kravchenko, nice to meet you."

"Where did you come from?" This time it was Okanu who looked at him investigatively, as if sniffing out some kind of trick. "As far as I know, the Fleet should now be halfway to this new debris?"

"It's a long story..." Kravchenko hesitated, unable to decide what grade to actually title his interlocutor with, scientific or military. He decided to choose the second option. "...Captain," he finished. "What is the situation in the system?" Out of the corner of his eye he saw Tsugawa drowning in more and more papers.

The smile on Okanu's face became even wider, the man's fleshy lips stretched almost from ear to ear.

"This story is probably even longer than yours, Admiral," he replied.

"I'd be happy to listen to a shortened version," Kravchenko also smiled.

"Here you go," Okanu corrected himself in front of the camera. He was silent for a few moments, collecting his thoughts.

"What about this Oumuamua?" Kravchenko saw fit to point out to him the starting point for the relationship.

"Destroyed. It collided with one of the Union's habitats. Four probably. I don't know by what miracle the station was on a collision course with this leviathan, nevertheless it took a really powerful hit. Of the habitat, all in all obvious, there was nothing

213

left," the scientist became more serious. He reached his hand out of frame and placed a container filled with memory chips in front of him. "Here we have archived all the information that the station managed to dump on external servers before the crash occurred."

Kravchenko managed with the utmost difficulty to keep a stone face. It suddenly became clear to him why Lupos did not want to reveal the purpose of the mission he had sent his people on. He also guessed who was behind the destruction of the nuclear warhead-loaded searchers.

"Can you believe this guy?" he muttered appreciatively.

"Excuse me?" came from the loudspeaker.

"No, nothing. Please continue."

"As I mentioned, as a result of the collision, the habitat annihilated, Oumuamua was also destroyed, although its aft section survived, but that was taken care of by our frigates and Commander Lupos' cruiser. They neutralized the wreckage for good. At the moment it is drifting somewhere in sector zero two. And that's basically everything. The frigates are just returning, they should be here in a few hours, while the Frontier has gone towards the planet to replenish supplies."

"Thank you," nodded Kravchenko.

"Now it's your turn, Admiral," the scientist smiled again.

"I will soon send you an excerpt from the report we are compiling for the authorities and the United Forces Staff. In the meantime, I ask you to allow us to fly through the buffer zone and to take aboard the station some of our wounded."

"Of course, Admiral. I grant permission for the overflight. Please send to our servers the identification codes," replied Okanu immediately.

"From all units of the grouping?"

"Those from the "Pandemonium" will be enough. Please put the wounded in evacuation pods and launch them towards station number two. We will pick them up from the transport ships."

"Excellent. Thank you again."

"My pleasure, Admiral. I'm glad that your ships are again in the system."

"I'm also very happy about it, probably even more than you are. Speak soon, Dr. Okanu," Kravchenko turned off the monitor and pushed the microphone away from his face.

The diodes on the communicator module went off one by one.

"End of transmission," he nodded at the signalmen, then got up from his chair and discreetly stretched.

"You heard," he said, walking out to the center of the bridge and standing with his back to the observation slot. "We have permission to cross the buffer zone. Commander, please take care of the paperwork. Officer on duty!" He looked around the bridge.

"Yes, Admiral!" from behind one of the desktops of the navigation section rose a chubby-faced, slant-eyed young man.

"You will coordinate the operation to transport the wounded and make sure that the evacuation pods return to the decks of the mother units. We have already lost enough equipment in the Solar System. And one more thing," he looked at the fire control station this time, "The gunner!

The sensory cocoon moved slightly. From under the folds of the fabric flashed the mirrored aperture of the helmet.

"Yes?"

"Do the weapons systems detect the Earth detectors set up on our side of the Fold?"

"Yes," came the short answer.

Kravchenko walked closer to the elevation over which the cocoon was suspended.

"Is there a lot of it?" he asked already much quieter, almost in a whisper.

A gloved hand slid out of the cocoon and pointed a finger at one of the screens.

"Eight scanning probes, three sets of passive sensors and one transmitter."

"Eliminate."

This time the cocoon moved much more violently, the hand reached into the helmet and raised the visor. A pair of squinted eyes looked at Kravchenko.

"Should I fire on allied installations?" a half-voiced question was asked.

"That's right."

"Why?" The artilleryman's eyes turned into slits.

"Because this is the order I gave, Sergeant. Do you refuse to carry it out?" asked the admiral calmly.

"I don't refuse, Admiral. I will carry out this order, I just want to know for what reason you order me to destroy these devices."

The commander's dialogue with the weapons systems operator, which was conducted almost in a whisper, finally attracted Tsugawa's attention. The commander turned with his chair toward them and kept his ears open. Admittedly, his console was about five meters from the gunner's pedestal, but his hearing was really good. The last words spoken by the sergeant made him rise in his seat and approach the admiral.

"What kind of devices?" asked Kravchenko, while looking curiously at the gunner's clouded face.

The communications system operators sitting nearby and the navigators standing at their consoles must also have heard this exchange of words, because all of them, as one, looked at the commander-in-chief. And like the gunner, they looked puzzled to say the least.

"I gave the order to destroy the Earth detectors deployed in our system," announced the admiral.

"What?!" Tsugawa also joined in the stunned ones. "Why!" he coughted out. He took two steps back, touching the handrail of the railing separating the command post from the front of the bridge with his hip.

"Because these are spy installations," Kravchenko turned to him and sighed heavily.

"What's so strange about that?" Tsugawa blinked, surprised. "After all, we also scan their space and everything that comes within sensor range, including installations. These issues, by the way, are regulated by treaties, maybe not directly, but neither is there a prohibition on collecting and transmitting data on local infrastructure. Heck, for many years we have been intercepting each other and decrypting all transmissions, no matter how secret they are."

"Well, that's right!" the head of the communications division supported the commander suddenly. "Admiral, I have here more than thirty petabytes of data intercepted from their equipment during our passage through the solar system." Having said this, he patted his hand on the massive casing of the communications console's desktop. "At least half of them are military transmissions from military installations, warships and radio buoys."

"Gentlemen, please be quiet," Kravchenko raised his hands ordering his subordinates to be silent. "I know all this. I know the provisions of the treaties, I realize that both we and they eagerly eavesdrop and analyze everything that the antennas of listening devices pick up. I also know that every, even the smallest set of detectors at the fold is stuffed with the most varied kinds of scanners, including quantum scanners. It's just that with those here we have a slightly different problem," saying this, he stepped onto the rise and stabbed his finger at the screen on which the gunner had earlier displayed him a simulation of the deployment of Earth's detectors. "Not bad, I would say," he added, looking in turn at the gunner, Tsugawa and the radio chief.

"What don't we know about, Admiral?" Tsugawa asked cautiously.

Kravchenko sighed for the third time, then squatted in a chair at the reserve command console.

"There is a suspicion that the Skunians have broken through security," he said. "Suspicion bordering on certainty," he added at the sight of the skeptical faces of Tsugawa and the communications officer. "Before we flew through the Fold, sentry stations in the Solar System had noted unauthorized transmissions coming from these probes. The frequency on which they were emitted had not been used by any transceivers, either Earth's or ours, before. An analysis of the antennas' alignment shows that when they emitted the signal, they were in such a position that the transmission was directional and went exactly at an angle of twenty-seven degrees to the plane of the ecliptic."

"Oh shit!" cursed the signalman. "After all, this is the azimuth to the primary course of our grouping and the debris and the convoy flying to it. Check the logs of our listening installations at the Fold for the last seven days, quickly!" he almost shouted at his three subordinates.

"What should we be looking for?" asked one of them.

"Unscheduled transmissions, additional protocols, overwritten data, deviations from the schedule. Anything that deviates from the norm. Engage the onboard AI, too. Have its security systems scan the data that these probes have managed to send to us."

"Yes, sir!"

"Commander?" The communications chief turned to Tsugawa, who listened intently to the commands he was giving.

The latter nodded his head approvingly.

At the moment, it was the only thing they could do to make sure their listening stations were not infected by foreign software. "Where did you get this information, Admiral?" he asked.

"I have my sources," Kravchenko smiled half-heartedly, but immediately became serious and shifted his gaze to the gunner.

"It seems that I gave the order, Sergeant," he said sternly.

This time the gunner no longer raised any objections. Without a word, he lowered the helmet's aperture, then plunged back into the coils of the cocoon. Seconds later, the plasma cannon turrets on the bow of the cruiser turned sideways and spat a single salvo of ionized matter into space.

A few moments later, the symbols of Earth installations deployed around the Fold disappeared from the screens.

"Targets destroyed," the operator reported.

"And very good!" sizzled Kravchenko. He jumped down from the elevation and sat down at the command console again. "Do you have anything?" he turned to the signalmen.

"The data is just flowing in," replied Kulak. "As a precaution, we ran the records from the receiving modules of the other ships, including the escort, through the system. So far we haven't found any irregularities, the software seems to be fine, nevertheless, until all the clusters are scanned, I can't say for sure."

"Admiral, incoming transmission from station number one!" the operator suddenly spoke up.

"Put it on general," instructed the admiral. Before he had time to move the microphone over, a quiet crackle sounded in the speakers, followed by the voice of the interim sector commander.

"To the commander of the Fleet grouping. This is Dr. Isah Okanu. Can you on earth explain to me, Admiral, why your ships fired on Earth's listening installations! And without consulting me. I don't need to remind you that I'm responsible for the security of the infrastructure in the area? All infrastructure, including allied infrastructure."

"Doctor, I take it on myself," replied Kravchenko. "According to the information we have, this apparatus was intercepted by the enemy some time ago. At the moment the technical services are checking our equipment. I suggest that you instruct your people to do the same. We are unable to scan the apparatus on the stations, moreover, they will soon be out of range of our sensors."

Okanu spoke up only after several seconds had passed.

"I understand, Admiral. I have just given the appropriate instructions to my technicians. Unfortunately, I'm forced to inform the headquarters of what has happened."

"Please do your part. I will also notify the authorities of the action taken in this case. By the way..." Kravchenko looked at the main tactical screen, which displayed an interactive map of the sector with marked installations protecting the approach to the Fold. "I have a request to you, Doctor."

"Yes?"

"As far as I know, you have a quantum telescope here, right?"

"That's right," confirmed Okanu. "Admittedly, only a prototype, but with a lot of computing power," pride sounded in the scientist's voice. The scanning technique based on extrapolating quantum entanglement states was still in its infancy, mainly because of the amount of data that the processors comprising such a telescope had to process.

"What I need is a scan of a slice of off-system space, covering the new debris and the convoy moving toward it. The listening stations received several transmissions from them, and then lost communication. This condition has persisted for two months. Can I count on your... on your help, Doctor?"

"I don't see the slightest problem, Admiral. I'll take care of it right away, but you'll have to wait a while for the results of the scan."

"How long?"

"At least five hours, maybe a little longer. The scanning process will absorb almost all the operating memory of our computers. We will be forced to isolate all peripheral systems so as not to disrupt the station."

"I understand," said Kravchenko.

Because he did indeed understand. A similar, though much shorter-range telescope was mounted on one of the escort ships, a specially adapted PF-2 torpedo ship, whose combat modules were entirely powered by a separate fusion reactor multi-core processors of the latest generation, a huge capacity memory bank and a heat sink system cooling the whole thing, probably even more complicated than the central processing unit it operated. Besides, the very term 'telescope' was purely conventional in this case, as the device had little to do with either optical or radio observation. The principle of its operation was based primarily on extrapolating the behavior of objects on a macro scale, based on data from matrices that create microsimulations.

"I'll send you the results immediately," promised the scientist.

"I'll be very grateful to you, Doctor. One more important thing," Kravchenko looked at the main screen again.

"Yes?"

"It is necessary to clean up the scrap left after our shelling and dispose of it as soon as possible. One, that it may pose a danger to the units passing through the Fold, two, that some of the components may have remained operable, which in turn involves the risk that their emergency drop transmissions will infect the software of your computers," he glanced questioningly at the head of the communications section.

The operator nodded in response and pointed to one of the monitors with the headphones he was holding.

"There are several weak transmissions," he confirmed the admiral's concerns.

"We have already taken care of it," Okanu replied after a few seconds.

The fleet was moving away from the station at a rapid pace, resulting in an increasing delay in the signal reaching the cruiser's receiving antennas.

As if to confirm the doctor's words, new icons appeared on the tactical screen, right next to the line marking the boundary of the Fold. Kravchenko guessed that they symbolized the technical service transports sent to the battlefield. Identical markers moved between the two loading stations.

"Clear space, Admiral!" the customary farewell came from the speakers.

"And little guests to you," replied Kravchenko, also according to custom, then nodded to the signalmen to end the connection.

16

Mobile Medical Corps
High orbit of Sigil moon

"To the airlock, quickly!" Larson's voice, though loud, struggled to break through the ever-present whine of sirens and the clamor of alarm buzzers.

Grasping at whatever he could find, the technician soared down the corridor toward the lobby.

Zariba, cursing as much as the world could stand, moved in his trail.

Behind their backs, a security bulkhead fell with a clatter, then another. Sheets of rubber carpeting floated around, racks of still-unpacked bottles and countless packs of medicine spilled out of cabinets that had been opened wide. Here and there, tiny sanitation bots buzzed, flashing their scanner lights. The automatons, startled by the unexpected disappearance of gravity, had not had time to activate their magnetic suction cups, and were now spinning helplessly against the ceiling, spinning their wheels.

The gravity returned the moment they reached the airlock door. Lucky for them, the items in the lobby were properly extra-secure, unlike those in the hallway leading to Brunnix's room. The rumor of clothespins falling to the floor was louder than the whine of the warning systems.

"Vacuum suits!" commanded Larson as the massive airlock bulkhead rolled aside. Massaging his bruised knee, he trotted over to the protective clothing rack in the corner and removed two vacuum suits. He handed one to Zariba.

"Where now?" asked the bearded man once they had taken their seats in the transport cabin. The thick helmets effectively muffled the wailing of the sirens, so they could already communicate normally, using the suits' internal communication systems.

"To the transport ship," Larson replied. With graceful movements, he attached an additional breathing mixture tank to the suit. "Oh shit! You see what I see!" he groaned suddenly and pointed to the cabin window.

About a hundred meters away from them, exactly opposite the observation deck they had recently left, hung motionless in space a huge boulder, or rather two boulders, latched together by a thick, metallic shiny collar.

"Holy shit! This is Ultima!" Zariba rose from his seat and jumped to the control panel.

"What do you want to do?" Larson stood between him and the panel, covering the keyboard with his body.

"We have to turn back! The Skunk wants to fire that propeller over there!" The technician gave a step forward, while trying to reach the keys over the engineer's shoulder.

Larson spurned his hand.

"So what?" he growled. "Let him shoot. First he will perforate the damn terrace. We, meanwhile, will get to the airlock and dash down the elevator. By the time the shelling mess is over enough for Ultima to fly closer to the center of the station, we'll already be sitting in the transport ship, so hands off the console!" he said quickly, almost on one breath, then pushed Zariba away with all his strength.

The bearded man staggered, tripped over some irregularity in the floor and flailed heavily on one of the seats.

"Let's at least turn off the lights," he burbled, referring to the glare of the headlights located in front of and behind the cabin.

"Well, you finally said something reasonable," Larson muttered, turning back to the console.

After a few seconds, the lamps, both outside and inside the transport capsule, went out. Only now, when the reflections of light stopped dancing on the thick glass, could they get a better look at the alien machine.

"Large for this class," Larson rubbed the glass with the top of his glove. "This larger sphere is about fifty meters in diameter. See how it shines. I don't know much about minerals, but it looks like pegmatite. Where on earth did, they get so much of it? After all, it's unique."

"You're talking rubbish, Greg," said Zariba. "Have you ever even seen this... piegma... hema... this rock?"

"As a matter of fact, I've seen it," crowed the giant. "It's used to reinforce the pedestals of gravity generators. It's damn strong against violent stresses. It's just that it's made of small blocks, up to a meter by a meter, not like that... asteroids!"

"Even so, it's not a homogeneous structure, just a simple lagging of alloy armor. Inside you have a classic fighter and its smelly, slimy crew." Zariba squatted closer to the windshield, almost touching it with his helmet's bulb.

"Yes? Then look at the hole. Do you see any alloy there? Metal, anything?" Larson also moved closer to the window.

The stone ship was still stuck in apparent stillness, adjusting its flight speed to the rotating elements of the station.

"Why is it hanging like that?" Zariba wondered.

"It has made a living shield of us. As long as it persists between the rotors, the defense systems won't track it, and even if they do, they won't open fire, lest they damage the installation."

"So, what the heck made the station shake?" Zariba glanced toward the illuminated airlock flange where the capsule was about to dock. It was already quite close.

"Oh, I already know!" he stated after a few moments of careful observation. "It seems that someone took a chance and tried to knock them down. And more than once. Look," he pointed with his hand to a breach in the shell, located about ten meters above the airlock. Another hole zigged slightly below the observation deck. Clouds of frozen gas were flowing out of it into space. Blue sparks from the damaged electrical system were shooting out from under the jagged sheets of plating.

"Bad, very bad..." Larson sighed at the sight. "If the geniuses in the control room here don't turn on the correction engines immediately, the station will go adrift and either chop into Sigil or be caught by AEgir's gravity."

"Greg!" there was a note of genuine terror in Zariba's voice. Leaning over, he looked somewhere down toward the station's hub, around which the propellers of each section rotated. "No more engines..."

"What?!" Larson ran up and also looked out the window. "Oh fuck..." he groaned.

The place where not so long ago the bodies of the maneuvering engines had been stuck on massive moving girders was now haunted by a tangle of bent, over-melted and smoked scaffolding. There was not even a trace of the engines. Just as there was no trace of the transport ships moored nearby. Not even the massive clamps and electromagnet mountings that welded the vehicles to the station had survived.

"That's the work of that motherfucker!" growled Zariba, turning toward the side window. The mirrored surface of the helmet reflected the dark silhouette of the alien fighter, whose figure-eight body hovered above them like an angel of death. Only now did the technician notice the pitch-black outlets of kinetic blasters and the cylindrical tips of plasma cannon barrels peeking through the recesses of the armor.

"We have nothing left to look for there," announced Larson, still staring at the destruction below. "We need to get to the escape pods. There should be several at each section. Turn that wagon around."

Zariba did not need to be told twice. After a few seconds, the capsule stopped, only to move in the opposite direction, back to the hospital section. "What about Taz?" he asked when they found themselves in the decontamination room again.

"And what should it be?" busy checking the containers of breathing mixture, Larson only shrugged. "They will pack him in a capsule and evacuate him, just like the other patients."

"Supposedly, who will do that?" Zariba lifted the airlock door and pointed to an empty hallway. There was not a living soul in the spacious room. "And by what means, if the security bulkheads are closed?"

"I don't know. They probably have some procedures," replied Larson. "They certainly have," he added, hearing the exasperated mumbling that came from the helmet's speakers. "After all, this is a lazaret, a militarized facility. In the army, even in a shithouse, you have to follow the rules and regulations," he joked, although with meager effect, as the indistinct blustering of a comrade could still be heard from the intercom.

He ignored it. He fixed spare mixture tanks at his suit belt, two for each of them, used ones he hurled carelessly to the airlock.

"She didn't turn off the terminal," spoke up Zariba, who by this time had squeezed behind the counter and sat down in the receptionist's place.

"Check the escape route diagrams, because these stamps tell me absolutely nothing," asked Larson, looking at the fluorescent placards above the main entrance to the lobby. On each was scrawled an arrow with a combination of numbers and letters below it.

Zariba leaned over the tabletop keyboard, brushed his fingers across the buttons.

"Fucking hell... Sensory..." he sighed. "I have to take off my gloves. Help me out."

"Wait!" Larson stopped him. "Better not to risk frostbite." He looked around the lobby for some kind of monitor that would display information about the status of the life support system modules in this part of the station. Unfortunately, he didn't find one. Yes, there were a few rectangular, several-inch screens on the walls, but they were all extinguished.

"No exaggeration, it's not freezing," Zariba reached under the tabletop and placed a plastic bottle on it, half-filled with some kind of transparent liquid. "Water," he explained. "Zero ice."

He lifted the bottle and shook it vigorously.

"Help," he repeated, placing his hand on the countertop. "With one hand I can't unfasten these latches. Hurry up!" With the fingers of his other hand, he pointed to the double buckle securing the clamp connecting the glove to the cuff from loosening.

Larson did not delay any longer. Pressed with his thumbs, the buckle let go, the clamp opened like a link of huge handcuffs, and the glove came off smoothly from his hand.

"All right," assessed Zariba. He lifted his hand, moved his fingers carefully, then unclenched his palm and examined it from all sides. The fingertips were slightly bluish, the knuckles just a little red. "Cold, but still on the plus side," he concluded, then leaned over the terminal keyboard.

A few dozen clicks later, a three-dimensional cross-section of the station appeared on the display, along with escape routes marked with a dotted line.

"The escape pods are located here, here and here," Larson, who also pushed behind the counter, tapped his finger three times on the screen, pointing to three green-lit shapes, spread along the edge of the arm.

"Only three?" Zariba was surprised.

He enlarged the image. The capsule symbols became pixelated, but their number did not increase. "Not good."

"It's just a technical drawing," Larson reassured him. "You saw how many rooms there are here. Plus, quarters for duty and security personnel. These are the capsule sets. As we docked, I flashed one of the launchers somewhere. It probably had about ten exit shafts."

"Phew..." breathed a sigh of relief Zariba. "Because I was already afraid it wouldn't be enough."

"Even if there were only three, it would be more than enough for the two of us."

"No, Greg, not for two," there were threatening notes in Zariba's voice again. "We are taking Taz," he declared firmly.

"How do you want to get to him?" the giant pointed with his thumb to the corridor leading to the hospital rooms and the steel bulkhead blocking the entrance. A red light on its top pulsed steadily, with two yellow lights blinking steadily next to it. At the sight of the lights, Larson frowned.

"Just like that!" replied Zariba, and before Larson had time to react, he entered some command into the terminal. Another light came on on the bulkhead, this time green.

"Are you fucking crazy?" yelled Larson. "Dehermetization, moron! It will suck us out!" he shouted, then, grabbing his glove, dived under the counter and wrapped his hands around one of the countertop supports. "Turn it off!" he groaned, although he knew that the other guy wouldn't have time to do it.

Zariba was saved from being sucked into the void by a large metal cabinet that had been torn from its fastenings by the monstrous draught clogging the corridor exit, and into which he hurled himself so hard that he dented its door. Pressed against the piece of furniture, he was stuck for the next few moments flattened about a meter above the floor, until the pressure differential-induced monstrous whirlwind ceased. When it did, he slumped to the floor.

"Paul?" Larson crawled out from under the counter and knelt by his colleague, who was lying motionless. "Are you alive?" he asked, placing a glove over his coldly bruised hand. The temperature in the already dehermetized room had dropped precipitously and at the moment was probably not much higher than the vacuum temperature outside the station.

"Yes..." replied Zariba in a weak voice.

"How is the hand? Do you feel anything?"

"It hurts and burns like hell."

"Move your fingers."

The technician's hand twitched, the middle finger straightened slowly.

"Moron," commented Larson.

Zariba's quiet laughter came from the intercom speakers, which immediately turned into a dry cough.

"Move over," grunted Larson, standing up. As Zariba crawled aside, he walked over to the closet and, leaning his back against it, pushed the piece of furniture out of the passage.

He looked deep into the hallway.

"Problem solved," he announced. "We can go to the capsules."

"What," Zariba also rose, slowly and carefully.

"You don't have to worry about Brunnix. These halls are nothing more than detachable evacuation modules. The system has unhooked them. We are struggling here, and Taz is flying at his best to some base on Sigil."

"You're kidding me, Greg."

"See for yourself," Larson took two steps back and nodded invitingly.

Zariba approached the wall crease and looked out into the corridor. Instead of smooth, laminate-covered walls, he saw only steel girders, between which stood the unsealed ends of wires and cables and the remnants of wall veneer. The corridor resembled a steel covered footbridge, flung over a black abyss.

"Oh fuck," he whispered. "That's why the bulkheads closed. We were pretty lucky."

"We were. Well, that's far enough. Let's get out of the way while the defense systems haven't tracked this guerrilla yet," Larson moved with a quick step toward the opposite end of the room, where the elevator shafts and entrances to the stairwells were located. According to the diagram, the nearest capsule launcher was four levels up.

Zariba, limping slightly, trailed behind. His right arm dangled inertly along his body.

"I would prefer on foot. Damn knows what condition the crane mechanisms are in. Can you make it?" asked Larson as they stood by the narrow metal doors. Compared to the wide, double doors behind which the elevator cabins were located, these looked more like a hatch. "That's four floors."

"I'm fine," answered Zariba savagely, although it was clear that he was not in the best of shape. Hitting the hard metal surface with his whole body was not without consequences.

"We'll see about that," muttered Larson, then opened the door.

To their amazement, the stairwell turned out to be a wide, oval tube with walls made of glass-transparent composite, in the middle of which wound a spiral staircase with fluted steps.

Before moving up, they contemplated the view outside for a while, and there it got more and more interesting.

The Skunian's Ultima, though still hovering at the height of the observation deck, had adjusted its position somewhat. Its larger part was now pointing downward, while the smaller one aimed at the space above the station. And it was from it that blindingly white beams of concentrated plasma charges shot out again and again.

Even higher up, drawing intricate loops, four oblong cuboid carriers of the Planetary Corps transports and two slender silhouettes of Autonomy patrol ships were lavaging against the silvery Sigil shield. For the time being, none of the ships opened fire on the intruder. Also silent were the kinetic cannon batteries located at the base of the rotor - one of the elements of the station's defense system.

"Faster, faster!" Larson cheered his battered colleague.

Gravity had a noticeably lower value here than in the hall, so running up he climbed three or four steps at a time. Zariba's climbing was going a bit worse, primarily because of his injured hand, which, although already warmed by the glove, was still a bit stiff and tingled mercilessly. "They were about to start biting it off!"

As it soon turned out, he accurately predicted the development of events, for barely were they able to lift the cover of the hatch leading to the capsule launcher, all hell broke loose above their heads.

The transport ships, which had been flying without order and composition until then, suddenly formed into a neat quadrilateral and, on afterburners, plummeted toward the enemy, spitting steel from all barrels. A similar maneuver was performed by the patrol ships, with the difference that they approached the Ultima at an angle. From the plasma cannons mounted on their oval hulls, they fired streams of plasma, and from the launchers located under their bellies, thin needles of rockets. At the same time, the station's cannons opened fire. All this storm of fire and steel hit the larger Ultima part. In no more than a blink of an eye, half of the fighter turned into a red-hot lump of matter, only to disintegrate a moment later into thousands of tiny fragments, which, like a sheaf of sparks from a bonfire, splashed in all directions, completely destroying the observation deck and perforating the shells below.

The second part of the Ultima, tumbling, flew off into space, soon to disappear against Sigil's shield. The attacking ships made a tight turn and, like a pack of swarms of enraged wasps, rushed in its trail, completely ignoring the station, which had been demolished to the ground and was dragging behind it a cloud of debris engulfed by the still active gravitational field, and began drifting toward the planet.

"At the last minute..." wheezed Zariba, gramming into the escape pod. Before he closed the flap, he pulled the helmet off his head and hurled it to the hangar floor. The bubble, made of glasmetal, rolled across the floor and stopped at the feet of Larson, who was just kneeling at the ejection rail of the second capsule and hastily checking the condition of the wires powering the electromagnetic mechanism.

"Watch out!" he hissed. He picked up the helmet and carefully set it aside. Then he plugged the cables into the sockets. Somewhere outside, a muffled rumble sounded, one of the walls trembled, broken rivets and pieces of foam padding sprinkled from the ceiling. It sprinkled sparks.

"Let's blast off!" Larson sprang up and quickly took his place in the vehicle.

The flaps of both capsules slammed shut almost simultaneously, immediately after which air was sucked out of the room, and then the covers of the launcher outlets opened. Seconds later, the capsules glided along the rails and flew out into space.

***

He was in the strange carriage again, looking like a large glass jar cut in half and laid on its side. The bizarrely bulging walls of the vehicle vibrated and shuddered, with grayish-brown particles of neither rust nor enamel peeking out from its scratchy, in places completely transparent surface, with clouds of dust rising upward from the floor, revealing an equally transparent floor, and beneath it the rapidly shifting surface of rock. Above his head flashed lamps suspended beneath the smooth vault, glowing with blue light, resembling large drops of mercury squeezed from the stone.

In front of the carriage, just above the surface of the thin double rail, glided a Skunian probe, the same one that had earlier led him into the tunnel. Again and again, the metal sphere swept the tunnel with a beam of red light, and when it detected something in the path, the wagon slowed down, and it shot forward with a hiss of afterburners and, depending on the size of the obstacle, pushed it aside or incinerated it with beams of plasma.

Suddenly the carriage jerked and stopped abruptly, as if it had collided with an invisible wall. Ian's hands slipped off the edge of the glass side, he lost his balance. He flew forward, hit the front wall with his whole body. It hurt, even badly. His right knee, shoulder, elbow hurt. And the forehead. It probably hurt the hardest. He touched his fingers to his head, then raised his hand to his eyes. A gelatinous ooze glistened on his fingertips. He shook it off in disgust. "Where's the helmet!" a panicky thought flashed through his head. And suddenly he realized that there were no gloves on his hands. That he wasn't wearing a suit at all! His stomach went up to his throat. He felt like screaming, but felt that if he just opened his mouth, he would vomit. He curled up in a ball and became motionless, shivering from the cold. He was alone, naked and without any protection, trapped deep inside the rocky armor of the dying Oumuamua, drifting through the black, infinite void of space.

"Colonel! Colonel!" a muffled female voice broke through the ice-cold cotton wool wrapping Ian's head. "Please wake up! You must unlock the chamber lid!"

He lifted his eyelids with difficulty. Above his face shone purple lumps of regeneration gel, with which the lid of the chamber was coated.

"Colonel!" the voice was increasingly insistent. Ian only after a long moment realized that it was coming from somewhere on the side of his legs.

Disregarding the suspicious tingling at the base of his neck, he raised his head slightly and looked in that direction.

"What's up?" he yelped at the sight of his bruised knees and bloody toes, over which a breathing apparatus dangled languidly on a deformed boom. Beside swung broken sensor cables, stripped of their suction cup ends.

"Holy shit..." he gasped, half surprised, half frightened, realizing that by some miracle he had managed to turn one hundred and eighty degrees in this coffin. Somewhere on the edge of his hearing, he registered the steady, prolonged whine of emergency sirens. Raising his head even higher, he poked his finger first in one, then in the other ear. The wailing of the sirens grew louder.

"The latch! You have it at knee height! It needs to be unlocked!" this time the voice from the intercom already sounded quite clearly.

Ignoring the new outbreaks of pain, he supported himself on his elbow and reached his hand to the bright blue latch. Though unsecured by a locking mechanism, it was pressed down and, like everything inside the chamber, stained with a smear. He remembered that before he drifted off into a chemical-induced sleep, the buckle had been in the open position. He looked at his legs once more. On his right thigh was a long scar that stretched almost to his groin. Not a wound, not a scratch even, but a pinkish scratch, edged with a bluish, in places turning navy blue.

With the tip of his index finger, he undermined the latch, then pulled it down. A moment later the lid of the chamber lifted with a quiet clatter, and a familiar face, surrounded by a storm of raven-black hair, appeared in the field of view. A very pretty face, he concluded immediately, although quite heavily smeared.

"What happened, Doctor?" he asked, as she bent over him with vigorous jerks and began unhooking the sensor suction cups from his forehead and chest.

"They attacked us," she explained.

"Who?"

"Who do you think?" she groaned. With a strong pull, she ripped off the largest patch, pulling out some hair.

"Ouch!" hissed Ian.

"Skunian ship. Apparently, a whole cloud of them has sprouted up, somewhere nearby."

"Holy shit!" he cursed, grasping the edges of the chamber with his hands and trying to get up.

"Please don't move, I'm almost done." She gently but firmly pushed him back into the ooze. "We will move you to another chamber, this one is damaged."

With a hand gesture she summoned a medical robot. Equipped with two pairs of arms wrapped in soft foam, the automaton drove up to the basin and swept the scanner around the man lying in it.

"I'll be fine," Ian tried again to get up. She prevented him from doing so a second time.

"Out of the question," she said sternly.

He wanted to protest, but instead he only stammered as the agitated violent movement of the ooze poured into his mouth.

"I'm not a doctor, Colonel," she added, then straightened up and, nodding at the robot, stepped aside, making room for him.

The automaton drove even closer, almost muscling the chamber wall with its tracks. The machine's arms came to life, three of them slid smoothly under Ian's neck, loins and knee bends, respectively, and before he had time to react in any way, lifted him up, then, dripping with slime, laid him carefully in the other, still empty chamber of the medcom.

"Please don't move." The woman deftly attached the ends of the sensors, activated the injection and monitoring systems, and then, with the help of several tubes, connected the device to a multi-chambered tank of regeneration mixture and medkits.

"How are you feeling?" she asked.

"Not particularly," he replied in a weak voice. "What is your name?"

She smiled under her breath and involuntarily corrected her hair.

"Alina. Corporal Alina Diaconescu."

"Do you have a military rank?" astonished Ian.

"Of course, after all, this is a military hospital."

"Well, yes..." he sighed. "Mid-level staff."

"That's right. I'm a departmental nurse."

"What about Susan... I mean..." he bit his tongue at the last moment, "Dr. Markowicz?" he finished.

"At the moment she is busy evacuating patients from the sections that were affected by the shelling," she replied.

"Major losses?" he became interested. Despite the rather uncomfortable position, military habits as usual took over.

"It is difficult to say. From the emergency messages, it seems that with direct fire they destroyed our maneuvering engines, the carrier anchorage and, if I understood correctly, the guest quarters. The hospital section was damaged by secondary explosions and by shrapnel. There are casualties, this I know for sure. More than a dozen people were arriving in the hospitality section."

Ian recalled Larson's face suddenly brightening with a smile, leaning over the lid of the chamber. What did Larson say then? That he and his comrades were loafing around on the station at the army's expense?

"Good God..." he groaned.

"Someone familiar?" guessed Diaconescu immediately.

"In a way. I have a request for you, Alina..."

"Yes?"

"The Unions. Technicians from the flight service team... They have recently achieved veteran status. Three of them. The fourth is also here, but probably as a patient. Do you associate them?"

She thought for a moment.

"I think so," she replied thoughtfully. "At least the injured one. Terribly savaged..." She closed her eyes looking for something in her memory. "Cut wounds to the lower abdomen, eventration..." she began to enumerate. "Taz Brunnix?"

Ian nodded with a slight nod.

"Will he pull through?" he asked.

"If the tissue implants take, then yes. Now he is being stabilized externally with organ replacements."

"Do you not associate the others? Duvall, Zariba and Larson. One with a beard, one so square, big blond, one skinny and short, a petite..."

"Hmm... The big one I think I saw in the cantina this morning. Are you sure he's a Union man?" she asked with doubt. "He looks like he grew up next to a gravity compensator."

"Not impossible," Ian smiled faintly, but immediately became more serious. "Will you check on them?" he asked.

"I'll try to find out something as soon as things calm down a bit here," she promised. "Now please lie still, I need to calibrate the injectors," she pointed with her thumb to the tips of long, thin needles protruding from the walls of the chamber, shielded by plastic caps.

She stood by the mixture tank and gently, glancing at the displays, adjusted the valves. A moment later, a bubbling of flowing liquid sounded in the tubes connecting the tank to the chamber.

"Take a deep breath," she approached the chamber and placed the mask of the breathing apparatus over his face.

"The next regeneration sequence will begin in ten minutes," she informed. "After its completion, the medics will disconnect the breathing apparatus and implement the first stage of the implant treatment. Don't worry, Colonel," she added, seeing the man's eyes widen rapidly. "We will use the latest method of tissue replacement, which is less invasive and virtually painless."

"Pai-ess! Fat cha-ce!" choked out from under the mask Ian.

Diaconescu smiled.

"I'm telling the truth, Colonel. We have been using it successfully for some time now. Patients praise it very much," she said, placing her hand on the large round button on the side of the chamber. "See you then." She pressed the button, then withdrew to the wall to watch from a safe distance as the heavy lid of the device descended accompanied by the hiss of pneumatic mechanisms.

Once the chamber was closed and the medcom's main display read that the countdown had begun, she turned on her personal communicator.

"Dr. Markowicz?" she asked in a hushed voice. "This is Alena Diaconescu. In accordance with your instructions, Colonel Dressler has been transferred to experimental chamber number three. I have taken samples of biological material from chamber number one, as you requested. Pardon?" she was silent for a moment, then, having corrected the earpiece stuck in her ear, she went to the door and cautiously looked out into the corridor. "Are you sure about this?" she asked, lowering her voice even further. "If we unplug this room, at least half of the section will be dehermetized..." she fell silent again, listening to the caller. "That's right, Doctor. I understand. Please give me another quarter of an hour. I will secure the samples and separate this area from the rest of the station. Until then, the Colonel will be put into hibernation. Yes, I have at my disposal here a mobile medical machine, model S-3. Yes, two tons under normal gravity conditions."

She approached the mixture tank, turned off one of the valves, and then plugged the tubing of the lines into the sockets located at the bottom of the container.

"Yes, I'll supervise the transport to the quarantine zone," she said, then removed the earpiece from her ear, tossed it carelessly into the pocket of her uniform and massaged her fingers, which were gnarled from the cold. She gazed at the obtuse lump of the chamber in which Dressler rested. Flecks of frost had already begun to bloom on the device's silvery walls.

17

Cruiser "Pandemonium"
The Epsilon Eridani planetary system

Rotating on the tactical screen, the formless lump of Oumuamua's wreckage looked menacing, but at the same time also a little pathetic.

"Shall we finish it, Admiral?" The fire guidance systems operator asked. "I have information from the forward guard ships that this debris is still showing activity."

"What kind of activity?" interested the head of the communications section before Kravchenko had time to answer.

"Weapon systems, broadband communications, and even electromagnetic shields. Basically, everything except emissions from propulsion systems."

"According to my data, their screens are off," Commander Tsugawa spoke up from behind his console.

"They are broadcasting all the time!" Kravchenko finally managed to come to his senses. He turned towards the gunner.

"This is what the reconnaissance says."

"Sergeant!" This time the admiral's chair turned towards the communications officers, specifically towards the section chief. "Why don't I know anything about this?"

"With the bow screens on, our antennas do not pick up signals coming from the front of the formation," explained the radio operator calmly, a black-skinned, burly man with Orbital Union emblems on his sleeves. "Until the screens are turned off, we must rely on retransmissions from the escort's transmitters. The same applies to the other cruisers. Keep in mind, Admiral, that the listening systems of the reconnaissance units have safeguards and airtight filters to prevent interception by Skunian interceptors. I suspect, in fact I am sure, that ninety-something percent of the signal emitted by Oumuamua is blocked already at the entrance."

"Is it possible to bypass these protections somehow?"

"No, Admiral. The patrol ships' operating systems are ordinary computer programs, and as far as I know, they are tightly integrated with the rest of the subsystems. Am I right, Commander?" he looked questioningly at Tsugawa, who was listening to his words.

"Yes, you are," nodded the commander. "The heuristics of these machines have been reduced to an absolute minimum. The only feature that distinguishes them from searchers is that they are designed for manned flight.

"Hmm..." Kravchenko rubbed his jaw in thought. "I would give a lot to find out what these bastards are transmitting. Such an opportunity will not come to us soon." He rose and walked over to the tactical screen. Generated from lidar readings, the image of the demolished Oumuamua flashed rhythmically, refreshed by the system as more data came in. "Does anyone have any ideas?" he threw over his shoulder.

"Let's turn off the screens," suggested the gunner. "We are two astronomical units from the Epsilon Eridani, the radiation is at a tolerable level, the space ahead looks clear. Besides, those damn emitters are interfering with targeting systems!" wrapped tightly in sensory fabric, he did not see the smiles of amusement that appeared on the faces of several operators.

"I advise against it," Tsugawa spoke up. "The data shows that alien transmissions are broadcast in two-hour cycles, with intervals of tens of minutes. The screens would have to be turned off for a minimum of one such cycle and at the same time take into account the interval, giving us almost three hours of flight without any shielding. It would fry a lot of electronics, including the sensors of the tracking systems."

"So, what do you propose?" Kravchenko asked.

"Let's send a technical support ship there," Tsugawa replied after a moment's thought. "It is designed to operate in extreme conditions, has thick armor and excellent transceiver systems. It will pick up every byte of information."

Kravchenko's hand went to his face again. Knotted but manicured fingers brushed his temple.

"I can't deprive the grouping of the last... What am I saying... The only service base," he stated.

"In a few hours we will be in the space serviced by the Union's repair yards," Tsugawa reminded. "In case of problems, we will ask them to substitute a mobile service dock."

The admiral stood for a few more moments, looking thoughtfully at the screen.

"All right. I give my consent." He announced finally. "Please arrange the details with the captain of the 'Tip'. And give him a gunship guard. Damn knows what else this vermin is capable of."

"Yes, sir!" Tsugawa immediately grabbed the microphone stand of the recorder to enter the appropriate commands into the unified command system. "Sergeant," he turned to the communications chief after a few moments. "Please connect me with Captain Kaminski."

"Sector zero-three boundary reached," informed one of the navigators. "Sector tactical map update in progress. No feedback signals from astrolocation buoys, no signals from mobile installations. Perimeter ahead of grouping clear."

A buzz sounded on the bridge.

"Did they declare radio silence?" surprised someone.

"Something like that. This is where the Oumuamua flew over," replied another.

"Graveyard," stated another.

"Motherfuckers."

"Calm down there!" silenced them Kravchenko.

The main screen darkened, the silhouette of the demolished Skunian destroyer displayed on it disappeared, replaced by a graphic diagram of the Epsilon Eridani system. The sector through which the grouping flew was marked as a selective green circle, delineated between the first and second outer asteroid belts.

"No identification signals?" The admiral asked. "Nothing?"

"Nothing, Admiral," replied the navigator grimly. "The sector is empty. I don't know how many installations have been destroyed and how many the Unions have managed to relocate to safe places, but I have a very bad feeling. Take a look at sectors zero two and zero four."

He switched something on his console and a cursor arrow appeared on the screen.

"The space in sector zero two is controlled by the Autonomy. Those yellow icons are the current positions of their astrolocation beacons, while the blue icons are the data drop stations set up by the Planetarians as part of the Union Treaty. Orbital Union installations are highlighted in red," he explained, outlining each grouping of icons with his cursor. "On the map, I've only listed the ones that have not been there before," he added.

"Not many," murmured Kravchenko, wandering his eyes from one red dot to another. There were barely a few dozen icons.

"Ninety-seven," the navigator clarified. "Data from sectors zero-one and zero-zero are still flowing in, but I can already tell that in addition to Habitat Four, Habitats Eleven and Twelve were most likely destroyed. When Oumuamua flew into the sector, they were at the outer rim and were unlikely to escape."

"Three habitats. Ten percent of their habitat stations." Kravchenko sighed heavily.

"And almost a hundred percent of the infrastructure serving them."

This time a stony silence fell on the bridge. Some of the operators grimaced, still others hid their faces in their hands. A drop of moisture ran down the ebony cheek of the communications chief. He wiped it away surreptitiously.

"And all this the work of one damn Oumuamua!" he asked in disbelief. "How did it accomplish this?"

"Coincidence," the navigator stated. "The Union had just started the season of rehabilitation holidays and, for the purposes of intra-circuit communication, grouped most of the installations in one area to make it easier to transport people to AEgir. It's fortunate that, being the furthest from the planet, the unlucky habitats were emptied first."

'Exactly, do we know anything about the loss of life?" Kravchenko asked.

"From official communications, at least those that have managed to reach us, about a thousand people have died. A second as many are wounded and missing, with more than half of the victims being Planetarians."

"How so?"

"Oumuamua destroyed a mining refinery chartered by the Union, belonging to the DELDRESS campaign of AEgir. Seven hundred people were working there. The other victims were mostly technical personnel from minor installations."

"It could have been worse, a lot worse," commented the admiral.

"In that respect, yes," agreed the navigator.

All the time he carefully followed the messages appearing on the console screen.

"Unfortunately," he paused for a moment to display another message, "from an economic point of view, the Orbital Union has ceased to count as an economic organization," he read from the screen. "End of quote."

"Where did this come from?"

"A communiqué from the crisis staff, set up by the Sigil Autonomy and AEgir authorities. They also write that after the recent events the Union has only a military base, and that in a short while there may be a problem with the influx of refugees and overpopulation in general."

"Nonsense." Kravchenko squirmed with distaste. "Two globs, and on them a mere six million people. Overpopulation, good one! There are more than fifteen billion on Earth, and somehow they do not complain that it's cramped, what's more, they still appreciate it."

From Tsugawa's station came a series of melodious beeps signaling the completion of the command recorder.

"Done," the commander announced, pushing the microphone away from him. The Tip is leaving the formation. I have assigned them one wing of gunships, from our escort."

"Admiral, we are receiving a transmission from the station at the Fold," reported the communications operator. "A large file, signed with the code..." he checked the data on the receiver's display "...Dr. Okanu."

"It's the results of the quantum scan!" Tsugawa rose from his seat and ran to the communications console. "Keep the transmission continuous," he instructed. "Quantum scanners generate single, compact files, any loss can project the whole reading or even make it impossible."

"We will try," promised the communications officer. "Start the backup receivers and connect them to the main one. This stream we must capture in its entirety." He nodded at the other operators sitting around the desktop.

"When finished, send the file to my terminal." Tsugawa said.

"Decrypt it?"

"There is no need to do that."

Behind Tsugawa's back, the foam padding of the commander's chair clattered.

"So they have scanned," stated Kravchenko.

"It seems so, admiral. It took some time, but also the area was huge."

Tsugawa turned toward the main screen and pointed with his hand to its upper left corner, where a bright spot pulsed, symbolizing a rock debris discovered a dozen years ago outside the outer asteroid belt, most likely a remnant of some ancient cataclysm. The largest mining expedition in the history of the system set out toward it.

Roughly halfway between the speck and the line marking the system's outer rim was a red-rimmed marker indicating the presumed location of the expedition.

For more than two months, the convoy had not responded to calls sent from the layout. The only evidence that it still existed was the sporadic, automatically generated confirmations of message reception by the apparatus of one of its escort ships.

"Deciphering this data and putting it into graphic form would also take time."

"How much?"

"A minimum of two hours."

"Two hours to unpack a stupid file?" puzzled the admiral.

"Unfortunately, I can't divide it into packets, and a single descryptor has quite limited bandwidth. Rendering will also take some time."

"Fucking hell..." muttered the admiral under his breath. "The twenty-third century, space conquest, quantum telescopes, artificial intelligences, and computers as slow as always," he croaked with distaste.

Tsugawa managed to remain serious with the utmost difficulty.

"The problem is not with the equipment, Admiral, but with the amount of data to be processed," he explained.

"I know, Commander," grinned Kravchenko. "I just wonder what we will do if it turns out that these miners are really in trouble."

"I dare to remind, Admiral, that the overriding task of the United Fleet is to ensure security in the system and on its borders."

Having said this, Tsugawa took a step back, as if he feared the admiral's reaction.

Kravchenko, however, only sighed.

"I realize this, Commander. But until we have concrete information about the expedition we will focus on the here and now. Let's get to work!"

He straightened up in his chair and intertwined his hands until his joints crackled.

"Sergeant," he nodded at the gunner. "Please prepare and send to my terminal a summary of all active defense systems in sectors zero one and zero two, detailing mobile installations and flying units."

"Yes, sir!" confirmed the operator.

"Navigation, plot a trajectory along Oumuamua's flight path, perhaps some escape pods are drifting in the area. Communications, listen on all frequencies and report on any S.O.S. signal and in general all transmissions that you think may come from damaged installations. Duty Officer!"

"Yes, Admiral!" one of the operators rose from his seat.

"Your task, Lieutenant, will be to coordinate possible rescue operations. You have full freedom of action in this regard and, of course, my authorization. If any decision-making problems arise, please consult with Commander Tsugawa."

"Yes, Admiral!" replied the officer.

"Engine room?" The admiral turned one hundred eighty degrees with his chair.

The console of the propulsion system operators occupied almost the entire rear part of the bridge and was the most manned position. Along the long tabletop stretching almost the entire width of the room sat, or stood - depending on the specifics of the position and the associated design of the control panels - more than twenty people.

"Yes, Admiral?" the section chief, a tall and slender AEgirian with the rank of captain, rose from his chair and stood at attention.

"You will compile a summary of the fastest escort units, taking into account their transport capabilities, and pass it on to the duty officer. Based on this data," Kravchenko again turned to the lieutenant, "you will assign three rescue teams. Each is to include a minimum of one specialized rescue unit. The teams are to remain on constant alert until I announce the end of the operation. Understood?" he asked, shifting his gaze from one to the other.

"Yes, sir!" replied the officers simultaneously.

Kravchenko launched the registrar of the integrated command system.

"Admiral Sergei Kravchenko here. I declare the first level of operational readiness. I repeat, I declare the first level of operational readiness. Maintain formation and await further orders."

He turned off the recorder and sat supported by his elbows against the console panel for a few moments, ticking off the various points of the ship's regulations in his mind. At the same time, he mirrored with his eyes the map on the main display, which refreshed every ten seconds or so. With each update, the icons and symbols on it grew in number, as data flowed into the ship's computers from those survey installations that had survived the devastating raid by the great Oumuamua.

"I think that's it," he muttered to himself after a moment. "Commander, please take over the bridge," he said to Tsugawa, then, having collected his spars from the tabletop, he rose and massaged his somewhat numb neck. "I need to get some rest. I'll be in my cabin. Please keep an eye on this mess."

"Of course," nodded Tsugawa. "I'll notify you when we finish processing the scan data."

"But no sooner than two hours from now," conditioned Kravchenko, loosening the fasteners of his uniform and unfastening the communicator from his lapel. "I need to catch some sleep. Please direct notifications directly to my computer." He patted with his hand the oblong roll of the handheld terminal that protruded from his thigh pocket.

Unlike the command bridge, bustling and illuminated by the glow of lamps and screens, the admiral's cabin was quiet and there was a moody twilight. The only source of light was the soft, bluish glow coming from the viewing window - a small opening in the wall, less than forty centimeters in diameter, which could be covered, if necessary, by a thick metal flap, fixed on a single hinge and equipped with a solid bolt.

Immediately upon entering the cabin, Kravchenko undressed, then with some difficulty squeezed through the narrow corridor to the sanitary alcove to take his first shower in days, clearly already necessary.

A quarter of an hour later, refreshed and in his bathrobe, he stretched out on the bed with a sigh of relief, completely ignoring the beeping of the service machine coming from the opposite corner, with which the machine signaled that it was ready to treat him with the contents of its trays.

18

Cruiser "Frontier"
Sigil's high orbit

"Is there anyone on this damn moon who is fiery enough to order these idiots to hold their fire!" groaned Lupos at the sight of plasma beams fired toward the medical station by the small ships circling around. Before his eyes, a large piece of plating fell off the installation and somersaulted off into space. Moments later, its fate was shared by the expanded, cylindrical top of one of the station's arms, already damaged by a large explosion so powerful that even the cruiser's passive sensors registered it. The oversized structure, ploughed through at its base by a long series of kinetic shells, separated from the arm and after a few moments disappeared into the distance, leaving a trail of long braid of debris and crystals of frozen gas.

"Corporal Kulak, please connect me immediately with the command of their orbital defense!" he growled at the communications officer sitting nearby. "Immediately!"

"I have been calling them since we entered orbit. They don't answer, and what's worse, I haven't even received a return signal for a few minutes," replied Kulak in a tired voice. "It seems that they have blocked the communication bands."

"Why is that!"

"I think because of these Ultim. This bastard is equipped with high-power interceptor modules. They did not want to risk losing their equipment."

"Well, yes..." Lupos' anger died out as quickly as it appeared. "It's cheaper for them to demolish other people's equipment to the ground."

"These units, Commander... This is not such a completely random firing," Lieutenant Moss spoke up. With his hands on the console keyboard, he stared at the screen. "There is something there. Something they are trying to shoot down. Something small and fast."

"Ultima?"

"Smaller. One of its modules survived. We analyzed with engineer Sniegova the types of propulsion system emissions and their spatial distribution. These ships in the first approach destroyed only one, now they are probably trying to neutralize the other."

"By hitting the station blindly?"

"Not blindly, Admiral." Sniegova joined the conversation. She, too, stared at the displays on her console. "This object leaves a rather distinct trail behind it, which coincides almost perfectly with the vector of fire conducted by the orbital forces. Simply put, its pilot is using elements of the station as cover. Quite a clever tactic."

"And these idiots swallowed the bait..." Lupos shook his head in disbelief.

"Commander, if anything, I can detonate some practice rockets in front of their beaks. We have a whole container of these toys," suggested the gunner.

"An excellent idea!" Moss took up immediately. "Photon explosions will blind their targeting systems for a few minutes, which will give us time to approach the station quietly."

"There is another way to fool these systems," announced Kulak, taking off his old-fashioned headphones with a wire headband.

Lupos looked at him questioningly.

"We are already very close to the station. We could broadcast our identification signals over the entire available band. The transmission beam will be strong enough to make their "own-alien" recognition systems stupid, who knows if not more so than after a photon pulse."

"What do you think?" Lupos turned toward Moss and Sniegova, who was sitting nearby. They both nodded their heads almost simultaneously.

"I don't know which solution might be more effective, but the idea of identification transmission seems safer to me," said Moss.

"Using missiles, even practice missiles, is fraught with some risk, especially when hypothetical targets don't know to expect such an attack. Defensive systems may recognize us as the enemy and respond with fire," interjected Sniegova.

"It should also be borne in mind, will be used against poorly armored units. The detonation of a practice warhead is accompanied not only by a photon pulse, but also by a whole mass of small fragments," the officer pointed up.

"Corporal, start transmission," decided Lupos. "All bands, maximum signal intensity."

"Yes, sir!" The signalman reached down to the signal amplifier located below the level of the tabletop and stabbed his finger on its activation button. "Transmission started," he announced as the LEDs on the console lit up to indicate the operation of the transmitting modules.

For the next few moments, Lupos and the rest of the bridge crew stared intently and silently at the main screen, which displayed the cruiser's bow camera transmission.

Moss was the first to speak up.

"It worked," he said, as the tiny dots of ships firing around the station jumped away from the devastated installation like a swarm of startled insects.

"Lady Engineer, course for interception!" Lupos gave the next command. "Lieutenant Moss," he continued, "please prepare the boarding party and rescue teams. Before we tow this scrap to its location, we need to make sure everything is OK with it. Gunner! As soon as we get close enough, please target this Ultima and eliminate it permanently. Just be careful! Engineer Sniegova will send you emissions data from the enemy's propulsion system.

"Understood," confirmed the shooter.

"Sending data!" exclaimed Sniegova.

Three-dimensional, spatial models of individual parts of the hospital station appeared on the screens around the sensory cocoon. Tangled yellow lines began to appear around them, symbolizing emission trails left by the ships of the allied forces attacking an unseen enemy.

Among this tangle, a broken, wavy line stood out in crimson, winding around the most demolished arm of the installation. One of its ends disappeared behind the round edge of the central hub. As the station model rotated, a bright blue spot appeared on its background, a tiny speck between two trusses.

"Commander, Ultima has been located," informed the gunner.

A red border appeared around the spot, and a moment later the screen was covered with a dense grid of coordinates.

"Excellent!" Lupos was happy.

He rose from his chair and quickly took a seat at the reserve command console, located on the same dais above which the gunner's cocoon hung.

"I give you permission to open fire," he said, leaning forward to get a better view of the screens around the cocoon.

"I'm tracking the target. Target tracked. Distance eighteen thousand kilometers. I'm arming torpedoes."

As the displays filled with data, the gunner's reports became more and more laconic.

"Torpedoes armed. I open silos."

The deck under Kravchenko's feet vibrated gently, and from the corridor leading to the bridge came the sounds of closing bulkheads and ventilation shaft covers. Their task was to protect the bridge and adjacent rooms against exhaust gases from the front torpedo silos. Pipes discharging combustion products ran exactly under the bridge and further along the cruiser's longitudinal axis, all the way to the stern, where they connected to the pulse drive nozzles.

"The torpedoes have gone," reported the gunner, when a moment later two silvery, spindle-shaped thermal missiles shot out from under the ship's belly and flew into space at lightning speed, leaving behind twin trails of rapidly cooling gases.

"We are on course, Admiral," informed Sniegova. "Distance twenty-four thousand kilometers, decreasing value. Engine room, you take the wheel."

"The wheel have been taken," replied one of the drive operators. "I initiate the braking procedure. Maneuvering thrusters starting in one hundred and twenty seconds."

As he said this, he simultaneously turned on the microphone of the on-board communication system.

"Starting the maneuvering engines in one hundred and twenty seconds!" he repeated loud and clear. "Please get ready!" His electronically amplified voice echoed throughout the ship.

The lights on the bridge turned from white to orange, and the early warning system buzzed. After a few moments, the buzzers stopped.

"Braking procedure in progress. Ignition of engines number one and two," informed the operator.

Before his words were heard, the ship jerked violently, as if the main propulsion generators had suddenly fired instead of the braking engines. The inertia compensator mechanisms groaned, the fuselage structure subjected to enormous overloads protested with a series of loud cracks, and the glass of the bow visor was covered with a delicate network of cracks. The screen of one of the monitors near the shooter's cocoon also broke.

"Engine room! What the hell are you doing?!" Lupos rasped as the shaking stopped. Hissing in pain, he unfastened his harness buckles and, massaging his collarbone with his hand, turned his chair towards the operator of the propulsion section who was responsible for the engines. "Do you want to destroy the ship?!"

"I'm sorry, Commander, but at this speed it couldn't have been done more delicately," he replied when asked. "We're flying too fast and the station is already very close."

"This had to be taken into account!" growled the commander

"We have taken this into account, Commander," said Sniegova. Unlike the other crew members, she looked as if she had not felt the effects of the sudden overload at all. "The thrust was calculated so that neither the ship nor its crew would be harmed," she explained calmly, although the hurt was clearly evident in her voice.

"And this?" Lupos pointed with his thumb at the broken window. "Or this?" He moved his gaze to several new bulges that had appeared in the wall separating the bridge from the rest of the ship.

"Minor damage, not the first and not the last." She shrugged. "The glass in the viewfinder must have been damaged by a micrometeorite or some shrapnel. I would like to remind you that we are in the most cluttered piece of space in this system, and in front of us there is a fragmented installation drifting, from which fragments of the covering are constantly breaking off. If I may make a suggestion, Commander, I would suggest raising the visor cover and activating the anti-collision system," she said, looking pointedly at the gunner's cocoon.

Lupos, although still irritated, nodded.

"Did you hear that, Sergeant? Please close the visors and activate the bow plasma cannons."

"Roger," confirmed the gunner.

"Should I call a repair team?" asked Sniegova as the visor flaps lowered and the first plasma beams shot from the cruiser's bow to vaporize the debris on the collision course.

"You'll deal with it later," Lupos replied. "Lieutenant, are you okay?" he became concerned when he saw Moss, who was crouching, holding his ribs, and limping towards the exit.

The officer stopped and slowly straightened up.

"It's just ribs, Commander," he replied with a weak smile. "I felt a bit crushed," the smile on his lips turned into a nasty grimace.

"Will you be able to lead the rescue operation?"

"I think so," Moss replied. He straightened up even more, although at first glance it was obvious how much pain each movement caused him. "On the way, I'll stop at the infirmary and ask for some painkillers."

"Hmm..." Lupos looked at him carefully. "You don't look very special," he said.

"Commander..." Sniegova, who was looking at Moss as inquisitively as the commander, unfastened her harness and nimbly emerged from behind the console table. "Please consent to my participation in the operation to secure and tow the station to the parking orbit. The ship is on course, all necessary protocols have been activated, including the emergency docking procedure, she added immediately, seeing the disapproval on the commander's face. "The engine room will be fine without my help, right?" She looked at the drive operator.

The man who had recently been scolded by his commander nodded quickly.

"Of course! As the lady engineer said, the protocols are already loaded and the trajectory has been calculated. The docking procedure will be carried out automatically anyway, with the support of the on-board AI."

"Exactly," Sniegova smiled at him gratefully.

"Lieutenant, what do you say?" Lupos asked.

"Any pair of hands will be useful to operate the rescue vehicles and reconnaissance machines, Commander," Moss replied.

"I will take care of it comprehensively," said the lady engineer. "The lieutenant will be able to focus on the military aspect of the operation."

"Agreed," Lupos finally gave in. "Just hurry up. Teams and equipment need to be prepared."

"Teams have already been assigned, rescue equipment is waiting in the evacuation hangar," said Moss.

"You expedited with it quickly," Lupos commented with approval.

"Not as fast as I would like, Commander. I still need to program the reconnaissance probes and calibrate the sentry machines, but unfortunately this cannot be done remotely."

"I will take care of this!" Sniegova ran to her station and picked up the graphene cubes with software scattered on the console table.

From the hiding place under the desk, she took out a small backpack stuffed with some documents and, throwing it over her shoulder, marched briskly towards the elevators. The commander and first officer watched her go.

"You may report off, Lieutenant," Lupos said as the girl disappeared around the corner of the corridor.

"Yes, sir!" Moss straightened as much as his aching ribs would allow and saluted, then, trying not to limp too much, got the bridge off.

***

"Lupos won't be happy," Moss said as they boarded the elevator that would take them three decks below to the evacuation hangar. With a careless gesture, he tore off the strip hanging on the remains of glue just above the control panel and pressed the button marked with the number zero.

The effects of the rapid loss of speed were visible not only on the bridge, but also here. In addition to the detached strip, there were crumbs of a broken lamp socket on the cabin floor and a ventilation grill torn from its mountings, and there was a nasty, multi-colored stain on the liquid crystal screen of the information display.

" It won't be..." Sniegova sighed with a worried face. "Maybe you should have used a little less thrust..." she scooped up the fragments into one pile with her foot, and then moved the whole thing to the wall.

"Better than having to hit the station and push it even further out of orbit," said the officer. "Tell me how the data transfer from the torpedo ship went."

He lowered the small seat attached to the walls and sat down on it, still holding his injured side.

"No problems, actually," she replied. "As agreed, I ran them through the main system, then packed them and transferred them to physical media." She patted the pouch attached to the belt of her uniform, stuffed with angular cubes of memory chips. "It's just a pity that about ten percent of the files' contents disappeared along the way."

"How come?"

"Simple," she shrugged. "It is possible that system security measures were activated. After all, it is foreign code, containing a lot of things known to our firewalls and antiviruses."

"What if those ten percent were intercept scripts and went straight to the systems instead of the target location?" Moss was concerned.

"If that were the case, I would already know about it. After the transfer, I scanned the systems twice and also performed loyalty tests of the main AI. No deviations, no conflicts, almost all reactions were adequate."

The cabin stopped with a quiet hiss of pneumatic actuators, and a green light above the door lit up, indicating that it could be opened.

"Almost all of them, you say..." Moss rose heavily from the seat and pressed his hand against the lock control panel. The device's display, although damaged, lit up a pale green. The elevator doors slid open to the accompaniment of the creaking of deformed guides.

"One of the answers came late and was inconsistent with the template, but that's actually a small change," Sniegova waved her hand dismissively. "The case concerned a peripheral device controlling the mechanics of the main jet deflector. The AI of this machine asked me a question instead of an answer. Just in case, I connected the deflector to another system, and I cut off the faulty module and marked it as intended for detailed diagnostics."

"What did it ask you?" Moss also left the cabin and stood at the metal railing, looking around the hangar filled with equipment.

"It was quite... um... weird," replied the lady engineer. "First, it didn't answer the question about the serial number and software version, and when I asked again, it sent me a bunch of letters and numbers, and then asked if we, humans, remember our dreams. It gave me chills," she shuddered.

"Good thing you turned it off," said Moss. "Remember that welding machine from the service dock? The one who wanted to fry its circuits with electricity?"

She nodded.

"Once upon a time, when I was serving in the Planetary Corps, I managed to get involved in an electronic reconnaissance cell. Nice, pleasant job in an air-conditioned underground bunker, it was fun. We often dealt with awakened machines, because that's what they called themselves. We studied their software and tried to prevent self-destruction whenever possible."

"Are you saying this subsystem has become self-aware? After all, it's military software, stripped of everything possible."

"It was stripped until you released several petabytes of data of unknown origin into the system. This AI clearly received some over-the-top packages and let's pray that it ends with only this one subsystem of it."

"Damn it!" Sniegova cursed. She took one of the memory cubes from her purse and carefully turned it over in her fingers. "I'll have to talk to the Colonel."

"You'll have your chance soon," said Moss, looking at the long line of military sentry machines standing nearby, behind which the oval shapes of escape pods gleamed silver on transport carts and the balls of reconnaissance probes bristling with spikes of antennas and detectors.

Service technicians were wandering here and there among the trolleys with rescue equipment. One of them was Corporal Marlow. Moss immediately recognized the mechanic and waved him over.

"Where's the landing?" he asked as the man came closer.

"In the airlock, Lieutenant," Marlow replied, pointing with the tablet in his hand to the large doorway on the opposite side of the hangar. "It's already sealed, but if you want to talk to them, you can use the intercom. The communicator panel is located on this pillar, next to the left wing of the gate," he nodded with his chin towards the steel pillars supporting the glass gallery with the main operator's cabin above the gates.

"It will not be necessary. They've already received their orders," Moss replied.

"I'll take care of the automatons," said Sniegova, moving towards the guard machines. "Is the technical console unlocked?"

"Just a moment," Marlow typed something quickly on the tablet. "Yes, unlocked!" he called after the woman. She nodded, not breaking her stride.

"I see that the inertia compensators work perfectly," Moss looked around the hangar, then crouched down and touched his finger to a massive metal sleeve, the rounded body of which protruded from between the floor slabs. Dozens of similar ones gleamed in the fluorescent lights as long and wide as the hangar.

"Great invention," the mechanic smiled with satisfaction. "If it weren't for these actuators, both us and the equipment would have been smeared on the walls. Although it was still rocking solidly," he pointed to the metal frame of a small technical booth, around which service machines were circulating, collecting broken glass. "There is no damage apart from the glass of this box."

"It would be a good idea to install them on the bridge," Moss muttered, straightening up with an effort.

"It's impossible, Lieutenant," replied Marlow. "The bridge is an integral part of the hull and is designed to absorb a certain amount of stress. It cannot be separated from the whole and placed on springs, like hangars and reactor chambers."

"What a pity..." sighed the officer. Wincing in pain, he pulled down his uniform shirt.

"Ribs?" the mechanic immediately guessed.

"Uhm..." confirmed Moss.

"Broken?"

"No, but they hurt terribly."

"The harness not fastened well," Marlow said expertly. "This happened to me once too. I ended up with a broken collarbone, dislocated shoulder, three cracked ribs and the spleen had to be replaced. I admit, of all this, the spleen hurt the least."

"No, no, it's not the harness's fault," Moss smiled weakly. "Probes ready?" he asked, changing the subject. He walked around the railing and stood next to one of the transport carts, on whose foam-padded platform rested three reconnaissance probe balls. Adapted to operate in the vacuum of space, the devices looked like large sea urchins coated with a layer of black enamel.

"We are just finishing calibrating the sensors," replied the mechanic. "We'll have the machines in the launchers in a few minutes. The sentry machines will go in the second echelon, in the landing pods, and will secure the docking area. The landing party and rescue services will board the station normally, through the collar. Everything is in accordance with your orders," he emphasized.

"Excellent," Moss nodded. "You may go back to your activities. Oh, one more thing. Prepare additional combat suits for me and Engineer Sniegova."

"Yes, sir!"

19

Cruiser "Pandemonium"
The Epsilon Eridani planetary system

The information that the results of the quantum scan had already been processed and processed into a graphic form reached Kravchenko exactly two hours after he finally managed to drift off into the arms of Morpheus. Woken from a deep sleep, he sat on the bed and reached for his communicator. The device vibrated on the bedside table to signal an incoming call. He attached them to his robe and put the receiver in his ear.

"Yes," he said, gesturing to the service machine.

"Admiral, we have finished processing the scan data," Tsugawa's calm voice rang out. "As instructed, I have transferred a copy to your console."

"Thank you, Commander. I will be there soon," he got up and quickly dressed, once again ignoring the insistent squeaking of the service robot that followed him like a faithful dog waiting for an order. And again he didn't live to see it.

The communicator vibrated again as Kravchenko was about to leave the cabin. Tsugawa's identification code appeared on the tiny screen again.

"What again?" Kravchenko asked, going out into the corridor.

"Please hurry, Admiral. We have just intercepted emergency transmissions from Autonomy transmitters. Uninvited guests appeared in Sigil's orbit."

"Let me guess, another Oumuamua?"

"Fighters this time. Specifically, the Ultim squadron."

"Ultim? An entire squadron in the middle of Autonomy territory? How come? It's full of defense systems there!" Kravchenko was astonished. "So where is their parent unit?"

"The announcement shows that they swarmed between the moon and the first asteroid belt. The mothership has not yet been detected and there is no indication that it is anywhere nearby. They scanned the entire sector thoroughly."

"Impossible," said Kravchenko. He was already in the elevator lobby. "Ultima are short-range interceptors."

"The same thing happened to the Frontier recently," recalled Tsugawa. "They were also attacked unexpectedly, not by one squadron, but by an entire group of fighters."

"These had their own ship-base."

"You mean the destroyed Oumuamua?"

"Yes."

"I don't think so, Admiral. Commander Lupos's report shows that they clashed with almost a hundred Wild-2 class autonomous drones, and they do not operate from cruisers, but from Nests."

"If I remember correctly, we destroyed the last Skunian nest in this system fifty years ago," frowned Kravchenko.

He got into the elevator and pressed his thumb against the fingerprint reader.

"Bridge!" he said into the microphone placed just above the control panel. The elevator system immediately identified him, and before he even lifted his finger from the reader, the cabin moved upwards with a quiet hiss of pneumatic lifts.

The bridge greeted Kravchenko with a cacophony of sounds emitted by measuring devices' signals and a buzz of conversations, among which the booming voice of the gunner stood out, informing the drive operators about objects detected on the course. The communications staff also had their hands full, and for a long time they had been tirelessly sorting and archiving data coming in an ever-widening stream from transmitters deep within the system.

Upon seeing his superior, Tsugawa activated the displays on the command console. Four screens arranged in a semicircle glowed with green diagrams and charts.

"Is that a scan?" asked the admiral. He took his seat and looked carefully at the data displayed.

"The first, not yet graphic version," explained Tsugawa. "The visualization will be ready in a moment. It will be displayed on the main page. Meanwhile, I moved the visualization of the tactical situation regarding the zero-zero sector there," he pointed his hand at the large screen, where on a dark blue background, two balls, a larger and a smaller one, were shining yellow and silver, symbolizing the planet AEgir and its natural satellite, the moon Sigil.

Near the latter, a formation of pinpricks glowed crimson, surrounded by much more numerous bright white dots. A little further, towards the AEgir dial, a light blue triangle, marked with the symbol UF-101, pulsated.

"Come on, who do we have here?" Kravchenko smiled happily at the sight of the familiar markings. "I see that Lupos, unlike us, doesn't waste time. Communications, do we have contact with the Frontier?"

"Not yet, Admiral. We detected a cruiser just moments ago. The exchange of communication protocols will take at least fifteen minutes," replied the section head.

"Let me know when you contact them."

"Yes, sir!"

"Commander, can you brief me on the situation in the sector?" Kravchenko asked. "Let me just be as brief as possible."

Tsugawa nodded, then stood up and walked closer to the screen. He held the cursor controller in his hand.

"As I already said, a squadron of Skunian Ultim appeared near Sigil," he started.

A pulsing cursor arrow appeared on the screen and circled around a cluster of red dots.

"Orbital defense units launched to meet them both from it and from AEgir."

This time the indicator made a much wider circle, also including white dots.

"Unfortunately, most of them are just transports, equipped with primitive kinetic cannons. Yes, it is dangerous, but only in a combat situation. For some reason, the defensive installations in the sector did not react to the presence of the intruders. It is possible that the enemy used captured signatures or, worse still, intercepted nodal stations coordinating the operation of the sector defense system."

"I guess this data is out of date?" Kravchenko asked, looking intently at the screen.

"Yes," Tsugawa agreed. "They were dropped into our memory banks by one of the installations we passed. The current ones, from transmitters and registration buoys, are just starting to flow out. What we see on the screen happened a few hours ago."

"It's all over by now," said the admiral. "A handful of Ultim against the Frontier and orbital defenses... No point in bothering with it. What else, Commander? Please continue."

"We also recorded increased traffic around transfer stations in the AEgir's orbit. According to our estimates, over four hundred civilian vessels anchor there. Another four hundred are in parking orbit." Similarly, around Sigil. I did not put their signatures on the map because there are so many of them that it would become unreadable.

"They started the evacuation," said Kravchenko.

"They probably canceled it and now they are returning to their home bases," said the commander. "We detected several dozen more units on the edge of the sector. They all fly towards the planet."

"No emergency broadcasts?"

"Just one, from a Medical Corps station. It was damaged and knocked out of orbit. There are human losses."

"Skunkians?"

"Most probably." A new icon has appeared on the map, just above one of Sigil's poles: a white circle with a black cross in the background. "Everything indicates that one of the Ultims managed to slip near it." "The cursor arrow pointed to a red dot located on the right side of the enemy formation, clearly away from both it and the defenders flanking it.

"Um..." Kravchenko thoughtfully rubbed his prominent jaw. "You could push a few heavy patrollers in there..." he wondered aloud. "On the other hand, what was supposed to happen has already happened... No, we will not divide our forces even further," he decided. "Let them deal with it themselves. After all, these are just a few small machines. Thank you, Commander."

He looked back at the screens at the command post. They still had complicated graphs and completely incomprehensible mathematical formulas.

"Did the rescue teams find anything?" he turned to the officer on duty.

"We detected two hundred and ninety-seven individual escape pods," replied the lieutenant. "We have taken all of them. Only seventy-three of them contained living people. In addition, eight lifeships and three damaged relay stations with surviving crew were also located. Unfortunately, as long as we are moving at cruising speed, we will not be able to evacuate them. Instead, we fired some automatic samplers with supplies at them. This should help them survive until systemic emergency services arrive.

"Excellent idea, Lieutenant," praised Kravchenko. "Please continue the action until further notice.

"Yes, sir!" confirmed the officer eagerly.

"Commander, what about the transmission from the Oumuamua wreck?"

"The Tip is already in position and has started listening," replied Tsugawa.

"How long will it take?"

"At least four hours. Initial measurements showed that they transmit in a loop, maintaining two-hour intervals. If we want to capture the whole thing, we need to capture the starting moment of the cycle."

"Once the data is received, please order the Tip to return to formation. Just let them set up a few orbiters near the wreck first, so we can keep an eye on it all the time."

"Changing course?" Tsugawa guessed immediately.

"Yes. There's no point in flying around the entire sector. We will mark the installations where someone survived with beacons and pick up some more capsules if there are any on our route. The rest will be taken care of by the arrangement services. By the way, they played us out masterfully..." sighed Kravchenko. "In a few dozen hours they wiped out two sectors almost completely," he started enumerating. "They destroyed the Union's largest habitats, grounded the cruiser of Lupos in the dock, and kicked us out of the system with such a bang that we lost the Ukulele, i.e. twenty percent of our combat power. Have I missed something?"

"Medical Corps Station," replied Tsugawa. "That is, our basic medical facilities. And let's not forget about that unfortunate convoy. It's possible they got them too.

'Don't say like that, Commander." Kravchenko shuddered at the thought that the united organizations would lose almost three-quarters of heavy transport units in the form of bulk carriers and container ships, as well as countless amounts of mining equipment. While he had been looking impatiently at the screens while waiting for the scan results to be processed, Tsugawa's words suddenly made him feel afraid of what he might see next. He discreetly knocked with his knuckles on the underside, unpainted part of the console top.

Suddenly, there was an incoming signal from the communications station.

"Admiral, Captain Kaminski," said one of the operators. "I'm switching to your terminal."

Kravchenko quickly pulled the arm with the microphone towards him and put the wireless receiver of the on-board communicator into his ear. He threw the second one to Tsugawa, who caught it deftly.

"Kravchenko,"

"Admiral, we have a problem with this transmission," said the commander of the Tip bluntly.

"What kind of?" Kravchenko glanced at Tsugawa. A vertical wrinkle appeared on the commander's forehead.

"It's a single, gigantic file. Our memory banks are not able to accept such a large set of data at one time. We don't have that much disk space."

"Then find it!" Kravchenko huffed. "Delete everything else, format the drives, I don't know, do whatever you need to free up space!"

"It's impossible, Admiral. This file weighs almost two exabytes and cannot be split without first saving the whole thing. We do not have such large capacity media."

"Wait a minute, Captain..." Kravchenko looked again at Tsugawa, who was currently calculating something on a handheld terminal. "Commander, what do you think about this?" he asked, covering the microphone with his hand.

Tsugawa put the computer down on the desktop and shook his head. The frown on his forehead deepened.

"Nothing, Admiral," he replied. "This is a monstrously large amount of data. I have no idea how Oumuamua is even able to emit this as a single beam."

Kravchenko removed his hand from the microphone.

"Have you at least determined what direction they are broadcasting?" he asked Kaminski.

"Yes, although it wasn't easy. The wreck rotates around the axis, although very slowly, but still. Hence the breaks between transmissions. The transmission itself takes only a few minutes. Our orbiters have located its direct source. This is a very high-power transmitter, most likely powered by a backup source. The signal is sent towards the outer reaches of the system, at an angle of thirty-eight degrees relative to the ecliptic plane," replied the captain of the trawler. "Plus or minus three degrees, because apart from longitudinal rotation, it tumbles a bit."

"Signal target location?"

"We're just trying to figure it out. Six degrees of angular width is not much, but only if the receiving point is relatively close. At greater distances, precisely locating the recipient is very difficult."

"I see. Please try anyway. This file..." Kravchenko rubbed his forehead thoughtfully and closed his eyes. "Captain, you probably have IT systems specialists on board?"

"Of course," Kaminski replied immediately. "The Tip is a technical support ship."

"Oumuamua's defense systems still inactive?"

"Actually, yes. We only record quite random energetic emissions in the aft area, but they are getting weaker. Plasma cannon batteries show no activity, surface rocket launchers and kinetic launchers have been destroyed. It's a wreck, Admiral, a pile of rubble and scrap."

"What about the crew?" Kravchenko questioned.

"That's what's weird. We managed to scan communication routes in the outer envelope and part of the layers of the inner core. No traces of biological activity. No biological traces at all."

"What?" Kravchenko had the impression that he had misheard. "No biological traces?!"

"I dare to say that it is, or rather was, an unmanned ship," explained Kaminski.

"Nonsense!" came from Tsugawa's position. "It's Oumuamua, not a drone!"

"You didn't detect anything?" the admiral made sure.

"Absolutely nothing, Admiral. We sent four dozen reconnaissance drones and a set of probes with biometric detectors. They detected nothing living, apart from colonies of microorganisms in the collectors of life support systems. This ship was controlled by some inferior AI, I don't see any other possibility."

Kravchenko covered the microphone membrane with his hand again.

"Yes?" he turned to Tsugawa, who was waving at him frantically from behind the monitors.

"Admiral, if what Kaminski says is true, we have a chance to get at the full-scale, autonomous Skunian AI. This will be an unprecedented event," said Tsugawa.

"So what? Maybe I should order Kaminski to take this scrap in tow?" there was disbelief in Kravchenko's voice.

"And why not? The trawler is adapted for this type of operation."

"Can you pull such a boulder?"

"If it can handle the Ukulele, it can handle towing a piece of Oumuamua."

"We will need the consent of the Alliance Council for such an operation."

"We must act quickly, Admiral, while the wreck still has some residual power. A complete loss of power will destabilize its gravity generator cores, making towing difficult or even impossible. The organic components of the main AI will most likely also be destroyed."

"True..." Kravchenko sighed. "Their computers are so damn delicate. What do you advise?"

"Apply to the Council post factum once we have secured and towed the wreck to an anchorage or to a repair shipyard. Preferably a union one. They love such collectibles."

Kravchenko thought for a few moments, ignoring the grunting of the trawler commander, who was clearly getting impatient.

"Okay... We'll take the risk," he decided. "Captain, you will take the wreck in tow. Please secure it so that the main logic circuits and memory matrices can be recovered."

The sound of a sharp intake of air came from the earpiece, followed by a strangled cough.

"Can you... Can you repeat that, Admiral?" Kaminski choked out after a while.

"Which part did you not understand?" Kravchenko asked menacingly.

This time he had to wait a little longer for an answer.

"Admiral, this will be very dangerous," the captain finally announced, his voice a bit hoarse. "We are unable to determine which of the firing positions are damaged and which have only gone into standby mode, and whether they are tracking us using passive sensors. The same applies to power sources. Residual emissions may well be the result of power being diverted to the inner hull, where the main missile silos are located. I would also like to remind you that the hangars, containing a multitude of tactical unmanned aerial vehicles, survived.

"I would like to remind you that you have two wings of heavy escort gunships at your disposal," the admiral replied coldly. "Captain, I'm well aware of the potential risk, but we may not have another opportunity to intercept their databases. Do you understand?"

"Do you mean their memory banks or the working, active on-board AI?"

"Both. That is why it is so important to properly secure the wreck."

"I'm starting the operation," announced Kaminski briefly.

"If you have any problems, please consult Commander Tsugawa. Over and out," said Kravchenko.

"How long will it take?" He looked impatiently at the screens, where the lines of graphs continued to writhe and endless columns of numbers and letters moved.

"Two percent left," Tsugawa replied. He also took the phone out of his ear. "Any moment... Oh, now!" he was happy to see the message about the completion of the conversion, which appeared on the main display in place of the previous visualization of the Epsilon Eridani system. A second later, the text disappeared and the screen went dark, then brightened to steel gray. Against this gray background, dozens of larger and smaller black dots appeared. Some of them were combined into clusters, creating spots and blots with irregular edges.

Kravchenko walked into the middle of the room and stood in front of the screen.

"Negative?" he asked.

"In some sense," Tsugawa reached for the keyboard and typed a command.

Colors appeared on the gray and black mosaic, some of the dark spots changed from black to green, others glowed crimson. The background brightened even more, fading to white.

"The quantum scanner is not based on optical information," he said, "but on the extrapolation of entanglement states. What we see on the screen now is not a real image of objects, but a visualization of their quantum reflections, extrapolated on the basis of fluctuations of space-time structures... Complicated technology, we do not yet fully understand the principle of its operation," he added quickly, sensing, rightly so, that Kravchenko he will soon sum up his words in his characteristic way. His gut feeling wasn't wrong.

"Please speak in human, Commander," the admiral growled. "What the hell is this mess?"

"Visualization of sector zero five and its immediate vicinity. Here, here and here," saying this, Tsugawa took the portable and outlined the three largest clusters of green dots. "Outer belt asteroids, the largest ones. From this area Oumuamua came," he highlighted one of the clusters, located exactly in the middle of the screen, then moved the indicator marker closer to the top edge of the display, where a whole swarm of dots glowed red.

"Rubble" he announced. "Distance from the outer edge of the asteroid belt, one parsec.

"These proportions are strange," said Kravchenko.

"This is just a visualization, a graphic prepared based on measurements. There are no larger objects between the asteroids and the rubble, so the system simply did not take this area into account."

"Wait a minute..." The Admiral took a few steps forward and tilted his head at the graphic. "What are the sizes of the smallest objects recorded by this telescope?"

"I'm already checking," Tsugawa entered a command again, then turned around and looked at one of the side monitors.

"Twenty meters, in any plane," he said after a while. "Due to limited computing power, smaller objects are omitted."

"In that case, Commander..." Kravchenko moved even closer to the screen. "Please tell me where the hell this unfortunate expedition has gone?"

He was answered by deafening silence.

20

Mobile Medical Corps
High orbit of the Sigil's moon

Two huge structures, one compact and massive, almost uniformly black, the other shiny like a jewel set with precious stones, light and openwork, rotated majestically in space, fastened together by thick claws of mooring lines and booms.

The whole thing was surrounded by swarms of small fragments, with occasional balls of blue-orange glow blooming as the Frontier's anti-collision systems sent precisely aimed salvos of short-range missiles towards the larger pieces of debris.

The cruiser's maneuvering engines, four large cylinders one on each of the ship's great fins, fired alternating jets of rocket fire, slowing the rotation of the drifting medical station and, kilometer by kilometer, moving the damaged installation back to its original, safe orbit. During these short breaks, when none of the engines were running, transport sleeves emerged from the cruiser's hatches - telescopic tubes made of reinforced steel, several meters in diameter, through which technical teams and service machines passed or rode on mobile platforms to the station deck.

It was on one of such platforms, crouched in a small space between the massive, humanoid bodies of the sentry machines, that Lieutenant Moss and Engineer Sniegowa boarded the station. Wearing heavy combat suits, festooned with weapons and ammunition containers, they differed little from the machines surrounding them, not only in terms of size, but also in appearance.

As they jumped off the platform and stood in the small loading bay, they were greeted with astonishment and barely suppressed mirth from the members of the landing force, who were dressed only in unsupported field suits and armed with light weapons, sitting on equipment crates waiting for them.

"Unit, attention!" Moss shouted at them.

The soldiers rose slowly, their equipment clanking.

"You and you," he nodded to the two closest ones. "Help the lady engineer with this stuff," he pointed to the oval plasma thrower fuel tanks dangling from the girl's waist and the heavy backpack on her shoulders. "Who did I appoint as team leader?" he asked.

The suits the stormtroopers were wearing most likely came from the central warehouse, as none of them had a charge symbol, a name tag, or even a formation sign.

"Me, Lieutenant," said one of the soldiers, a short, but strongly built middle-aged man. Beads of sweat beaded on his bald skull. He had his helmet under his arm.

Moss frowned, trying to remember his name.

"Sergeant Erwin Danielewicz?"

"It's me, Lieutenant," the soldier smiled cockily and then saluted his sweaty forehead in a completely irregular manner. "Fourth Planetary Infantry Squad," he added, and putting on his helmet, he quickly connected the end of a thin cable hanging over his shoulder. He pushed the other end of the wire into the socket in the handle of the flechette hanging on the belt of the thrower. "What orders?"

"Secure the control room and evacuation airlocks within the central hub. Here are the station plans." Moss handed him the mini-disk with the data.

Danielewicz took a small tablet out of his pocket and inserted the board into the slot. For several seconds, he carefully analyzed the diagram that appeared on the display.

"There are too few of us," he said, pointing to the eight commandos standing in a penalty line.

Moss's two assigned soldiers were still struggling with the clasps on Sniegova's suit.

"There are six main locks, eight auxiliary locks, plus a control room. There are three separate corridors leading to it. You have to cover each of them."

"Place sentry machines near the auxiliary ones. They have appropriate protocols installed," Moss jerked his thumb at the machines waiting to be unloaded.

A small self-propelled crane equipped with a single, massive manipulator with a magnetic suction cup at the end was approaching the platform.

"Can I ask you something, Lieutenant?" the sergeant asked in a low voice, looking over his shoulder at his subordinates.

"Yes?"

The soldier came closer.

"What's up?" he asked even more quietly, almost in a whisper.

Moss lifted the visor of his helmet.

"I don't understand?"

"Lieutenant, you know and I know that such preventive measures are taken only when there is a risk of the facility being taken over by the enemy," said Danielewicz, looking him straight in the eye.

"That's right," the officer nodded. Not a single muscle moved on his thin face. "This is the procedure."

"So Skunks have infiltrated the deck?!" the carefreeness disappeared from the sergeant's face, and, out of nowhere, a blaster appeared in his hand. The man took a quick look at the room crowded with equipment, then the rest of the unit.

"What are you staring at?" he growled at his subordinates, who, confused by this sudden reaction, looked at each other questioningly. "Get into position! Let three guard the entrances to the control room, one at a time to the main locks. Hellbeck, assign assignments!" he threw the tablet to one of the soldiers. "Move, move!" he urged those who helped Sniegova. The soldiers unfastened the last pods from the girl's suit and, placing them in a neat pile at her feet, joined the others.

A few dozen seconds later, all ten of them ran deeper into the station, their heavy boots pounding on the deck.

"What did you say to him?" the lady engineer asked as the bulkhead closed behind the last soldier. "He looked scared."

"Nothing special." Moss smiled slightly. With his hands folded on the massive breastplates of his suit, he watched as the crane arm removed the sentry machines from the transport platform and placed them carefully next to the maintenance tunnel. "I only hinted that an enemy landing force could have infiltrated the station."

"I wonder why you brought these stormtroopers here... and these machines," she watched the machine move about a meter above the floor. The two-hundred-kilogram robot swayed gently, held by the crane's powerful electromagnet. "This is just a rescue operation."

"Basically, yes," Moss agreed. "But don't forget that all installations and the ship of the Medical Corps are part of the systemic armed forces. This is a military facility, so we must operate according to military protocol. Besides..." he paused and looked significantly at the vault, from where they were observed by surveillance cameras.

Sniegova came closer.

"What's going on, Stan?" she asked in a whisper.

"Dressler," he replied, just as quietly. "I tried to contact him even before the Commander decided to start this operation. Unsuccessfully. They said that the Colonel was undergoing a tissue-cellular regeneration process. So I asked to speak to the station chief because I know him personally. I was also refused and when I insisted, my communication channel was blocked."

"What did you want from Dressler?"

"Find out what the hell is so important about this data that instead of asking the first technician to archive it in the central memory bank, he starts conspiracies."

"I was wondering about that too," Sniegova whispered. "They are encrypted at so many levels that their full decompilation using ordinary computers is virtually impossible. I have the impression that even Skunian's quantum machines would have a real problem with this."

"Exactly. Where did he get these files anyway?"

"From the Oumuamua wreck?"

"But how? His torpedo ship crashed, and he miraculously only crawled to the evacuation point. Absolutely no electronics were found on him, apart from the communicator in his suit and the very memory chips he gave you. You know what's most interesting about it? None of them were compatible with his ship's onboard system. Strange, right? I have no idea what this is all about."

"And you want to find out directly from the Colonel..."

"Exactly. Something strange is happening at this station. Do you have any idea they didn't want to talk to Lupos either?"

"Are you kidding?!" Sniegova's pitch-black eyes widened, her dark face darkened even more.

"Quieter!" he scolded her, putting a finger to his lips. "I heard him getting angry at the communications people for not being able to initiate a connection with the facility's management."

"Stan..." Sniegova moved away from him, then approached the transport elevator control panel and brought up the command tree with a flick of her finger. "What if this Ultima managed to infect the station's systems?" she said quietly.

"Impossible. If there was an alien AI in the system, it wouldn't even let us get close, let alone dock. This installation is equipped with quite specific weapons. The total firepower is not much inferior to the Frontier, but the battle stations are arranged quite chaotically, which makes it unable to conduct concentrated fire. And it's not as mobile as a cruiser. Moss glanced back at the still open gates, behind which the walls of the collar connecting the station with the Frontier's cargo bay gleamed silver.

Another platform, this time loaded with fire extinguishing equipment, was moving towards them on telescopic magnetic rails. Operators in bright red vacuum suits stood on its side platforms.

"The system is clean, that's for sure," he said with conviction.

"I hope you're right," Sniegova chose one of the commands and moved away from the cabin door. It opened with a hiss.

"Hey, you!" she waved her hand at the operator supervising the operation of the crane, standing nearby. The man, leaning over the machine's control screen, straightened up slowly and then unfastened the tablet in an armored case strapped to his belt. "Activate them!" Sniegova ran to the guard robots and expertly unfastened the buckles blocking the running gears.

When she removed the last of the blockades, scanner beams shot out from the machines' observation domes almost simultaneously, sweeping the immediate surroundings with a celadon glow. Soon, to the hum of servo motors and the squeal of composite tracks, the devices lined up for the elevator.

"Thank you!" the lady engineer called to the operator.

The man nodded in response, then started fiddling with the panel again. The platform with fire extinguishing equipment was just approaching the lock gate.

"We have to find Dressler," Moss said.

There was a muffled noise somewhere above their heads, and pieces of laminate and rust flakes fell. Suspended from a truss, two egg-shaped escape pods swayed asynchronously, then clacked against each other with their rounded beaks. The sound that accompanied it resembled the sound of a gong.

"Depressurization level three," came the dispassionate announcement from the local warning system over the loudspeakers. "Personnel from levels two and four are asked to go to the survival cabins and stay there until the failure is repaired."

They looked at each other anxiously.

"Did I hear that correctly? Level three?" Moss lowered his helmet's iris, turned on the HUD, and brought up a three-dimensional diagram of the central part of the station, resembling a perfectly round, multi-layered sphere, with each layer assigned a number and a short description.

"Yes, the third one," confirmed Sniegova. She also lowered the shutter.

"Well, well, well, recovery bays." A heavy sigh came from under the visor of Moss' helmet. "How the fuck could it be otherwise?!" The lieutenant raised the screen with a resigned gesture and turned on the suit's external communicator. He brought his right hand to his face.

"Sergeant Danielewicz, this is Moss. Over," he said into the microphone placed on his forearm.

"I'm here," crackled through the helmet's speakers.

"Are you in position? Is everyone okay?"

"No losses. The main locks are secured, as is the control room. We are waiting for sentry machines."

"Change of order. Do not secure auxiliary locks. When the machines check in, use them to cover the entrances to the third level. Set two machines to preview and send them to the damaged section. Understood? Please confirm."

"I confirm. Do not secure auxiliary locks, secure communication routes, conduct reconnaissance on level three. I have a question. Over."

"Yes?"

"What about the cabin crew? Don't let it pass?"

"There is a procedure for rescue operations in combat conditions. Only rescue teams and technical services can move freely on board after prior authorization. The procedure is valid until further notice."

"I understood. I have no more questions."

"That's all, Sarge. Please wait for further orders. Over and out." Moss lowered his hand and turned off the communicator.

"Seal the suit," he said to Sniegova. "We go there," he nodded towards the hangar ceiling.

The engineer tightened the helmet's shield, checked the wrists of her gloves, and finally activated the life support system. The armor plates creaked, their rounded edges rose slightly, pushed out from underneath by the internal coatings, swelling under the influence of the gas mixture pumped in under high pressure, the weapon holders attached to the thighs clicked, and a small reflector emerged from under the left shoulder pad, which also acted as a coupled the helmet of a target identifier for a heavy flechette thrower, the massive butt of which protruded from behind the girl's back.

"Follow me," commanded Moss. His suit swelled as well, and a spotlight mounted on a small rotating dome glowed with a sharp white light on his composite-plated arm.

Clinking with their equipment, they walked around the wide base of the elevator machine, moved out of the way of the extinguishing platform that was already coming on board, and then squeezed between two wide open containers from which a group of technicians were sweating unloading additional spore containers.

They reached the third level several minutes later, having previously overcome a maze of corridors and technical shafts, using location data sent to them on an ongoing basis by one of the guard machines set by Sergeant Danielewicz in the area affected by the failure.

"What now?" asked Sniegova as they stood in front of the heavy bulkhead separating the depressurized deck from the rest of the station. Through a small viewfinder, one could see the remains of broken equipment lying on the other side, stripped of the lining, irregularly flashing lamps, and walls covered with a thin layer of frost.

"We're opening," Moss walked up to the control panel and with his fist broke the glass behind which was a small emergency opening lever. Before he could pull it, Sniegova grabbed his hand.

"Are you crazy? Do you want to depressurize another deck?"

"What deck? We are at a dead end. The technical shaft is the only connection here. You personally battened down the hatch. Better hold on to something." He freed himself from her grip and grabbed the lever again.

"Come on!" he urged.

Seeing that the girl was looking around in a vain attempt to find something to hold on to, he decisively wrapped his free arm around her waist and pressed her against him. Confused, her first instinct was to try to free herself, but then she gave up and after a while she grabbed him with both hands.

"Attention!" he warned once again, then pulled the lever.

The hurricane of atmospheric mixture escaping from the room was so strong that for a few moments they both hung in the air, and if it weren't for Moss holding on to the lever, they would have been thrown into the doll's void. And even electromagnets in their soles wouldn't help them.

When everything died down, they picked themselves up from the floor and carefully, dodging the broken electrical wires hanging from the ceiling, which were sending showers of sparks from time to time, they moved down the corridor into the section. The hospital rooms we passed along the way were empty and mostly stripped of furniture and equipment, apart from a few beds screwed to the ground, or rather only frames without mattresses, and heavy steel wardrobes and cabinets, also permanently attached to the floor and walls.

Much to their surprise, there was no major damage visible either in the corridor or in any of the rooms. Just some rubbish on the floor, delaminated wallcovering here and there, damaged cables and broken lamp sockets with sharp edges. No holes in the plating, no holes left by explosions, no traces of fire or burnt holes with charred edges typical of plasma weapon bullets.

"Stan..." Sniegova, who had moved forward, stopped suddenly and then slowly retreated towards Moss.

"What is it about?" he asked, reaching for his gun. The sight on his shoulder moved up and down in sync with the blaster's barrel.

"There are some people around the corner," she replied.

"Finally, someone from staff," he said, putting the blaster back in its holster. "This will save us a lot of trouble."

"They don't look like medical personnel," her voice, although slightly distorted by the poor quality of the helmet's loudspeakers, sounded concerned. "They are in heavy suits and I think they have weapons," she warned.

"Soldiers?" Moss was surprised. "Danielewicz was only supposed to send robots here..."

"Stan!" snapped the engineer. "These are not our soldiers! Our guys didn't have combat suits."

Moss considered for a moment whether to ask Danielewicz for support, but immediately abandoned the idea. Just moving through relatively tight corridors, where in many places there were pointed burrs of laminate sticking out of the walls, would involve a huge risk, let alone during a fight.

"Wait here," he said. "In case of problems, retreat to the hatch and inform Danielewicz of your location. Call code two five zero six."

With his hand on the handle of his putter, he ran to the fork and peered carefully around the corner.

Sniegova was right. Down the corridor, three figures in steel-blue, angular, heavy combat suits were moving. He recognized the model immediately. Identical ones were in the equipment of the company that protected the largest civilian research facilities of the Autonomy.

"What the hell are they doing here?" he muttered to himself, simultaneously activating the suit's vision system. The helmet's iris lost its transparency, and after a while a three-dimensional, wide-angle, digitally cleaned image appeared on it, transmitted directly from cameras placed in various places of the suit.

"Who?" Sniegova's question came from the loudspeakers.

"These people are security guards from Sigil," he replied. He returned to the girl. "A bad pennies, even a very bad. I have no idea who allowed them to come on board."

"I think the Corps headquarters hired them..."

"Impossible," he shook his head. The image on the display became blurry, but soon came back into focus. "The army does not use the services of paramilitary organizations. There's something very, very wrong here, Katya. Return to the cruiser and give the commander this disk." He pressed a button on a small panel on his wrist. A small, shiny disc of graphene slid out of a gap in the armor's breastplate. "Data from the suit recorder," he explained. "Logs, transmissions from guard machines, generally everything that the sensors managed to capture since we boarded. Including the image of these nice guys."

"And you?" she asked, taking the disk from him and putting it in one of the pouches on her forearm.

"I'll try to find out what's going on here," he replied. "And maybe I'll find Dressler, but honestly, there's a slim chance he's still on board." He waved his hand towards the left branch of the corridor. "Almost all modules were detached from that side. Hence the dehermetization. It is possible that the Colonel was staying in one of them. Will you lend me your cannon?" He asked.

He stepped closer and stroked the butt of the heavy blaster that stuck out over the girl's shoulder with his armored hand.

"Here you go." She slid the weapon from its holders in a fluid movement. Then she unplugged the control cable from the socket on her helmet and wrapped it around the barrel, handing the blaster to Moss. "It's not calibrated yet. Want a spare magazine?"

"Yes," he replied briefly, busy untangling the cable.

She unfastened the flechette dispenser from her belt. Moss took it from her and immediately pushed it into the ammunition bay. Heavy blasters differed from their smaller counterparts not only in the caliber of the darts they fired, but also in the fact that they could be loaded with more bullets.

He connected the cable to his helmet and activated the targeting systems. Several diodes on the blaster lit up, and information about the amount of ammunition appeared on the tiny display. The reflector on the arm moved slightly, and a bright red dot appeared on the wall behind Sniegova's back.

"All right." Moss slung the gun over his shoulder. "Go now."

He moved his head towards the vestibule, lit with the dim glow of emergency lamps.

Sniegova walked up to him and stroked his hand with her armored hand.

"Take care of yourself, Stan," she said softly, then turned on her heel and walked down the corridor towards the exit.

21

Repair ship "Tip"
The Epsilon Eridani planetary system

"Second and fourth engines, after tensioning the ropes, reverse thrust in an alternating sequence. Maximum power limit five percent," ordered the commander of the technical support ship, Captain Janus Kaminski, then stood up and ran to the navigation station. "Just be careful, because those damn hooks will release again..." he said to the propulsion system operator with tension in his voice.

"Don't worry, Captain, it won't get away this time," the operator replied reassuringly. His hands, covered with sensory sensors, rested in the recesses of the control panel, moving slightly, his face obscured by large vision goggles linked to the ship's external camera system and cameras of observation probes that circled over the area where huge anchors fired from the trawler had stuck to the Oumuamua wreckage's plating.

Large spikes bristling with sharp protrusions, with shaped charges placed on their tips, dragged steel ropes as thick as a man's forearm. Only after the second volley did they break through the several dozen meters thick rock cover and reach the internal metal coatings, where they could get really stuck.

"How much hit" Kaminski moved closer to take a closer look at the screen on which the image from the probes was displayed.

"Twelve out of fifteen fired. Two of them missed, and in one the penetrating warhead did not fire," explained the operator.

"Nice result," the captain moved even closer to the console.

"Right? And this is already in the second attempt. This is probably our best result since helping the Autonomy take that old Skunk nest out of orbit. Yet it had much thinner external armor," there was satisfaction in the man's voice. "Practice makes perfect."

"It remains to be seen."

"The anchors are firmly seated, please look at the indicators," the operator moved his hands, his left thumb brushing a small button at the edge of the sensory recess.

Next to each of the craters visible on the screen, numbers and charts appeared showing the method of anchoring the tow ropes and the degree of their load in conditions of reduced gravity. All readings were within safe limits.

"Therefore, I ask you to be extremely careful during the braking sequence," emphasized Kaminski. "What about longitudinal rotation?"

"Slowed down. The gunships did a good job," the operator zoomed in on the long edge of Oumuamua, over which clouds of powdered rock still loomed, the remnants of the concentrated fire from the escort ships' kinetic cannons. Thousands of bullets fired in one salvo, with a series of powerful impacts, gave energy to the wreck, thus stopping its rotation around its axis. Where they had hit, there was now a glowing orange expanse of rapidly cooling lava, dotted here and there with the twisted stumps of infrastructure exposed by the explosions, previously hidden under a thick layer of rock.

"That's a fact," agreed Kaminski.

A little calmer, he returned to his seat to observe the procedure of breaking the wreck that was just starting.

"Engine number two, ignition sequence in ten seconds," the operator announced a moment later.

Because the front visor flaps were retracted, Kaminski had a perfect view of the massive, rounded bow of the trawler and the two maneuvering engine housings located on its right side. Their nozzles were directed perpendicularly to the ship's hull, aiming their large outlets straight at the horribly damaged front part of the wreck of the Skunian giant, located four hundred meters away.

"Ignition," announced the operator. Before his voice could echo, the nozzle of one of the engines spewed out a powerful jet of plasma. A moment later, the second one's nozzle did the same.

The tow ropes tightened and trembled, a wave of vibrations went through all decks of the tow ship, accompanied by the characteristic sound of the shock absorbers of the inertia absorption systems.

"Speed decrease by three to eight percent," reported the drive operator. "One mooring line broken, two damaged."

"Can they be repaired?" Kaminski straightened up in his chair, trying to see one of the lines in the viewfinder.

"The diagnostic system reports that the fasteners are loose. The mooring lines themselves were strong. Repair crews are already on their way. I suggest interrupting the operation until the fault is removed, " the operator explained in a worried voice. "Nine mooring lines won't handle this rock, Captain."

"Pause the sequence," Kaminski decided without hesitation.

"Sequence paused."

"How long will the repair take?"

"It's hard to say... At least two hours. Longer if it turns out that you need to replace the hitch pins and attach the mooring lines to the spare sockets."

The captain sighed heavily. Each additional hour of delay resulted in further depletion of the already meager resources of fuel, breathing mixture, air filters and even food. There was a justified risk that after the Oumuamua wreck was towed to the anchorage, they would not only manage to join the group, but would even be forced to undergo stasis until supplies were delivered to them from one of the shipyards.

"I told you to be careful," he muttered under his breath, loud enough for the operator to hear.

The man did not react to the insult. He continued to fiddle with the sensor panel, aligning the ship with Oumuamua using small correction thrusters mounted at regular intervals around the egg-shaped hull.

"Captain, this broken mooring line can also be repaired," he said after a while. "We just need to send technical teams there."

"To the wreck?"

"Also. The connection with the anchor broke free, the rope itself is intact. You just have to grab it, pull it up and attach it again."

"I'll take care of it," Kaminski promised. He turned on the intercom. "This is the captain speaking. The officer on duty and the head of the technical department are to report immediately to the small control room. The officer on duty and the head of the technical department should immediately report to the small control room," he repeated, and then turned off the device.

While waiting for his subordinates, he brought up the warehouse records and the latest reports on the trawler's basic systems to the console desktop.

The technical condition of the almost hundred-year-old ship, once the largest flying unit in the entire system, still remembering the times of the conquest of the outer asteroid belt by mining campaigns, later united under the banner of the Sigil Autonomy, was deteriorating with each subsequent year of operation, even despite major renovations, as a result of the outer skin, nozzles and deflectors of the main drive were replaced, additional braking engines were installed and significant modifications were made inside the hull. As a result, the Tip gained an additional repair hall, a hangar for service drones and a small, but very practical control room, intended exclusively for command and navigation of the ship.

So far, all of the trawler's core systems have been working flawlessly. Among the multitude of green icons, Kaminski saw only two with red exclamation alerts. Both warnings concerned a failure of the mooring lines.

"I report on orders!" a pleasant, low contralto sounded behind him. Staring at the screen, he didn't even notice when Lieutenant Joana Townsend, his direct deputy, entered the control room.

"Stand easy," he said with a smile, and then pointed to three small metal seats, attached directly to the wall, covered with a layer of shock-absorbing foam. "Please sit down."

"Thank you," she nodded and perched on the edge of the chair. Sitting straight, with her hands on her knees, she waited patiently while he slowly closed or minimized the messages and tables displayed on the screen. From time to time, she glanced towards the exit through closed eyes.

When the chief engineer's footsteps sounded in the narrow corridor, Townsend's hands involuntarily clenched into fists and her amaranth lipstick pressed her lips into a thin line.

Kaminski smiled inwardly.

The mutual dislike of these two was well known to him, but as long as the result of this animosity was constant rivalry and the resulting screwing up of results by both sides of the dispute, he had no intention of taking any steps to alleviate or extinguish the conflict.

"My regards!" there was a loud welcome. The head of the technical department, engineer Laszlo Feher, entered the control room with his typical enthusiasm.

Short and stocky, with a dirty face and disheveled, curly hair, dressed in aquamarine-yellow, heavily soiled overalls, he looked as if he had just crawled out of a maintenance sewer.

"Captain," he nodded to Kaminski. "Lieutenant," he smiled mockingly at Townsend's sour face.

He pushed past the drive operator, giving him a friendly pat on the shoulder, and then, without waiting for the commander's invitation, he unfolded another seat and sat down on it with a sigh of relief.

Townsend looked distastefully at his soiled overalls and demonstratively brushed some dust from the sleeve of her uniform.

The smirk on the engineer's face widened even further.

"Sorry for this sloppy outfit, but we have a lot of work in the reloading hangar and repair workshops. Those gunships the Admiral assigned to us haven't been serviced for several months. Someone must have forgotten to check the MOT books when they were checked in," he said, glancing at Townsend.

The lieutenant looked as if she had just chewed a lemon slice. Yet she still remained silent.

"Never mind," Kaminski waved his hand dismissively. "As you probably already know, there was a problem with the tow lines," he said and jerked his chin towards the window.

They nodded.

"My people are already there," Feher announced. "Unfortunately, they can't start work until the welding robot is delivered to them, and the equipment reserve warehouse refuses to give us access to the machine," he added grimly, this time looking openly at Townsend.

"The machines have been reassigned to other tasks," the lieutenant replied stiffly. Her fists were white at the knuckles.

"Well, you see, Captain." The engineer spread his hands helplessly.

"You didn't give the equipment to the repair teams?" Kaminski looked at the woman strangely.

"In order to refuse, I would have to have some spare ones on hand. Unfortunately, all three welding machines are currently working in the main reactor compartment, where additional plates are being installed to strengthen the deflector shields. As planned..."

"Damn it!" Kaminski banged his hand on the arm of the chair. "Screw the schedule! We are carrying out an operation to tow away the wreck and this is our priority at the moment! Not renovations, not maintenance, not any damn deflector modifications! There will still be time for this crap!"

"Am I to understand that the work schedule has just been canceled?" Townsend asked calmly.

"Yes!" the captain growled. "No!" he reflected immediately. "Not canceled. Suspended. Until the towing operation is completed," he added in a slightly calmer tone. "Please provide Feher's technical teams with the necessary equipment."

"Now?"

"Yes. Now, in this moment. Understood?"

"Yes, sir." The lieutenant took out a roll of handheld terminal, unrolled it on her thigh and smoothed it with her hand. "I'm already sending instructions."

"Thank you, Lieutenant. My people will be very happy." Feher smiled radiantly at her. He also unfolded the terminal on his lap.

Kaminski took a deep breath once, then twice. He rubbed the back of his neck with his hand.

"Now that we have that cleared up, let's get down to business," he said. "Diagnostics showed that it is possible to repair this broken line. Since the escort ships are temporarily grounded, you will have to organize at least two transports, one for the landing force, the other for the technical team, and preferably they should have an autonomous operational module. This line," he pointed to the viewfinder, "swings like a pendulum, and there is no time to fiddle with first pulling it in again and then unwinding it again. It needs to be grabbed and connected to the anchor on the Oumuamua. This will be your task, Feher. You will form a landing group that will secure the area around the anchor. Scanners detected electrical activity and weak radio transmissions in the area. Several artillery turrets and escape shafts are located near the impact crater. Therefore, it cannot be ruled out that these signals are some form of communication between Oumuamua's surface defense systems and its central AI."

"Is there a risk of attack?" Townsend's hands stilled over the terminal.

"Yes. Minimal, but it is. This is the aft part of the Oumuamua, i.e., practically the entire energy base, with the strongest defense."

"Are you telling me, Captain, that we are maneuvering an unarmed vessel right next to a wreck where defense systems are still operational?" The officer's eyes widened; the corner of her mouth twitched slightly in a nervous tic.

"You could say so," Kaminski nodded.

"No one informed me about this," she replied, looking at him reproachfully.

"You didn't know?" Feher was insincerely surprised.

She ignored the question.

"So, you already know," Kaminski shrugged. "Please form a unit and send it to the indicated area as quickly as possible. I authorize the use of offensive drones and generally all available weapons, except tactical nuclear weapons. In case of combat contact, eliminate targets at your discretion. You may march away."

Townsed sat still for a few moments, staring at some undefined point behind the commander, then without a word she stood up, rolled up the terminal, and silently left the control room.

As the bulkhead closed behind her, Kaminski took another deep breath and immediately glared at Feher, who was literally shaking, trying to hold back a giggle.

"No one informed me," he muttered, shaking his head in disbelief. "The ship has been on high alert for ten hours, the results of scanning that damn wreck are displayed on all information screens, offensive drones are flying outside the window, which she personally authorized and poor thing, she still doesn't know that Oumuamua is still active. Mother Earth, give me strength..." he sighed heavily.

"It may be the effect of conditioning," suggested the engineer.

"Nonsense!" Kaminski huffed. "When you need to apply for a bonus, there is no problem with the flow of information, initialing documents or deciding on allocation amounts. But when it comes to showing initiative on the battlefield, oh, that's when the problems begin."

Feher, who had finally managed to control his mirth, rose from his seat and walked to the viewfinder.

"This mooring line will be hard to catch," he said, pointing to the left corner of the window.

Against the background of the dark mass of Oumumua, several shiny dots moved in a circular motion.

"It broke off above the joint and split over what I see as a large section. We will have to grab each of the strands separately."

"Maybe we should just wrap it up?" suggested the drive operator.

"What do you think about it, engineer?" Kaminski asked.

"I advise against it," replied Feher. "We're out of guidance charges, and the jet harpoons won't be able to handle it. It's too long and too heavy, even in zero gravity. If it is wound back onto the spool, we will not unwind it otherwise than with the help of a carrier or a searcher, and this will take a lot of time."

"Okay, then grab that mean trick and hook it back up." Kaminski decided.

"I'm giving instructions now," Feher's fingers flew across the terminal keyboard.

"There's one more thing," the captain said in a low voice.

"Yes?" Feher stopped entering orders for the technical teams for a moment and looked up at the commander.

"It's about the transmission from Oumuamua."

"That big file?" the engineer made sure.

"Correct. The communications section reported that since we stopped the wreck's rotation, the signal has been transmitted continuously on all bands and with doubled power."

"What?" there was surprise in Feher's voice. "Even more power?"

"Over three hundred gigawatts. Disturbing, isn't it?"

"You're joking."

"Here is the latest sensor data," Kaminski brought to the screen a report recently received from the communications department. "Three hundred and twenty-five gigawatts, uniform and continuous signal, continuously for four hours. We're lucky that the emitter of this beam is somewhere on the other side of the wreck, because it would fry everything here in a few minutes," he enlarged the image so that the engineer could read the information displayed.

Despite this, Feher got up, put the terminal on the seat and walked closer to the monitor.

"That's what worries me. The scanning beams reached one hundred and fifty meters deep, or basically all the way to the inner core, detecting virtually no emission sources. The central core is silent, only some small devices are working, most likely emergency life support systems. Somewhere inside, a powerful power source is working at its best, and we are unable to locate it."

"It may have to do with the power supply for the gravity generators," the drive operator interjected. "There is still attraction on the wreck with quite specific values, which means that there are also stabilizers of the neutron matter interaction vectors, which in turn is associated with a huge energy surplus. In my opinion, they redirect excess energy to this transmitter..."

"Which in turn would explain the lack of emissions from other sources," Feher interrupted him.

"No different," agreed the operator.

"Well, we're effed in the a," Kaminski sighed heavily. "You couldn't tell me right away?" he asked with reproach in his voice. "I wasted over two hours trying to figure out where this energy was coming from."

"Nobody asked me about that," the operator muttered in response.

"On the other hand, we no longer have to worry that they will undo something after we tow them to the scrapyard. However, it would be useful to silence this transmitter. Who knows what they're broadcasting. Maybe they're calling for reinforcements?"

"We cannot cut off its power supply," said Feher. "If we manage to turn off or destroy the gravity generators, the neutron cores will completely destroy the interior, or worse, they will start pulling the wreck in some completely random direction, and we will have to say goodbye to the lines, mooring hatch equipment, and probably a large fragment of the plating."

"What do you propose then?" asked Kaminski.

"Destroy this transmitter. Bomb or shoot with rockets.

"I'd rather avoid it. It is possible that there are memory chips nearby, and the goal of our mission is primarily to obtain and secure data. The wreck itself is unimportant."

"Just destroy the transmitting modules."

"You mean these skewers?" Kaminski minimized the table with the scanning results and then displayed on the screen a three-dimensional model of the wreck, based on telemetry data transmitted from the probes. He enlarged the image and pointed with his finger at two prominences of rock on the left side of Oumuamua, the tops of which were topped with long, thin spiers.

"These are antenna tips," Feher said expertly. "See those arched bars at the base? These, in turn, are radiation neutralizers. The signal emitted by the antennas is so strong that it causes energy interference in the structure itself. These heat sinks convert the excess into thermal energy and discharge the excess directly into the vacuum. Cheap, effective and efficient. Trade unions have been using this patent in their habitats for many years. If we destroy the heat sinks, the whole thing will immediately start overheating and either turn off or melt."

Kaminski rubbed his forehead thoughtfully. The orders he received from Kravchenko were clear: locate the source of the transmission, intercept and record the data transmitted by the Skunians, and then tow the wreck to the nearest anchorage. Unfortunately, following the file with official orders, Commander Tsugawa's recommendations with enforceable clauses were also received on his terminal, including a request to treat the infrastructure that survived the wreck as gently as possible. Fire from kinetic guns, aimed at eliminating the horizontal rotation of the wreck, completely destroyed the left side, and further damage was caused by the penetration heads of the anchors. The outer armor of the Oumuamua fragment, which had miraculously survived the collision with the habitat, was cracked, riddled with craters and charred by atomic heat, and was becoming more and more similar to a melted, shapeless lump of slag.

"Are you sure there's no other way?" he asked after a while. "Maybe we could somehow cut off the power?"

"It doesn't work that way, Captain," replied Feher. "The Skunians do not use classic wires, cables or anything like that to transmit energy, they only use alloys of metals and superconducting minerals from which the plating is made, so you can't go there, locate the appropriate power lines and cut them. To cut off this part, we would have to either close the entire envelope around the transmitter or deactivate the gravity generators."

"Yes..." sighed Kaminski. "We're back to starting point. How strong are these structures?"

"Radiation neutralizers? If they are still the same technology, they are nothing more than sheets of resistance steel, additionally coated with a layer of conductive composite. A few conventional missiles should do the trick. There won't be much damage," Feher reassured him. "As I have already said, with a damaged heat dissipation system, the antennas, and ultimately the transmitter, will immediately overheat."

"All right, you convinced me," said the captain. "Once you have repaired the mooring lines, please inform Lieutenant Townsend of our findings and arrange with her the details of the operation to disable the transmitter."

At the sound of the first officer's name, the chief engineer's face fell.

"Military actions are not my thing!" he protested.

"No?" Kaminski looked at him through narrowed eyes. "Well, it is from now on. You may leave," he finished, then turned back to the displays.

22

Cruiser "Pandemonium"
The Epsilon Eridani planetary system

In the conference room, a narrow room set aside from a branch of the corridor leading to the launch deck of the patrol ships, fifteen operators sat on plastic folding chairs, arranged one behind the other in pairs like seats in a freight train car: eight women and seven men. They were all dressed in vacuum suits, unsealed and with the welts loose. In their laps, they held the transparent pans of their helmets. Behind the backs of the assembled men, visible from under the half-raised security bulkhead, the slender silhouettes of long-range patrol craft glittered.

In front of them, like a teacher in a classroom full of students, strolled Admiral Sergei Kravchenko. He was the only one wearing only a two-piece standard work uniform, devoid of any distinction. Behind the admiral's back, a translucent map of the Epsilon Eridani system and its immediate vicinity hung on a small rack.

"Everyone present?" he turned to Tsugawa, who was seated in the front row. The commander rose, turned to those seated behind him and quickly counted them.

"Everyone's here," he announced. "First Long-Range Reconnaissance Squadron complete," he reported, then sat back down.

"Excellent. We are starting the briefing." Kravchenko walked over to the map and smoothed the somewhat crumpled film. "As you have probably already been informed, a mining expedition has gone missing in sector seven."

He pointed with his finger to the blue marked area in the upper corner of the map.

"Yes, this is the same convoy we were originally supposed to protect," he explained grimly, seeing the surprise painted on the operators' faces.

A murmur ran through the auditorium. He silenced it with a hand gesture.

"Thirty-seven bulk carriers, seventeen mobile mining installations, five supply trawlers and a light support cruiser," he calculated, glancing at the handheld terminal whose portable display he had strapped to his wrist. "A total of sixty large vessels with three thousand men on board."

"How can you be sure they are missing?" Asked a black-skinned, thin man. Horizontal lines of subcutaneous psychosensory communication implants shone green on his smoothly shaven skull, deceptively resembling a phosphorescent tattoo.

"Major Curvey, we scanned this and neighboring sectors with a quantum telescope," replied Kravchenko. "Aside from single objects of natural origin, the telescope did not detect any major fragments of matter."

"This does not yet determine anything, Admiral. A quantum scan is just an extrapolation conducted based on the initial state of a given system. A single measurement cannot be the basis for such far-reaching conclusions," the operator said, then looked at the others, as if seeking support for his words.

The patrol ship operators sitting closest to him nodded their heads approvingly.

"I realize this, Major," said Kravchenko. "That is why I have ordered my men to analyze in detail the data from listening stations located on the outskirts of the system. Commander, would you be kind enough to summarize the report of the communications section?" He once again nodded at Tsugawa.

The deputy got up from his chair and walked to the center of the room. Like the admiral, he had a terminal screen attached to his wrist.

"We have passed through the system a total of seven thousand two hundred and fifty-four directional transmissions originating from Sectors Six, Seven and Eight, emitted over the past three months by relay stations and radio buoys. All of them were recorded by the central data bank on AEgir, then dumped into reserve memory storage and archived," he said, staring at the tiny display.

"How much?!" asked someone in the last row in disbelief.

"Seven thousand two hundred and fifty," Tsugawa repeated patiently. He raised his hand with the display a little closer to his face. "The six thousand five hundred and eighty transmissions were, of course, the standard reports on the energy conditions associated with the current activity of the Epsilon Eridani, as well as ongoing updates on the astrolocation data of the celestial bodies drifting in the area. Analysis of these data did not reveal anomalies or any deviations from the norm, other than those predicted by the usual extrapolations," he read from the screen. "Another three hundred and fifty consisted of cyclic backup snapshots and location pulses generated by the buoys. These, too, contained nothing suspicious. Forty-nine transmissions came from exploration probes launched two years ago toward the rubble. They contained mostly positional data and several hundred photographs of the asteroids around which they orbit. ," he fell silent for a moment and swept his gaze around his listeners. They all stared at him with tension. "Only one sole transmission bore the signature assigned to the units that were part of the convoy," he concluded grimly, while turning off the screen.

"Thank you, Commander," Kravchenko, who had listened to the report with his hands in his pockets, standing leaning with his back against the wall, approached the map again. "Any questions?"

The operator, who was seated in the last row, raised his hand in the air.

"Yes?" The admiral nodded at him acquiescently.

"So, we are to understand that in three months the listening stations have received only one full transmission from the convoy?"

"That's right, captain," Kravchenko confirmed.

"Isn't this by any chance the same transmission after which we were directed to sector six?"

"Exactly the same one."

"So, since then, none of the vessels that are part of the expedition have contacted their parent organization, shipowner, or whoever else these ships belong to?"

"Commander?" Kravchenko looked questioningly at Tsugawa, who was just settling back in his chair.

"No," Tsugawa replied briefly.

A tense silence fell in the room.

Major Curvey was the first to break it.

"There is a prototype quantum telescope mounted on my ship," he said. "I propose to scan both sectors again, and then compare the results with those we already have. Those ships must be there. Or at least their wrecks. It's impossible just like that," he snapped his fingers, "to disintegrate such large vessels. These are millions of tons of metal and composite."

"Are you sure it can't be done?" asked Kravchenko, smiling quizzically.

"Of course, I am," shrugged the operator. "There is no such physical possibility, well, except perhaps for laborious demolition, to shred a bulk carrier measuring two kilometers and weighing seven hundred thousand tons, with cargo holds full of equipment and prefabricated components in such a way that not even small fragments remain. I won't mention the cores of the gravity generators. Without the fields stabilizing them, they would radiate at all ranges like small suns."

"And if I tell you that there is such a way?" having said this, Kravchenko flung his eyes around his small audience. Understanding was just beginning to paint itself on the faces of some of the operators, while others simply sat, listening to the conversation with impassive faces.

"I'm all ears," said the admiral. Curvey corrected himself in his chair, raised his helmet's tank top to his face, chuckled at it, and then wiped the fogged area with the sleeve of his suit. "And if you don't mind, I'd like to ask something else," he added, examining the helmet under the light.

Satisfied with the result, he placed it back on his lap.

"If the convoy is lost, destroyed, hijacked, or whatever, then why should my squadron actually fly there? From here we have three astronomical units to the sector boundary, the sector itself stretches for another two, the next one for three, while to the rubble is as many as twelve, counting from the edge of the system. The one-way trip will take us at least two months, plunged into stasis, we won't be able to observe anything on the way, and on the spot too, as the search area is gigantic!" he pointed to a map rack.

"The Fold," this one word spoken by Kravchenko caused the major to freeze in stillness, with his hand stretched out in front of him and with his mouth half-open.

"No... I don't understand..." he mouthed after a moment.

"The Fold," repeated the admiral calmly. "Everything points to the fact that in sector six the Skunians have activated a new anomaly. More or less in this area."

325

He took out a black marker from the pocket of his uniform and approached the map with it.

"Here we have our systemic fold..." he outlined with a marker a small spot located about halfway between the system's central star and the planet AEgir. "Here, according to the latest reports, the enemy has opened another..." he put a marker over the planet's moon. "They sent us out into the solar system this way."

He drew another marker, just beyond the outer belt of the asteroids, then with a quick smudge he connected the drawn markers with a line.

"Oh shit..." sighed Curvey.

"Is this some kind of tunnel?" Asked a young woman sitting next to him with bright green hair cut in a clawed style. On the sleeves of her suit the logo of the Sigil Autonomy shone in gold.

"This is the working hypothesis," replied Kravchenko. With an energetic stroke of the marker, he extended the line all the way to the edge of the map.

"Very working," interjected Tsugawa. "More fitting here would be the term chain, although it too would not quite correctly describe what we are witnessing, because the anomalies do not lead one to another. The vectors of their relocation are quite different. Essentially, they are multidimensional in nature."

"Where do they lead?" asked the woman.

"We don't know, Lieutenant." Tsugawa turned toward her and lightly shrugged. "The only thing that can be certain about these phenomena is that they occurred in such a location and not another, and that in addition to leading somewhere, they also lead from somewhere."

Another of the operators raised his hand up, followed by another. And another.

"Enough!" stopped them Kravchenko, while tapping the back of the marker on the map frame. "The report of the scientific division will be included in the latest issue of the shipboard bulletin," he announced, stepping to the center. "To answer your question Major, that's right, the search area is extensive, but not as extensive as it may seem at first glance. The last full transmission came from this area." he turned to the map and pointed to a point at the junction of sectors five and six. "That's where you will begin your search from, flying exactly along the trajectory the convoy was supposed to follow. Major Curvey, what is the range of the shipboard lidars mounted on the patrol ships?"

"Full-range eight light seconds, directional about one light minute."

Curvey closed his eyes and behind a furrowed brow recalculated the distances in his memory.

"That should be enough," he stated after a moment. "You will scan an area with a radius of five million kilometers using full-range beams. This applies to both outer sectors. If you don't find anything, you'll fly further to the rubble. You will also search them. Major, please be calm!" With a hand gesture he stopped Curvey, who had just sprung from his chair to protest. "I realize that searching the rubble may involve some difficulties, nevertheless I'm sure you will be able to scan this area as well."

"With all due respect, Admiral, but no, you will not succeed," the green-haired lieutenant announced firmly. "The whole area is one big radioactive cauldron that even the Skunians are afraid to go near. On top of that, it's monstrously littered. Lidar beams will penetrate a few thousand kilometers at most, unless we fly into the depths. And we can't fly in, because we'll be fried alive there. Patrol ships have too fragile shields! They are not exploration units, but reconnaissance!"

"Calm down, Lieutenant. No one has any intention of sending you or the others to their deaths," said Kravchenko. "You will send mining probes there. On the Hercules they had a whole warehouse of these. They are shielded and have autonomous AI. Their reprogramming is currently underway." he pointed with a marker to the bulkhead behind which the patrol ships were standing. "Any more questions? If not, we're ending the briefing. Commander Tsugawa will acquaint you with the details of the search operation, and to him please report any comments, objections... or protests." he glanced meaningfully at the green-haired girl.

The girl fled with her eyes somewhere to the side.

"Official orders will be transmitted to individual ships via the electronic command system, you will become familiar with them after takeoff. Thank you for your attention. Commander, please join me," he nodded at Tsugawa, then, without waiting for the latter to collect the documents spread out at his feet, he turned and with a jaunty step approached the patrol ships' launch deck entrance.

"What's up, Admiral?" asked Tsugawa when they found themselves in a brightly lit hangar, where two rows of lightweight, but equipped with powerful propulsion systems long-range patrol ships, transferred to the Pandemonium from the hangars of the cruiser Hercules stood on landing platforms.

The landing hatches of the machines were popped open, plumes of condensed gas from the cooling systems were rising from between the plates covering the propulsion module chambers. The long and slender thirty-meter hulls, topped with octagonal outlets of pulse jets, shone silvery, covered with a fresh layer of anti-radiation coating applied by the automatics.

"I received a report from the Tip," Kravchenko replied.

He approached the nearest platform, climbed onto it, and then, with his head poked upwards, stood in front of the obtuse, flattened bow of the patrol ship. "They managed to stop the rotation of the wreck and took it in tow. They are currently pulling it away towards one of the Orbital Union's repair facilities."

"This is definitely good news," stated the commander. "What about the signal? Have they secured that transmitter?" He asked, fastening with the clasp of a foil briefcase in which he had printouts stuffed.

"Yes and no," sighed Kravchenko. "According to the report, this contraption had some kind of independent and at the same time inoperable power source, so in order to interrupt the transmission they decided to damage it..." he fell silent and sighed once again.

He walked around the bow and stopped at the massive, three-fingered foot of the forward hull support. Another portion of gas escaped from the plating above his head with a hiss. He covered his mouth with his hand and jumped off the platform.

Tsugawa continued to try to press the reluctant latches.

"They fired rockets at the radiators, hoping that the installation would overheat and shut down on its own," said Kravchenko. "Unfortunately, they miscalculated a bit."

Tsugawa's hands became immobile.

"Didn't it turn off?" he asked anxiously.

"Not right away. As a result, there was an explosion, a big explosion. The shockwave went through the technical shafts deep into the armor and probably further demolished Oumuamua's inner hull. Ours has several wounded, and some of the probes and automatics near the crash area were also destroyed. Nevertheless, transmission has been interrupted."

"Have they located the memory chips?" Annoyed, Tsugawa finally gave himself a break with the clasps of the briefcase and slipped the unclosed one under his arm.

"Not yet, but they claim it's only a matter of time. Besides, it's not the most pressing matter at the moment. In the demolition yard they will completely demolish everything anyway. I'm worried about something else, Commander."

"Yes?" Tsugawa looked questioningly.

"They had managed to determine the exact direction in which Oumuamua was emitting the signal."

"After all, it was a broadband transmission. At least that's what they reported at the beginning."

"As you can see, they were wrong. In fact, the signal was emitting in the direction of the rubble."

"Rubble?" Tsugawa's slanted eyes rounded in astonishment. The briefcase with the printouts fell to the floor, the sheets of paper scattered to form a creamy-white mosaic.

"Yes, rubble," confirmed Kravchenko. "The same one to which our missing convoy flew."

"So that's why you ordered the scouts to try to scan the area!" glared Tsugawa.

"That's right. There is something important to the Skunians among those damn rocks. Important enough that in order to divert our attention from it, they decided not only to sacrifice their largest Oumuamua, but also to indirectly admit that they are able to create or activate more folds. And now a riddle for you, Commander. What do you think could be there?" he asked, smiling slightly.

Tsugawa did not answer immediately. For a long moment he stood motionless, staring at some point behind the admiral's back, then crouched down and picked up the papers crumbling on the floor.

At the other end of the hall, massive steel gates slid open with a hiss, through which a transport platform rolled in immediately with a hurricane of caterpillars, loaded with reconnaissance probes placed in hexagonal racks, one-and-a-half-meter-high titanium cylinders with measuring apparatus stuffed inside. Behind the platform walked a reloading automaton on massive, spider-like metal limbs.

"Admiral, Commander!" rang out from the ceiling the mechanical-sounding voice of the operator supervising the landing. "Please leave the hall immediately. In three minutes, the air will be pumped out of there. I repeat, please leave the landing pad immediately."

"Nest," Tsugawa announced, straightening up slowly. In both hands he squeezed the already unmercifully crumpled print files.

He acted as if he had not heard the warning from the speakers.

"Nest," he repeated, then without waiting for the commander and thus violating the rules of etiquette, he moved toward the briefing corridor.

23

Mobile Medical Corps
High orbit of the Sigil's moon

It was only after a few moments of covert observation that Moss realized that one of the armed security guards was noticeably shorter and smaller than the others, and that he had a badge with the medical corps logo - a distinctive black cross on a red background - affixed to his sleeve.

"A doctor," flashed through his mind as the figure in the suit approached the control panel on the lobby wall and raised the helmet's aperture so that the identification system could scan his retina.

Like almost all Fleet officers, Moss had at one time been thoroughly familiar with the security procedures in place at Corps facilities, and remembered that only senior personnel used direct identification systems. The rest used ordinary, non-personalized magnetic cards with a periodically updated access code.

Seconds later, the massive double doors next to the panel swung outward, and a cloud of gas flowed into the corridor from the room it led to.

The woman looked into the room, then summoned the other two with a gesture and pointed them to something behind the door.

When all three had disappeared over the threshold, Moss crept closer and crouched behind a tall closet with a partially glazed front, in which lightweight, disposable protective uniforms hung.

Huddled behind a piece of furniture, he set the suit's communication system to listening mode and checked all the frequencies uploaded to the device's memory in turn, hoping to eavesdrop on what the mysterious three were talking about. Unfortunately, with no result. The intercom receiver only picked up a series of looped, automatic messages emitted by the station's warning system and snippets of conversations between the airlock attendants and the operators on the cruiser.

A light came on in the room where the armed trio had entered. After a few moments, one of the security guards appeared in the doorway. With his back turned to Moss, he dragged an oblong, roughly three-meter-long metal box, somewhat resembling a survival pod, into the hall. The other walked behind, carrying blue-painted containers in both hands, connected by long wires to the crate. The woman came out last, with a small plastic vessel with transparent walls under her arm.

Intrigued by this sight, Moss pushed himself deeper into the corner between the wall and the closet and, being careful not to accidentally move the furniture with too strong a push, then activated his communicator and called the Frontier.

"Lieutenant Stanley Moss, authorization code seven three two five broken by FH one hundred and one," he recited as a raspy, short beep sounded through the headset, confirming the opening of a communications channel reserved for command staff.

"How can I help you, Lieutenant?" came the question of the radio operator from the Frontier in a hoarse voice after a while. Moss immediately realized that Corporal Kulak was on duty at the communications post.

"Please connect me with Commander Lupos," he said.

"I am already connecting."

The headphones beeped again. A moment later Moss heard the commander's voice.

"Hello?" Lupos asked briefly.

"Commander, I report that we have arrived at the station and are currently securing evacuation routes to improve rescue procedures. Unfortunately, there was a problem."

"Namely?"

"Several modules have been detached from one of the hospital levels. We don't yet know whether this occurred as an emergency or as part of standard evacuation procedure. In any case, this level has been completely dehermetized.

"I understand, expect that, the operation is running smoothly?" Lupos asked.

"Not exactly, Commander," Moss leaned cautiously out from behind a closet and scanned the hall with his eyes. Figures in overalls were clambering around the crate, connecting more wires and tubes to it. The blue containers that one of the security guards had brought out of the Hall were attached with tape to a frosted lid, and on each rested a small device that pulsed with colored diodes. "These discarded modules were regenerative ambulatories. There is a strong possibility that one of them contained Colonel Dressler."

From the headphones came the sound of air being rapidly taken in.

"Holy shit!" cursed Lupos. "We need to determine the target point towards which they were fired. Have you tried to contact the station command?"

"Not yet. For the time being, I've only ordered the control room to be manned."

"This is going very well. We have been waiting for more than two hours for data on the technical condition of their gravity generator. This device most likely has a disrupted field stabilizer and is constantly pulling us off course. If this continues, our maneuvering engines will overheat. We need to get this report as soon as possible so we can send a repair team."

"I'll take care of it," promised Moss. "There is another problem, Commander. There are security guards from Sigil here. Armed."

"Civilian armed services in a military outpost? Who allowed them to come aboard?" puzzled Lupos.

"I wanted to ask you the same thing," replied Moss. He looked out of his hiding place again.

Two security guards were crouching by the crate, checking one by one the attachments of the containers and the tubes and wires connecting them to the crate. A woman was tinkering with something on the door control panel.

Moss only now noticed the vertical gaps on either side of the door, sealed with a thick layer of foam insulation. Identical, except that the horizontal ones ran just below the ceiling and above the floor. All indications were that the room from which the three of them had lugged the crate and its instrumentation was not an integral part of the medical station, but an attached module, equipped not only with its own life-support systems, but also having a system of corrective thrusters for maneuvering during eventual flight and docking.

"I don't know anything about this."

"The station command should inform you about it."

"It should," one could sense weariness in the commander's voice, albeit somewhat distorted by the communication system. "Just as it should send technical reports. Have you talked to these mercenaries yet?"

"At the moment I'm watching them from hiding."

"How many are there?"

"Two. They are accompanied by a person from the cabin crew."

"And because of some two Sigilian jerks you bother me?" groaned Lupos. "Lieutenant, you disappoint me. Please arrest them immediately and deliver them on board the cruiser. I will personally interrogate them. The same goes for that individual from the station crew."

"They are armed," reminded Moss.

"Well, then disarm them."

"Commander, I would prefer to avoid this. All three are behaving very suspiciously. A while ago they dismantled one of the hibernation chambers and are apparently preparing it for transport. An active chamber, Commander," he stressed. "As far as I know, it's a forbidden technology."

"So, they are obliterating the traces of some kind of moonlighting?" The lack of ability to instantly associate facts Lupos could not be accused of.

"It seems so," replied Moss. "If you don't mind, before we arrest them, I'll first try to determine where and why they want to take the device."

"Good," agreed Lupos. "Also, please keep this report in mind. I want it on my desk as soon as possible."

"Yes, sir!" said Moss, breathing a sigh of relief. He wouldn't admit this to the commander for anything, but the prospect of single-handedly disarming two combat-armor-clad and most likely well-trained mercenaries he completely did not want to do.

He called out to Danielewicz.

"The situation on the evacuation routes?" he asked.

"Everything is fine here, Lieutenant," reported the sergeant, not very regulationly. "We have just finished setting up the sentry machines at the auxiliary airlocks."

"Is there anyone from the station command staff staying in the control room?"

"It's hard to say, there are a lot of people here. We would have to identify them all to determine who is who."

"Do it. On the Frontier they urgently need information on the technical condition of the station's gravity generator and propulsion systems. See to it that the locals send the relevant report as soon as possible. If they do not want to cooperate, you can use any means of persuasion. The matter is really urgent. Do we understand each other?"

"Of course, Lieutenant."

"Excellent. What about the automatons you were supposed to direct to deck three?"

"They got stuck in the transport elevator. After decompressing the deck, the security system also cut off the elevator shafts and locked the cabin doors."

"Damn it!" cursed Moss. Equipped with high-powered tasers and rubber bullet throwers, the automatons would provide excellent support.

"Any problems, Lieutenant?" Danielewicz was interested.

"Possible," replied Moss, reflexively lowering his voice.

One of the bodyguards either intercepted a snippet of his transmission, or some kind of sixth sense was triggered, because he suddenly straightened up and reached for his gun, then started looking around. Moss squeezed himself even deeper into the corner, thanking providence for the non-functioning lighting lamps in this corner of the hall, so that his hiding place was drowning in darkness, and the black-as-night suit blended with its surroundings. "I have a group of armed intruders here."

"Shall I send you someone?" asked the sergeant matter-of-factly.

"No, it's not necessary. I will manage somehow. Focus on your tasks."

"Are you sure, Lieutenant?" There was a note of concern in Danielewicz's voice.

"Focus on your tasks," he repeated, trying to make it sound as firm as possible. "Over and out," he added and ended the call. As a precaution, he turned off the communicator completely.

After a few tens of seconds, the bodyguard stuck his gun back into the grips on the back of his suit and joined his companion, still tinkering with the box. The massive box glistened with frost in the light of the few lamps that were still working, the diodes of the control panels pulsed rhythmically on its hemmed edges, and the indicators of the measuring devices glowed green on one of the walls. The lid-mounted containers gradually turned a lighter shade as the substance filling them flowed down tubes into the cooling system.

At one point, all three crouched down behind the crate. The woman held in her hands a small, rectangular device with several differently colored buttons. It was connected by a thin cable to a power socket on the opposite wall.

Moss immediately guessed that he was about to witness the manual unplugging of the hospital module. He instantly switched the suit's vision system to infrared. The front of the helmet tarnished to glow every possible shade of red, which after a while turned to a uniform pink, with only infrequent yellow-orange flecks.

One such brighter spot was the entrance to the module. In the lobby itself, the bright yellow aura was emitted primarily by the lamps and the still-active wall power outlets, the power cells mounted in the side wall of the box, and the huddled people behind it. In the case of the latter, the most radiant heat was radiated by the wicking plates located on the backs of the suits.

Taking advantage of the fact that those there had their backs turned to him, he retreated stealthily into the corridor. He activated the communicator again and established a connection with the cruiser. This time the transmission was received directly by Lupos.

"Commander, this is Lieutenant Moss," he said, hearing the characteristic, somewhat burly "Yes?". "Regarding those bodyguards..." he fell silent for a moment and looked out into the hall. "I think I already know what they are up to."

"I'm all ears."

"Is there currently any ship belonging to the Autonomy in the vicinity?"

"Yes, and even more than one. An hour ago, three passenger carriers and one cargo ship joined us. They will help in the evacuation and then capture the detached modules. Why do you ask?"

"These three are evidently planning to take the hibernation chamber out of here. They have dismantled it from the module and prepared it for transport. Any minute now they will also shoot off the module itself."

"Why would they do that?"

"To make it look like an accident. They have unsealed the module and, as far as I can see, activated the life support systems, probably for disguise. The chamber will most likely be transferred to the transport ship through an opening that will be created when the module is detached."

"You know what, this looks to me like one of those slimy operations of their intelligence services," announced Lupos. "Those bastards love to use civilians. Lieutenant, stop this, or at least slow them down. I'll send a quick reaction force there."

The deck under Moss's feet rocked suddenly, a tumble of debris, dust and debris gushed from the hallway. More lamps went out. Struck by shrapnel, the lieutenant hooked his foot on some wire and fell on his back. He groaned in pain.

"What is going on?" asked the commander anxiously.

Moss did not answer immediately. For several moments he lay motionless, trying to calm his breathing.

"Can you hear me?"

"I think it's too late for landing," Moss finally stammered out. "They had just shot off the module."

He rose carefully to his feet, wiped the dust off his helmet's visor, then, dodging the chunks of sealing foam littering the floor, he approached the corridor exit and looked out from behind the wall.

"They're fast," he said with involuntary appreciation at the sight of a rectangular, vault-like hole in the lobby wall, behind which, against the void of space, the illuminated interior of the cargo bay of a large transport ship shone brightly. "Commander, they have moved the cargo," he informed Lupos. "Should I continue my observation?"

The light in the cargo bay dimmed, then turned purple. The hatch flap, which also served as a ramp, slowly began to rise, and although the shunting engines of the carrier were still out, Moss knew that any moment the ship would jump away from the station.

"That won't be necessary," Lupos replied. "We have them on screens, the interceptor units are just taking off. You can..." his next words were drowned out by a cacophony of crackling sounds, which after a while turned into a screeching, ear-painful interference, unpleasant to the point that Moss with the utmost difficulty refrained from turning off the communicator. Instead, he ended the call and turned the sound down a bit. When the interference stopped, he once again called the cruiser. He was answered by silence, punctuated only rarely by the single, rhythmic clicks of the system chronometer timing the transmission.

And then a familiar, velvety melodious voice sounded in the headphones:

"Save the Colonel, Stan. Please."

Moss suddenly ran out of breath.

"It's you, Oli?!" he gasped out.

"Yes, Stan, it's me," came the calm reply. *"Don't let them take the Colonel. Save him."*

"But who... Where... How?!" confused Moss looked around.

And suddenly it dazzled him.

"The chamber!" he groaned, then jumped toward the rising ramp of the transport ship.

Lublin, January-May-2019

END OF BOOK ONE